AB NEGATIVE

An Alberta Crime Anthology

Edited by Axel Howerton

Coffin Hop Press

ISBN: 978-0994737809
ISBN-13: 0994737807
Paperback Edition:
July 2015

Published Worldwide by
Coffin Hop Press
Calgary, Alberta
Canada
www.coffinhop.com

PROUDLY CANADIAN

iv

For Alberta,
Femme Fatale and Beautiful Dame.
Mother of Us All.

CONTENTS

INTRODUCTION

Death.

Whether it comes at you in an explosion of violence, going *gentle into that goodnight*, getting bit by the wrong damned mosquito, or *walking spanish down the hall*, it's the same everywhere you go, and it's tough all over. Even way up in the Great White North… dead is dead, baby. There ain't nothing you can do about it.

The stories collected here under the title *AB NEGATIVE* all have something to do with death. They all examine one side, or the other, of *The Big Sleep—The Long Adios—The Dark Forgotten*—whatever you want to call it. Some of them focus on the here and now. Some of them delve into the past. Some of them even jump into some strange future. Some get cozy. Some keep it noir as midnight. Some fall somewhere in between, and some make their own damn rules. Just like Albertans. And that's the other thing they all have in common:

Alberta's best crime writers, writing crime stories set in Alberta.

What else do you need to say, eh?

Enjoy.

Axel Howerton
Calgary, Alberta, Canada
June 2015

MURDER ON THE MALL
RANDY MCCHARLES

I was nursing my fourth cup of joe, people watching on Stephen Avenue Mall, when two mooks shuffled down the pedestrian-only pavement and wandered into Willie's Western Wear across the street. For the past two hours I'd been marking everyone who entered Willie Makowchuck's boutique for wannabe cowboys, but these two stood out like last month's leftover pizza. Both were late teens, early twenties, which was nothing special for Calgary's urban cowboy scene. But, while Willie offered leather boots and felt hats for ages nine to ninety, these two wore neither. The tall, emaciated blond wore torn jeans, which was about as cowboy as he got, and a bright pink and yellow t-shirt that advertised SpongeBob SquarePants. His shorter companion sported greasy dark hair, greasier dark pants, and a t-shirt advertising God knows what. It was red and black and featured a rabid donkey's head with great curling goat horns. The word badass was stamped underneath in some kind of heavy metal font.

My gut told me this was it. If SpongeBob and Badass didn't fit the bill, I'd turn in my PI license.

Setting my half-finished cup of hot Irish on its Pegasus Pub and Eatery coaster, I tapped the display on my iPhone and turned up the volume to my earbud. Back when I was a cop, homicide division, we never had such toys. They were available, but the public outcry of big brother watching made them impolitic to use. A career change from public detective to private detective had its advantages.

Despite the tiny display, the webcam I had set up behind Willie's counter gave me a clear view of the two stooges sneering at the merchandise as they wandered up to Willie. Oh yeah, these were the guys I was after. At this rate I'd have the job tied up before dinner.

Then the back of Willie's head suddenly blocked part of the shot and I swore under my breath. From this close, the eighty-year-old storeowner's hair didn't look as thin and greying as reality declared, but if he inched much further to the right, that was all the footage I'd get.

"You got our money?" Badass drawled. At least he sounded like a cowboy.

"Bug off," snorted Willie, the sound a bit muffled as he was facing away from the microphone. The old man shifted left, and I got a clear shot of SpongeBob grinning like an idiot.

"That ain't polite," SpongeBob said. "You'd better apologize to my friend."

"I'll tell you what I told him." Willie's raspy voice grew loud with anger. "Bug off."

"You need us," Badass said, his face a scowl. "Ain't

no one else gonna keep them vandals from breaking up yer fine merchandise." He flicked a finger beneath the brim of a white cowboy hat displayed just within view of the shot. The hat shifted on the manikin's head. Badass's scowl deepened and he flicked his finger harder, causing the hat to flip up and off the manikin, out of the camera's view.

Willie snorted again. "The only vandals I see are you two. Get out of my store before I call the cops."

"Ohh," said Badass. "I'm so scared."

"We're pussycats," SpongeBob said, "compared to the bad boys we seen hurting your neighbours."

"Really?" said Willie. "You're pussycats are you? Then how are you going to stop these bad boys you're talking about?"

Badass glowered at his companion. "He's a pussycat. I can take care of your problem."

Willie began coughing and his head shook. Was the old man having a seizure? Then I realized he was laughing. Sometimes with old people it's hard to tell the difference.

"I opened this store in 1956," Willie growled. "You two prairie oysters hadn't even been born yet. Hell, your parents hadn't been born yet. And I ain't never had trouble I couldn't handle myself. So you get the hell out of my store before I show you what trouble really looks like."

SpongeBob was no longer smiling and Badass looked ready to provide some nice evidence for the camera. His fists were out of sight below the counter, but I could see them clenching in my mind's eye.

"You're an old fool," SpongeBob said. "Consider our protection service terminated. Maybe we'll come back after you've learned your lesson."

3

"Protection service!" Willie shouted. "You're just a couple of brainless thugs. You come back and we'll see who needs protecting."

The look in Badass's eyes suggested that something might happen then and there. Something nasty for Willie if I couldn't get inside his store in time. I'd never lost a client and I didn't feel like losing one today. I was already rising out of my seat when SpongeBob put a hand on Badass's shoulder and turned him toward the door. I doubted that SpongeBob was the brains of the outfit, but he had just demonstrated that he had more going for him than Badass.

Willie Makowchuck had hired me to sort out his protection problem because the police don't get interested until a crime has been committed— money out of pocket or damage to the store. Even then, the mere $100 a week protection money these two punks had demanded wouldn't put them high on police radar. Whoever their ringleader was, he wasn't dumb. $100 was chump change, not enough to get anyone's attention. But if they extorted ten shop owners, that's $1,000. And there were dozens of mom-and-pops along Stephen Avenue. Expand the operation to Tenth Avenue, and they could pull in ten grand a week and still the cops would have bigger fish to fry.

Of course, the more mom-and-pops you extort, the more likely you'll hit on someone like Willie, an ornery bastard who wasn't gonna let some punk kids rob him of a dime, never mind a C-note.

I smiled at the thought that this gig sure beat taking photos of straying husbands.

The two wannabe felons stepped out into the bright afternoon sunshine and blinked as their eyes adjusted. Willie was as cheap with light bulbs as he was paying extortion threats. The few lamps inside his store couldn't be more than forty watts. I'd had to adjust my webcam for almost nighttime lighting.

Grimacing, I swallowed that last of my fortified coffee and threw a pair of Lizzies on the table. Forty bucks. Almost half of that was tip, but I'd sat there long enough that the leggy server deserved it. I was just pocketing my iPhone and preparing to follow SpongeBob and Badass to their next victim, when an explosion echoed along Stephen Avenue. I watched, stunned, as SpongeBob toppled to the pavement, a dark splash of red staining the sea fungus's yellow smiling face.

Less than a second later I scanned the street for the shooter. People all along the avenue lay flat against the pavement. Those who hadn't dropped were still running toward the shelter of nearby shops. There were even a few who darted past my street side table into the Pegasus Pub. I just sat there. It was too late to hit the ground. If another shot was coming, I would have heard it already.

There were only two people on the street stupid enough not to duck and cover. I was one. The other was Badass, who just stood there, white-faced and staring at his partner in crime's corpse.

There should have been a third person– the shooter. Possibly he was lying on the pavement, hiding in plain sight. Or had the shot come from a window above one of the shops? The only person I could be certain hadn't fired the gun was Willie. The old man's thinning hair had been bobbing in front of the webcam as I pocketed my phone. And now he was stepping through his shop's front door, looking first at Badass and then at SpongeBob, lying on the sidewalk in a growing pool of blood. Then he looked across the avenue at me, as if I had fired the shot.

I raised both of my hands and waved them, as if to say, "Look, no gun."

Willie only muttered and produced a cell phone from his pocket. I could see him punch the keypad three times.

Badass seemed to suddenly notice Willie. Perhaps he heard him speak into the phone. I should have been able to hear him myself; for the first time all afternoon the street was quiet, save for a few people gawking about from where they lay on the ground, whimpering. Then I noticed the music emanating from speakers outside the pub. I'd been there so long I had tuned it out. Loverboy was singing *The Kid is Hot Tonight*, obviously not about SpongeBob. Next I heard sneakers pounding on pavement; Badass was making a run for it.

I should have stayed in my seat. Perhaps even ordered another hot Irish. God knows I could have used one. If Willie didn't outright tell the police about my involvement, my webcam behind his counter would get their attention. They'd want to see the footage. Then they'd want to know what the hell I thought I was doing there; when I left the force, it wasn't exactly on good terms.

That's what I should have done. Instead, I clamped my Elkhorn Fedora onto my head and started at a fast walk down the pavement toward City Hall, the direction Badass had gone.

Following the punk was no problem; Stephen Avenue was still mostly deserted. And for a badass he wasn't much of a runner, even when frightened for his life. I hadn't gone half a block, however, before people began crowding back into the street, now more interested in finding out what had happened than being afraid of it. I picked up my pace so that I wouldn't lose my quarry.

A siren sounded up ahead followed by flashing lights, then a police car wormed its way out from a wall of pedestrians. I pulled up against a stone storefront as it went past. Murder was one of those bigger fish that occupied the police.

Looking back up the avenue, I spotted Badass turning south down First Street East. I sprinted to catch up, then turned cautiously at the Glenbow Museum and walked at a normal pace along the sidewalk behind a trio of pedestrians. Badass's running had slowed to a fast walk. Kids these days. Raised on soda and video games. As he reached Ninth Avenue and the side entrance to the Glenbow ConocoPhillips Theatre, the walk light began to flash. Badass picked up his pace. As did I. If I had to wait for the next light I'd lose him for sure.

Badass made it across the street and was continuing south on First when the walk signal ended. I was still in the crosswalk. Horns began blaring even before the traffic light turned green for the one-way traffic. Badass looked back and frowned at me even as I reached the curb. I immediately turned right toward the Calgary Tower and hid myself behind the corner of the One Palliser Square building.

One of my first purchases when starting out as a PI was a reversible overcoat from Abercrombie & Fitch, off-white on one side and some ugly hue of brown on the other. I quickly pulled off the coat and reversed it. Whatever that brown was, it truly was god-awful. I also pulled off my crushable Fedora and stuffed it into a pocket.

Stepping back around the corner I continued south on First Street. To my profound relief, Badass was still in sight.

I wasn't even sure I needed to follow him. Willie hadn't hired me to look into a murder. Murder was the reason I had quit the police. Well, one of the reasons. Whoever said, "You seen one dead body you seen 'em all," hadn't a clue. After three years in homicide I still got ill viewing a corpse. When transferring out became difficult, I quit. I'd had more death than I could stomach.

But Badass was the only lead. He may not have committed the murder, but he knew the victim and he might know who had pulled the trigger. Of course, SpongeBob or even Badass could be on file with the police. My iPhone had a good image of Badass. But if they weren't on file – many young criminals drifted from city to city – the police might have nothing. Except an ex-cop with black marks in his own file. They'd love that.

I shook my head at the thought and then realized that Badass was no longer in front of me. Another black mark for my own copy of that file. Stepping double time, I hit Tenth Avenue and spotted him heading west on the south side of the street. Then he was gone. Following, I found the spot where he'd disappeared. It was a narrow entrance to a brick walled watering hole called The Seedy Bar.

The name was well deserved. For starters, the lighting was almost non-existent, much worse than Willie's cowboy boutique. In this place, forty-watt bulbs hadn't been invented yet. After my eyes adjusted, I guessed that the furnishings had been bought at auction from an older, possibly condemned seedy bar: ripped seat leather stinking of stale beer; ratty carpet with holes in it, possibly made by real rats; and something deemed art by a blind person adorning the walls.

The clientele was sparse, looking disreputable and undesirous of notice, never mind company: hitched up shoulders; baseball caps, likely stolen from gas station attendants, pulled low over furtive eyes; and glass beer steins clutched in tight fingers.

Badass might think he was hiding among them, but his t-shirt was one of a kind. The back also had badass stamped across the bottom, just below the image of a donkey's generous behind. The dark-haired teen clutched a glass stein, already mostly empty. A second sat on the counter in front of him.

I took a seat at a small table slammed hard against a curtained window. A busty blond floozy took my order. Somewhere in her thirties, she might have been pretty had she gone easier on the drugs and the booze. She returned a moment later with a none-too-clean glass mostly filled with a beer-like substance. I paid with cash and sat there, not touching the drink.

My plan, before extortion had morphed into murder, was to follow the two bullyboys from Willie's back to their base of operation. Take photos of everything and everyone along the way, and make two copies, one for the police and one for the thugs. My theory was that if they knew that the police had all the information they needed to find and arrest them, that they would move on to another city. As a private investigator it wasn't my job to arrest criminals. I'd been hired to get them off Willie's back and this seemed as good a way as any.

Of course, that all changed when SpongeBob took a bullet.

Halfway through his second glass, Badass pulled a phone from his pocket and punched a number. Calling his boss? The conversation was short and whispered. Badass's hand trembled and his eyes were wild. Definitely his boss.

A few minutes later the floozy was still giving me dirty looks when Badass downed the last of his second beer and made for the door. I tipped an invisible hat at her and then pushed aside the edge of the almost black curtain to peer outside. Badass was standing out front staring at his watch.

Then a beat up Chevy Impala skidded to the curb and Badass climbed in. I was out of my seat and out the door in an instant, but the Impala had already pulled out into traffic.

Looking the other way, I spotted a taxi and waved at it. The taxi didn't have a passenger, but it didn't slow down either. There was nothing for it; I jumped out into the street. Brakes squealed. Oil burned. Black smoke filled the air. The taxi driver rolled down his window and swore a blue streak at me. Some of the words I didn't even know.

I ignored him and climbed into the passenger seat.

"What are you doing?" he cried. The driver wore a length of bright yellow cloth wound tight around his head and had a Middle Eastern accent. "I have a pickup."

"Follow that car!" I said.

"You are an idiot," he said. "I have a pickup."

"I reached into my wallet and threw a handful of Lizzies at him. "Now you don't. Follow that car."

"You are still an idiot," he shouted, but hit the gas anyway. The ID attached to the visor displayed his photo, driver number, and a name–Bindar Dundat. Sounded more East Indian than Middle Eastern.

I couldn't see the Impala, but Bindar turned his taxi

south on Centre Street and there it was, two blocks down and turning east onto Twelfth Avenue. In no time at all we were also on Twelfth and only half a block behind.

My iPhone chimed and I did a stupid thing. I answered it.

"Galloway!"

I recognized the voice. My old partner at Homicide.

"Kowalski. It's good to hear from you."

"Don't give me that friendly crap. You fled a crime scene."

"I'm following a suspect." I didn't tell him it was one of the few suspects who couldn't possibly have pulled the trigger.

"You're not a cop anymore," Kowalski growled. "At best you're a witness. But it never is the best with you, is it? Now get back here!"

"I would. But there's still this suspect."

"Let the police deal with him. You're not the police."

"Yes," I said. "But the police aren't following him. I am. I'll be there as soon as I can." I hung up.

The phone chimed again. This time I was smart; I ignored it.

Badass turned north onto Macleod Trail and went straight through downtown, passing within four blocks of SpongeBob's cooling corpse outside Willie's Western Wear. The taxi driver, oblivious to the murder, followed hot on Badass's heels.

Once past the Fifth Avenue lights and onto Memorial Drive, Badass kicked it into high gear, going over a hundred in an eighty zone. My taxi started falling behind.

"They're getting away," I said.

"They're speeding," Bindar answered.

"You haven't watched many crime shows, have you?"

"I love a good crime show." Bindar showed me a wide grin. "Especially the chase scenes. Yet it amazes me how no one loses their license. I have coworkers who have driven over the speed limit. They have lost their licenses and now they clean toilets."

I looked into my wallet and found it notoriously lacking in Lizzies. I was going to lose this puppy after all.

Bindar ignored me and got onto his car radio, speaking in some language that sounded a lot like me trying to get a word in edgewise when talking to my captain back when I was in Homicide. My driver was probably contacting the police to take me off his hands somewhere.

He turned south onto Deerfoot Trail, even though I saw no sign of the beat up Impala, and sped up to one hundred kilometres per hour and not a centimetre faster. The Seventeenth Avenue exit came up and he took it, turning east toward Forest Lawn. Was he taking me back to his place for coffee?

At Twenty-Eighth Street he turned into Radisson Heights. Up ahead I could see another taxi ambling past older houses with faded paint and chipped sidewalks. Two blocks later my driver turned left onto Fifteenth Avenue and pulled over to the curb. About six houses ahead of us sat the old Impala.

"How?" I asked.

"With a little help from my friends." Bindar tapped his radio. "You get out now?"

I threw him the ten and two fives I still had in my wallet. "You guys are greatly underrated."

He shrugged and pulled out into the street.

The neighbourhood was quiet, though I could hear loud music from a block over. Rap, if you call that music. Otherwise the place could be a ghost town.

I strolled a little way along the sidewalk and then crossed the street and leaned against a wobbly fence where I had a good view of the house behind the Impala, whitewashed and with a lawn that needed cutting. A few pieces of trash lined the front wall like modern art. The Impala's engine pinged as it cooled.

My phone chimed and I looked to see a familiar number. "Kowalski," I said in greeting.

"Galloway! I don't see you giving your statement to Sergeant Evans. Where are you?"

"Stuck in traffic," I said. "Rush hour."

"It's not even three in the afternoon!"

"You get out much, Kowalski?"

"You get down here before I put out a warrant for your arrest."

"Again?"

This time it was Kowalski who hung up. I smiled.

Stakeouts can be boring. I'd done a few as a cop. More as a PI. But never standing out in the street in plain sight of the place I was watching. There were a lot of curtains on the windows. They could be watching me right back. And in greater comfort. A few hours went by. Well. It was probably a few minutes; it just felt like hours. Before I knew it I had walked across the street, up to the front door, and was knocking.

A biker-looking dude answered the door. He wore a skull and crossbones muscle shirt and his face was a rat's nest of hair. Tattoos covered his arms. One of them said, "MOM." He stared at me like I was a Jehovah Witness selling pamphlets.

Badass came up behind him along with two other

guys about the same age. Maybe this was a high school barbershop quartet, graduated and gone bad.

"Tough luck about SpongeBob," I said.

They all stared at me.

"Who?" asked Biker.

"Your blond friend with the SpongeBob t-shirt."

Two of the quartet vanished, leaving Biker and Badass in the doorway.

"You're him, aren't you?" asked Badass. "You shot Kevin."

I shook my head. "I was there and saw it go down. I'm helping the police." It wasn't a lie. The police didn't want my help, but I was helping them anyway. "Any idea who would shoot your friend?"

Both of them shook their heads.

"Come on. He had to have enemies." I gave biker-dude a penetrating look. "You have enemies. Perhaps someone you were extorting?"

Two jaws dropped.

"You might as well come clean. The cops know all about your little racket, and will be less gentle than me when they show up."

Two jaws remained dropped.

"How's this then? You give me the list of businesses you were shaking down and I'll find out which one of them is gunning for you." I gave them my trademark smile.

It had occurred to me during the taxi ride that someone less civic minded than Willie might have found a cheaper and more permanent way of solving their extortion problem than hiring a PI.

"Seriously," I said. "If I can find you so can they. And they'll be no friendlier with you than they were with Kevin."

Two minutes later the door closed and I had a list of downtown businesses in my hand. This is why Kowalski and I didn't get along back when I was a cop. And after. Kowalski is a brute force kind of guy. Many cops are. They don't believe in the soft touch. Seeing it in action is even worse. Kowalski would never simply ask for the list. And watching me do it, he'd be spitting teeth. Maybe it's some kind of religious thing.

I scanned the list but nothing stood out. No one puts down front for the mob when registering their business. I'd have to check them out, all twenty shops. It was then I remembered that I'd been dropped off by a taxi and that my Yaris was parked downtown. I really didn't feel like hoofing it down Seventeenth Avenue trying to hail a cab and I'd already softened these guys up. I knocked on the door again.

"Excuse me, but I don't suppose I could borrow your car?"

It took less than a minute of additional song and dance to get the keys – these wannabes really were green – and twenty minutes of driving before I was downtown at the Sixth Street Parkade using my credit card to pay for parking.

Fortunately, biker-dude's list was in extortion order and started three blocks west of Willie's crime scene. Beginning with a couple of innocuous boutiques in Eighth Avenue Place, I worked my way east.

Nothing felt out of place at any of the shops. A cop has a nose for these things. You don't lose it when you leave the force. Then I stood outside a grimy storefront called Archaic Antiques. I didn't know about the goods inside, but the grime outside the building certainly felt antique. My nose was tingling.

Stepping inside I found old furniture and shelves

filled with brass knick-knacks in desperate need of polish. There was a counter with no one behind it, but as I moved about the place the floor creaked and a curtain moved revealing what looked like a has-been gorilla straight from the WWF, except that he was wearing an Oxford shirt and dress slacks instead of wrestling trunks.

Not wanting to waste time, I moved up to the counter and ran a finger across its surface, collecting dust. "Got anything more recent?" I asked.

He just stared at me. Perhaps he didn't speak English.

"I'm not really into old stuff," I said. I winked at him.

"Who referred you?"

So the gorilla did speak English. "Joe," I said.

"Joe who?"

"Does it matter?"

The gorilla frowned, a straight band of skin and eyebrow running across his forehead. "We're closed."

"It's only just past three in the afternoon."

"Special holiday," he said.

"Right," I said. "SpongeBob SquarePants Day."

The frown became more intense.

"Maybe I'll come back tomorrow," I said and left the shop.

Ignoring the other suspects on my list, I walked the remaining block and a half to Willie's Western Wear. SpongeBob was gone, just a dark stain on the sidewalk remained to commemorate the lanky youth's death. Police tape was everywhere and several uniforms were cautioning gawkers away.

"Where have you been?" Kowalski demanded before I was even within proper berating distance.

"Oh, you know," I said. "Following suspects,

generating leads, chatting with a killer."

"You're not a cop anymore," Kowalski growled. "Not that you were much of one when you were."

"Well, that's a matter of perspective, I suppose. How are things going here?"

Kowalski snorted. "Mr. Makowchuck is ready to see you hang. When he hired you to chase away protection punks, he didn't think you'd kill one of them to do it."

"I didn't—"

"Of course you didn't." The big cop smiled. "Not even you would be that stupid."

I decided to accept the compliment. "Did you figure out who Kevin is?"

"Who?"

"The kid in the SpongeBob shirt."

Kowalski didn't answer, but he scrawled something into his notebook. "I want your webcam recording."

"Of course you do, but you don't need it."

My ex-partner grunted. "We need it to track down the other guy."

"He's at 1579 Twenty-Eighth Street in Radisson Heights along with three other gang members. But none of them saw the shooter."

Kowalski ground his teeth and made another note. "And you did?"

This wasn't going well, not that I'd expected it to.

"I didn't see him either. But he may work down the street at Archaic Antiques."

"And you know this because..."

"Because he doesn't smell right."

"Never hold up in court." Even a brick-head like Kowalski respected a cop's sense of smell.

"I think I can lure him out," I said. "All I need is the bullet calibre that killed SpongeBob."

"I thought you were done with homicide. Couldn't stomach it anymore."

"Yeah, well. This thing hit me in the face and not by my choice. I'm in it now and I may as well finish it."

Kowalski snickered. "Sorry to break it to you, but you're a civilian."

"Which is why I can finish it. You try and a good lawyer could argue entrapment."

Kowalski shook his head. "Your funeral. Doc says it looks like a 357."

"Gotcha."

I turned around and headed back to Archaic Antiques.

The gorilla looked more annoyed than surprised to see me. "What?"

"Joe sent me back. He doesn't want to wait until tomorrow."

"Get outta here."

"Joe wants to know if you have anything in a 357."

"What?"

I pushed myself against the counter and leaned in. You got a 357 handy? Joe?"

The gorilla's right hand dropped beneath the counter. My instinct was to reach for my holster, which of course wasn't there since I was no longer a cop. Besides, I had enough nightmares; I didn't need more by walking around with a widow maker in my pocket. Gorilla's hand was coming back up so I grabbed the nearest thing handy, a brass and green glass banker's lamp, pulling it so hard that the cord popped from the wall plug and the light went out. I could see gun metal in the gorilla's clenched hand. He was whipping it over the counter. I heaved the lamp, smashing it into his face, and the gorilla swayed backward but didn't let go of the gun. Neither did he fall down. He was a big guy and had taken some hits in his day. Well, that's what I get for bringing a lamp to a gunfight.

Twisting the lamp in my hand I hit the gorilla again, this time with the heavier brass base. Another sway, but he still didn't go down, and his gun hand was wavering in my direction. This time I hit his hand. The gun fired, but it had swung toward the side of the store. The bullet hit something, but I was too preoccupied to see what. There were noises behind the curtain. Reinforcements. I was going to have to take the gorilla's gun away from him. Fast. But how? I'd bit off more than I could chew and I knew it.

I raised the lamp again, ready to take another swing, when the street door burst open. Kowalski's voice shouted, "Stop! Police." Then the pitter-patter of many hard-soled shoes pounded into the shop.

The sound of the gorilla's gun hitting the floorboards was barely audible above the thumping of my heart.

Then I heard Kowalski laugh. The first time I'd ever heard the calloused cop laugh. "I always said you were trouble, Galloway. But for once it's paid off."

"Yeah, well, buy me a cup of joe and we'll call it even."

A friend of mine had once said that a homicide cop was in it for life; you could leave the job, but the job would never leave you. I'd laughed at the time. I wasn't laughing now. The nightmares were bad enough, but it looked like the job might still be in my blood. The only bright side was that I'd managed to solve a murder without coming within twenty metres of the corpse. Put that in my file, Kowalski. Even so, this private investigator gig wasn't going to be as easy as I'd hoped.

FREEZER BREAKDOWN
SUSAN CALDER

Freezer Breakdown Party
Jim & Rhonda Wellington's back yard
336 Baker Street
Today, July 11, 3:00 PM to whenever
Last evening we discovered our freezer bit the dust.
The contents are thawing.
Friends, neighbors & relatives don't let the food go to waste.
Come share the spoils: burgers, casseroles, desserts & more.
We virtually guarantee no salmonella poisoning

I grip the door knob, reread the invitation dropped in my mailbox and know I should attend on account of the promise I made to Mother, as she lay dying, the night I killed her.

"Vincent," she rasped, her pale face drenched with sweat. "When I'm gone." She coughed. "You'll never ... manage ... alone." She slumped back on her chair, eyes closed. "Promise you'll marry."

Three days after Mother's death, Lorraine showed up at my door, holding a casserole dish. She wore a T-shirt with *Calgary* in rope letters across her chest. The slight bulge of her eyes made me wonder if she had hyperthyroid disease, Mother's more benign affliction. I guessed Lorraine to be in her late thirties, about ten years younger than me.

She shoved the dish into my hands. "My sister Rhonda, down the street, asked me to bring you this quiche. She says she's sorry about your mom. I'm sorry, too, even though I never met her. Or you, before today. Rhonda's husband, Jim, also sends his condolences. He says you and he talk about hockey sometimes. You told him you sculpt little hockey players out of modeling clay. That is so cute."

I shifted the frozen dish from hand to hand.

"I like hockey." Lorraine toyed with her ponytail. "Naturally, being from Toronto, I root for the Leafs, not the Flames. I moved west last month and am staying with Rhonda and Jim until I find work. They say the job market's hot here, but it's not as easy as I'd thought."

I rested the dish on my belt to reduce the numbness in my hands. "What work do you do?" I asked to be polite.

"I'm a pharmacist," Lorraine said.

Out of nervousness, I snickered at the thought of Lorraine's access to medications that could have done Mother in. The funeral had taken place that morning and I was feeling giddy, having apparently gotten away with murder, so I made a joke. "A pharmacist?" I said. "I wish I'd met you years ago." Like all my humor attempts, it stank.

Lorraine's eyes narrowed. "Men." Her knuckles shot to her hips. "Jesus Christ, what's the matter with you guys? Your mother is barely cold and you're already flirting." She glared at me, her nose pinched with hatred.

I was hooked.

Now, as I carry the Wellingtons' party invitation into the house, it strikes me that their freezer expired a week to the day after Mother did. Coincidence? Shivers run up my arms. Or is Mother manipulating from beyond the grave? If that's the case -- and I wouldn't put it past her -- there is only one way Mother will let go. I will try to grant her dying request, even though I dread an afternoon of partying with my neighbors more than I fear salmonella.

In my bedroom, I search my closet for decent clothes. Soon I'll need to do laundry and dust and learn to cook something other than frozen prepared dinners. I pass over gray pants and shirts and haul out the clothing Mother always selected when she set me up with her friends' daughters, who were invariably too sweet for my taste. Mother said this polo shirt highlighted the silver in my hair. With my personality, I will have to rely on my looks, which women seem to find appealing. The salty colleague I had a crush on for years said I reminded her of a bland George Clooney.

My knees waver as I recall Lorraine's glare. As a precaution, before leaving for the party, I take an extra dose of my low blood pressure medication so that when I meet Lorraine I don't faint.

Murmurs waft from behind the Wellingtons' house.

The party is underway.

A man and woman and two boys sweep up beside me. I stifle an impulse to run.

"This must be the place," the short round man says. "I don't know these folks from Adam, do you? But who can say no to free grub?"

"And no cooking for me tonight." His skinny wife giggles.

I follow them through the gate to the back yard full of men and women chatting and laughing. Children chase each other around the grownups. I scan the faces and flower beds and spot a familiar shape: Jim Wellington, beer bottle in hand, expounding to three other people. Blood drains from my head. The woman leaning against the patio pillar is Lorraine. Her hair, worn down today, caresses her shoulders.

Jim spots me and raises his beer. "Vincent." He beckons with the bottle.

I approach; avoiding Lorraine's gaze, and recognize the man and other woman from my weekday C-train commutes. A curly-haired toddler stands between them. At the sight of me, the girl clutches the man's bow leg. Jim offers to get me a drink. I shake my head. Liquor makes me woozy at the best of times.

Jim nods at the man. "Do you know the Gables-- Marty and Cathy--my next door neighbors?"

"Yes," I say, as Marty answers, "No." He extends a freckled hand.

"Marty, we see him every day." Cathy turns to me. "Did anyone ever tell you that you look like George Clooney?"

Marty pats the child's head. "This is our daughter, Amanda."

I freeze. Mother's name.

The child buries her face between Marty's knees.

"Amanda's shy with strangers," Cathy says. "She's especially bad with men since she hit the terrible twos."

"Vincent," Jim says. "You've met my sister-in-law, Lorraine."

Lorraine's tanned face darkens as she whispers hello. She wears a scooped-neck blouse, flowing skirt and sandals.

"So Vince," Marty says. "What color is your car?"

I turn away from Lorraine. "Pardon?"

Marty grins. "Jim, here, read an article that claims the color of a person's car reflects his personality. What's yours?"

"Brown," I answer and wonder if that is correct. In the first place, I'm red/green color blind. In the second, the car belonged to Mother. I don't have a license. Mother always said I have no mechanical skills.

"I wanna go home." Little Amanda tightens her grip on Marty's leg.

"Not now, dear," Cathy says.

"I wanna go now."

Cathy forces a smile. "We missed our nap this afternoon and we're feeling cranky."

"Now." The brat stamps her foot with each word. "Now. Now."

Good God, I think. Lorraine is under forty. What if she wants children? Marriage is a prospect I can almost imagine, but fatherhood?

"What are we discussing?" A voice shrills in my ear. Joyce Lalonde, my neighbor from across the street, edges between Lorraine and me.

Jim finishes his sip of beer. "We're discussing the color of Vincent's car."

"Oh Vincent. I didn't recognize you out of your

business suit." Joyce's fleshy hand touches my arm. "That red shirt looks lovely with your salt and pepper hair. I am so sorry about your mother. I saw Amanda practically every day, out driving her car, which, of course, was green." Her fingers press my skin. "Amanda's death was such a shock. I talked to her the very day it happened and she looked the picture of health."

Joyce told me all this three times at the funeral.

Cathy looks at me. "Was it sudden, like a heart attack?"

"Diabetes," Joyce replies. "Such a cruel disease and so difficult to control."

Mother controlled it admirably. That Friday night, as usual, she watched The Big Bang Theory. Normally she cackled through the stupid jokes. The recorded rerun sent her nodding off. As she snored in her armchair, I stabbed her thigh with a needle. She woke up instantly.

"Vincent, what are you doing?" Her eyes gaped. "I've already taken my insulin. Get me a chocolate bar. Quick."

"Insulin shock," Joyce explains. "An accidental overdose." She digs her fingers into my arm. "You meant everything to your mother, Vincent. That must comfort you a great deal. The day she died, Amanda was on the sidewalk in front of your house, peering anxiously up the street. She said you were late from work and you never stayed late without phoning. She was so worried that something had happened."

I had stopped off at the craft store to check out their new supplies. By the time I arrived home, Mother was frantic.

"Mother," I said. "I'm forty-seven years old, the top systems analyst at the bank and only half an hour late."

She patted my arm. "Next time you'll remember to phone?"

I brushed off her hand. "Forget it and I don't want any dinner."

"Vincent, don't pout," Mother said. "You used to do that as a child when you didn't get your way."

"When did I ever get my way?" I stomped up to my room.

The hockey figurines on my shelves seemed to echo Mother's taunt: Child. I grabbed Giordano, my favorite, and hurled him to the window. He crashed to the floor, shattered into pieces.

"Your mother's name was Amanda, too?" Cathy strokes her daughter's hair. "Interesting how old fashioned names come back into style."

Rhonda Wellington joins the group. "Vincent, I'm so glad you came. Doesn't he look handsome today, Lorraine?"

The sisters' shared glance makes me wonder if this party is a set up to get me together with Lorraine. It isn't all about you, Vincent, Mother used to say.

"I'm surprised so many turned up," Rhonda says. "Especially after that silly salmonella joke Jim put on the invitation."

Damn. The smiley-face should have clued me in that it was a joke. You have no sense of humor. Mother was dead, but I couldn't get rid of her voice.

Rhonda holds out her plate. "Sweets, anyone?"

Joyce Lalonde pats her belly. "They look tempting, Rhonda, but I'm saving myself for your casseroles."

"I want a cookie," squeals Amanda.

"No, honey." Cathy's hand strokes intensify. "You'll ruin your dinner."

The girl reaches up to the plate. "Gimme."

"You know how sugar makes you hyper."

"Come on, Cathy." Rhonda lowers the plate. "One sweet won't kill her."

The child grabs two Nanaimo bars and shoves them into her mouth.

Rhonda raises the plate to adult height. "Are the rest of you sure you don't want some?"

"Well, since you've twisted my arm." Joyce takes a square and bites. "Mmm. You'll have to give me the recipe."

"They're simple to make and freeze well," Rhonda says.

"Speaking of freezing," Jim says. "I read an article on cryogenics."

"Jim." Rhonda glares at him and looks apprehensively at me, as though Mother were lying somewhere in frozen suspension. I had her cremated, in accordance with her wishes. Every morning, as she scanned the obits, she used to tell me cremation was neater than burial.

Rhonda's glare fades, but its presence has made me long for a glimpse of her sister, Lorraine, concealed behind Joyce's bulk.

"I want more cookie," whines Amanda, her mouth ringed with chocolate.

"You've had enough," Marty says. "If you don't behave we're going home."

"No." The toddler stomps.

The night she died, Mother begged me, her voice

fading. "Vincent. Chocolate."

"No," I said. It was the first time I recalled saying it to her. "No." It felt good.

Mother's eyes widened, as she grasped my intent. "Vincent?"

Little Amanda screams.

Marty picks her up. "I'm sorry, Rhonda, Jim." He ignores his daughter's kicks to his thighs. "We have to leave."

Amanda slaps her father's mouth.

Marty peels off her hand. "We might come back later, after she's had a nap. Nice meeting you Lorraine, Joyce, Vince."

Rhonda looks at Jim. "I think it's time you fired up the barbecue. I'll pop some casseroles into the oven. Joyce, would you mind giving me a hand?"

They leave me alone with Lorraine. My knees weaken. I edge toward the pillar for support.

"Vincent." Lorraine coils a strand of hair around her finger. "I've wanted to apologize for my behavior the other day, when I dropped off the quiche." Her fingers glide to the chain around her neck. "You see, I recently broke up a long-term relationship – that's really why I left Toronto -- and I was angry at him, angry at all men and blew up at you. I'm sorry. I mean, my God, you'd just come from your mother's funeral and were naturally bereaved."

I clutch the pillar. My head spins.

"I know what it's like to lose a parent," Lorraine says. "My dad died last year. A stroke. Just like that, he was gone. I never had a chance to tell him ..."

Lorraine stands in freeze-frame against a blur of party guests. I picture Mother's final moments: her body

28

collapsed, a film of water coating her skin. My hand gripped her fingers, my body trembled as my rage dissolved into the horror of what I had done mingled with a fear that Mother was right. How could I manage without her?

I had tried, twice. When I was twenty-nine, I rented a bachelor apartment. One night, I found myself crawling around it, searching for the door. Somehow, I stumbled across the hall to my neighbor's place. A month later, Mother brought me home from the psych ward. Ten years ago, I bought a condo with a view of the Bow River. I wound up on the balcony, itching to jump.

With Mother gone from my life, what would happen?

"Vincent." Lorraine straightens her skirt. "What say we grab a casserole and bring it to your house to heat?"

I scan the fuzzy crowd. "Isn't the food for the party?"

"There's more than enough for this mob," Lorraine says. "We'll take the store-bought stuff. It's better than Rhonda's cooking. Did you really like that quiche she sent you?"

I let go of the pillar. "Now that you mention it --"

"You can show me your little hockey players."

"I don't think so, Lorraine."

She fingers her necklace. "We'll steal a bottle of Jim's home-made wine."

"Uh ... Uh ... Ah."

"Pardon?" She leans closer.

I inhale her flowery perfume. Eyes closed, I see yellows, purples, oranges and reds. Reds? Was that possible? I blink my eyes open. The party guests come into focus.

"What type of wine do you prefer," Lorraine says. "White or red?"

"You choose, Lorraine, I'm color blind."

She laughs. "Vincent, I didn't know you had a sense of humor."

Sweat streams down my forehead; my body grows spongy; legs liquefy. I reach for the pillar and touch Lorraine's soft hand. *Red wine or white?* I'm color blind. I get it.

DEVIL'S DUE
AXEL HOWERTON

Darkness crowded the streets like a fog in this part of town, where broken streetlights stayed broken, and the night was still a thing to fear. A thing that filled all the places that people dared not go at two AM. The black challenger crept through the dark unseen. A smooth metal panther—curved hood swooping down with blood-red lines—seeking out a path with its nose down to the earth.

The car moved slow, rumbled quiet, gliding easy to the curb, low animal-growl cutting to absolute silence in a heartbeat.

Devil eased back in the soft leather of his seat, staring down at the screen of his phone, the blue glow filling the inside of the car with its hollow warmth. He ran his thumb up the screen and watched the lines sail by, before they hit rock-bottom, bounced, and settled on that

one last word.
  Rabbit.

Duncan saw the black beast as it came to rest outside, and knew it at once; by the chrome demon that sat atop the black-powdered grill, grinning death out into the night, and by the one tiny blue light that sparked up through the darkness, lighting the face of the man behind the wheel. The *bad man*. The *boss man*. Duncan ran for the stairs at the back of the house. Rabbit had to know. Rabbit had to hide. Run away, Rabbit. Run away and hide. Devil's come to call. Devil wants his due.

"Devil! Rabbit! Devil is here! Rabbit!"

Rabbit was sitting at the stained formica table, in what passed for a kitchen, when Devil let himself in through the back porch door.

"Yo, Devil! 'Sup, man?" Rabbit was as thin, pale and filthy-nasty as the table he sat at.

Devil looked around the room with open disgust. Take-out containers, empty bottles, assorted garbage and half-rotten food covered every surface.

Rabbit was decked out in his usual white trash dealer scrubs: designer jeans that were three sizes too big for his bony ass, dirty white undershirt that hung on him like an old rag, a pristine ball cap with an unbent brim that looked as if he'd just swiped it from the Jersey City at the mall, white-framed designer sunglasses, and brand-new oversized sneakers so barely-tied that he could have kicked them off like beach sandals. He grinned and flashed his gold-tooth grill—a smile that was an exercise in pointless spending—five grand of gold fence lining a maw full of blackening meth teeth. The worst part was the stench. It was like an open sewage drain every time Rabbit opened his mouth.

"Maid's week off, I guess?" Devil ventured, leaning back against the cleanest of the counters, hoping it was far enough to diffuse Rabbit's stinkmouth.

"Hahaaaaaaa! You's a funny motherfucker, Devil. You know that? Hey yo, Dunc! You hear what Devil said, man? Maid's week off and shit. Hahaaaa."

Devil fixed Rabbit with cool green eyes, calculating the distance—the physics—if he had to make a move. He pushed off from the counter and took a few steps around the kitchen as Rabbit stretched his skinny legs out from a worn out folding chair. "I've been hearing stories, Rabbit," he said casually, as if he might be wondering where the pop-tarts were hidden, "I hear you haven't been following the rules."

"Ahhh, no, man. Not me, D. You know I live by them rules, dawg. Ain't that right, Dunc?"

Devil raised an eyebrow towards the corner of the room, where Duncan stood nervous in the doorway. Tall and thin, but with a middle-age pot-belly. Dirty wisps of yellowed hair, acne like a fourteen year-old sugar fiend. Duncan's teeth were nothing but a memory. Poor, sad, old Duncan. Fifty? Sixty year-old crackhead loser? Some of these chicken-heads you couldn't tell. They went from 20 to 70 in the space of a year. Working as a lapdog to a twenty year-old wannabe. Duncan just nodded, wide-eyed, and kept his mouth shut. They said he wasn't all there. Rabbit called him *retard*, like it was some kind of hilarious joke between them, but Duncan was smart enough to keep his mouth shut, which was more than could be said for Rabbit.

Devil put his eyes back on Rabbit. Skinny little Rabbit with the glittering shit-mouth.

Rabbit squirmed under the glare. "Yo, D. I don't

know who you been talkin' to, but that ain't nothing but bullshit, man."

"You didn't sell to a kid from Manning?"

"*Ernest* Manning?"

Like there was another place full of kids called *Manning* anywhere nearby.

"Somebody told me they saw you and Duncan walking dime bags up there."

Rabbit flexed his skinny arms by shoving his hands deeper in his pockets, thinking his hoodrat ink would prove his status as a badass. Rail-thin arms covered in eighth grade doodling—probably scratched into him in that same filthy kitchen, by some tweaker with a rusty second-hand rig.

Rabbit hummed and hawed, rolled some imaginary chew toy in his mouth, jangling against that metal barrier that held his teeth in place.

"Hmm. Ahhhhh, wait, man. That the new Manning? Up at the top of the city, by that new LRT? Got that pool up there, all the sexy mommies go get their hot yoga on?"

Devil didn't bite.

Duncan was sweating like a pig on the spit, tucked up against the door frame, hiding like a spider on the wall. Feeling the rage. Feeling the danger. Rabbit should be hiding in his hole. Devil wants his due. Rabbit playing tough like a big bunny. Big bunny gets the horns. It was hanging there between Devil and Rabbit, hanging in the air like a Sword. Swinging in the air. Sword of Davos. Damos. Damascus. *Goddammit, Duncan.* All those brains and no future. No past. Nowhere to run to. Run, little Rabbit. Sword of *Damocles*. That's the fucking ticket, man. Devil was watching. Devil wants his due. Rabbit never should have messed with the Devil. Mess with the Devil, you get the horns. Devil. Devil. Devil could see him twitching back there, waiting. Waiting for the station to change. Waiting for the man. Waiting for the hits to begin.

"Hey, Rabbit." Duncan croaked out from his corner, "We were in Strath... Strath... Strathcona, at the train... meeting the Chinaman... China-man... Chinese man... That Chinese gentleman..."

Devil turned slow to take in Duncan's performance, watching the tweaker sift through his powdered brain, lost in some other universe, dangling at the edge of the black hole between his ears where his brain used to be. Here he comes, laughing and proud when he finally found what he was looking for. Poor, simple, wasted Duncan.

"Fong. Fong. His name was Fong!"

"Yeah, man." Rabbit laughed with him. "Sure you right, Dunc. Larry Fong. That's the motherfucker."

Devil still wasn't buying the story, even with doper Duncan chiming in. Of all the cops Devil kept in his pocket, Sergeant Clayden was the most solid. He'd picked up a mouse in the field behind Manning—some senior, called himself Trix. Just some kid, usually dealt in stolen soccer-mom vicodin and ADHD pills. Clayden caught him peddling hash to thirteen year-olds. Trix fingered rotten-mouthed Rabbit. You couldn't make this shit up if you tried.

"There are rules, Rabbit," Devil said, measuring his cadence to match his steps across the room.

"There are rules for a reason." Dropping the baton down his leather sleeve and into his palm as he kept his eyes locked with Rabbit's.

"What are those rules, Rabbit?"

Rabbit, for his part, was too stupid to do anything but keep playing his part—Play Hard, *Be* Hard—that's what all these white trash wannabes believed. They used to get stoked up on Eminem and reruns of *Scarface* on cable. Now it was *Breaking Bad* and *Grand Theft Auto*. They never seemed to understand the deeper meanings of these cautionary tales. They were face-value kind of thugs. *The World Is Yours*, Tony Montana. Rabbit truly believed he had the makings of an unstoppable Machiavellian drug kingpin. A couple grand in his pocket every week and he was Jesse Pinkman calling everybody bitch, rolling hard in his Pontiac Grand Prix. They never seemed to catch the episodes where Pinkman got beat down, or tortured, or contemplated putting a bullet in his own mouth. Meth made them stupid. Meth was a plague. Devil wouldn't touch it. Wouldn't sell it. Still, dealing was a business, and you needed feet on the street. Most of Devil's pyramid was solid, but then here comes Peter Cottontail and grandpa meth-brain. Rules didn't matter once you messed with that shit. Nothing mattered.

"Yo, D. I told you. Ain't nothing' but a thang. We ain't broke no rules."

"That's not what I asked you, Rabbit. I asked you what *are* the rules?"

Devil stepped within arm's length, pressing one leg against Rabbit's, imposing his presence, but keeping those thankful layers of leather and denim between them.

"*No kids. No Mamas.* I get it, man. But it weren't me." Rabbit smiled wide, flashing his golden gate again.

"This isn't the first time." Devil said, staring down into Rabbit's nasty face, that foul breath floating up like smoke. "This is strike two, isn't it?"

Rabbit's nostrils flared. He sat up fast—straight and rigid—throwing off the yoke of his seconds-worth of strife and repression. "Strike two, strike three… who gives a fuck? Y'know what, man. Fuck you. We don't need your shit, man. We out. Me and Dunc, we's gonna start our own outfit." Rabbit getting tough. Play Hard, *Be* Hard. Yet making sure that he wasn't on his own. *I* turned to *We* and multiplied his idiot-courage.

"Start your own outfit, huh? With what product, you hoodrat piece of shit?" Devil's hand tightened around the stick, and the muscles in his forearm turned to iron.

"We gots connections, yo. Everybody sick of your bullshit, Devil. You and your fucking rules, and your baseball shit. This ain't the U.S. of A, man. Nobody gives a fuck about baseball 'round here, motherfucker."

"I guess not," Devil shot back, knuckles white around the grip of the baton. "You obviously don't get the metaphor, Rabbit."

"*No kids. No Mamas*" Rabbit sing-songed, swinging his fingers through the air like Bugs Bunny conducting the cartoon symphony. "Fuck you and fuck your strikes, and *fuck your mama*," Rabbit snarled. "Meta-suck-my-dick—you sad, old, Fonzie-boot wearin' motherfucker!"

A tight smile curled up at the corners of Devil's mouth. "Wow. You don't like my boots, Rabbit?"

Rabbit was leaning back, arms wide. *Come at me, bro.* Showing off his cool demeanor to Duncan, withdrawing his mock-respect, paying no attention to Devil as one of those Fonzie boots hooked the leg of the chair. Rabbit crashed to the floor, Devil standing over him, sneering down in open disdain. Devil hefted one steel toe into the small of Rabbit's back and flicked his wrist out from the cuff of his jacket, the expandable baton snapping to attention in his hand. Rabbit curled up into his natural state—squealing with his hands up, begging for mercy. Devil twisted into each crack of the stick like he was swinging for the fences. He kept the beating measured, like everything else he did, an equal number of strikes to the legs, the torso, the shoulders. He kept the head for last, saving one quick snap for that hideous metal guard-rail, feeling it give way to the rotten teeth beneath it, Rabbit sputtering blood and screaming.

The last shot was meant for the back of Rabbit's head, right in the soft spot at the base of his skull—put him down for good. Devil swung his arm back, coiling the muscles, ready to strike down with every ounce of fury that coursed through his veins.

"*Out… Out of the cradle endlessly rocking. Out of the mocking-bird's throat…*"

Devil's arm reached its apex and held there.

Duncan was sitting against the doorjamb, arms wrapped around his knees, rocking back and forth.

"*Out of the ninth-month midnight. Over the sterile sands, and the fields beyond, where the child… where the child… where the child, leaving his bed, wander'd alone, bare-headed, barefoot…*"

Devil stood straight, staring at the idiot weeping against the door, a cascade of words flowing from him like a prayer, but it wasn't a prayer. It was Whitman. Like Mister White taught in eleventh-grade English. Mister White with the shaggy writers hair and the tweed coat with the elbow patches. Mister White who taught

Devil—Adam Deville—to appreciate the irony of a good pun, pointed out the exceptional curves of Lacy McDonough's sweet ass, and the secret rebellion of Whitman's barbaric yawp. Mister White, who slid young Adam his first joint in a copy of *Leaves of Grass* that still sat on Devil's shelf.   What ever happened to Mister White? Rumors. Innuendo. Whispers of woe and tales of teacher-gone-wrong. Some sixteen year-old squeeze and he was never heard of again.

"Out from the patches of briers and blackberries, from the memories of the bird that chanted... chanted... it chanted to me... the bird that chanted to me..."

Hide in the light. Hide in the hole, Duncan. Leave the Rabbit in the field and hide yourself away. *Shine! Shine! Shine! Pour down your warmth, great sun!* Dream of the past. Endlessly rocking. Rocking the cradle. Robbing the cradle. How did you get here, Duncan, how did you fall so far from the light? Far from the light of that great sun. Endlessly rocking. Endlessly rocking.   Devil-Deville-Devil-Deville. *Day come white, or night come black.*

Devil looked down at Rabbit, at the moaning heap of broken flesh at his feet, and felt nothing but disgust. The fury was gone. The purpose was stalled. Devil stepped back, grabbed up a filthy-looking t-shirt hanging on the back of a chair, and wiped clean the baton, the cuffs of his jacket, his boots.

"You're lucky, Rabbit. *That* was strike three. Now you're out."

Devil turned to Duncan, still mumbling meter in the corner and crouched down in front of him, lifted his chin with a finger and looked deep into the wild eyes of a terrified child.

"Duncan."

"O' Darkness! O' in vain!"

"Duncan. I'm not gonna hurt you. Listen…"

Duncan curled tighter into himself, twitching and rocking and trembling.

"O' I am very sick and sorrowful!"

Devil put a gentle hand on Duncan's back and finished the section, *"O' troubled reflection in the sea. O' throat. O' throbbing heart, and I singing uselessly, uselessly all the night."*

Duncan stopped moving. He turned his face up, blotched skin mottled and pale, eyes red and full of tears.

"Devil. The boss man. The devil man. *Deville.* Devil's coming Rabbit. Run." Duncan whispered.

Devil stood, stunned by the sound of his name coming from Duncan's cracked lips. His real name, seeping from between those black tooth-stumps like a curse, and he saw the letters in front of him, the inscription in the front of *Leaves of Grass*:

Adam,

A man, yet by these tears a little boy again.

A reminiscence sing!

-D. White

D—Duncan.

Duncan had gone back to his endless rocking, his reminiscence of better days and quieter lives. *"Fuse the song of my dusky demon and brother.* Demon brother. Demon. Devil. *Deville.*

Devil felt the swell of the waves pushing against his chest, and the inside of his skull. Confusion and raw emotion. Indistinct and unfiltered. How did he not recognize Duncan? White? This wreck of humanity cowering in front of him. And what had Devil become that he stood over a man he once valued and admired, like a demon of fury and vengeance. What had Devil done to bring Duncan White to this end, a foul spectre of what once was? Devil backed away to the door, looking to the chaos he had made, a pile of broken flesh, and the empty ruin of a tragic soul. Put them together and you'd still be short a man. What was left in the world for men like these? Rabbit would just continue on, hurting people, breaking rules, a plague upon the earth. And Duncan would sit in his corner, broken, and waste away into nothingness. *Out of the cradle. Endlessly rocking.* The chaos had to end.

Duncan was still twitching, twisting into the abyss. *Out of the cradle.* Endlessly. *Endlessly rocking.* You're gone Duncan. Long gone and far away. The devil man. The bad man. The boss man. Devil wants his due. Poor little Rabbit. Run away. Far Away. Back to the past. Back to the cradle. Back to the days before it all came crashing down. To the days of youth and wisdom-lost. All those girls with all those lovely smiles. All those girls, Duncan. All those Devils. All those drugs and nightmares and pain. Bad little Rabbit. Bad little Duncan. Devil-Deville-Devil-Deville. Now you pay the Devil. Pay the Devil his due. Bye-bye bad little Rabbit. And bye-bye Duncan.

Devil worked a kink out of his shoulder as he stomped across the brown lawn back to the car. He pressed the button on the key fob without pulling it from his pocket, popped the trunk, and carefully wrapped the baton in a chamois and tucked it into a corner of the empty trunk. The poem repeating in his head, something long-forgotten, dredged up from the bottom of the ocean of his mind, thick with weeds and clogged with rust and salt, but still intact and unchanged in 150 years.

My own songs awakened from that hour,

And with them the key, the word up from the waves,

Climbing in behind the wheel, slamming the door against the night, Adam Deville—Devil to the whole wide world—let the metal and leather hold him tight like a blanket. He sat, staring out across the hood at the little chrome devil that sat atop the front grill, a tiny gargoyle grinning out into the night. An avatar to show the world what he'd become. Devil. Demon. Destroyer of men. He stared at his hands on the wheel, at the blood around the nails of his thumbs. It was five minutes by the dashboard clock, before he'd regained the composure to fire up the engine and rumble away from the curb.

The word of the sweetest song and all songs,

That strong and delicious word which, creeping to my feet,

(Or like some old crone rocking the cradle, swathed in sweet garments, bending aside,)

The sea whisper'd me.

MOVABLE TYPE
A CRESCENT CITY SHORT STORY
S.G. WONG

It didn't look like much to Ria. Maybe twelve by twelve of workspace hidden behind the house proper. The sunset, filtered through bright pink cherry blossoms, cast shifting shadows through the lone miserly window. She watched dust motes dance slowly in the still air.

The old man glowered. "Think you're a right Abercrombie, don'tcha?"

"Hardly, Mr. Ying. Know-it-alls don't make good reporters."

"Bah. You think I'm just bumping gums, eh? But you're wrong. This is a career-making story and I'm givin' you the chance to grab it and run with it."

Ria eyed him narrowly. "Well, you've gotta admit it's beyond most people. Frankly, not a lot of our readers will care how their paper gets printed. They just want to read about world news or the latest show business gossip."

"Bah. What are you, twenty? I can't tell with you people. Too old to be so dumb, anyway, especially in this business."

"It's rude to ask a lady's age."

"Maybe for you *gwai*. Not for us Chinese. We're obsessed with aging." He peered at her suspiciously. "Didn't you say you were born in Crescent City?"

Ria gestured dismissively. "Yes and that's neither here nor there. Can we get back to your so-called invention?"

"Fine, fine. Then pay attention." He puffed up his chest. "I can typeset a standard newspaper in half the time it currently takes. Your readers may not care how their news gets printed. But they certainly do care how quickly it gets printed."

Ria scribbled quickly in her notebook. "When did you do this?"

"Twelve years ago."

She faltered to a stop. "And how is this an exclusive now?"

He glared. "I'm giving you proof."

"Of what?"

"That I know what I'm talking about."

Ria shook her head. "And what exactly are you talking about then?"

"A revolution in printing."

Ria cocked her head to one side. "You got a printing press hidden in here somewhere?" She gestured at the piles of greasy machine parts, the stacks of paper schematics, and the grimy worktable. "I gotta say, all I see is a hobby workshop inside a garden shed."

"For gods' sake, girl, what are they teaching reporters these days? Haven't you been listening?"

Ria silently counted to five. "So what's this proof I'm supposed to have?"

"Have you never visited the printing room at the Herald, Miss Monteverde? Seen the typesetters at work? Listened to the printing presses? Felt the heat? Tasted the ink at the back of your throat?"

Ria shook her head. "My editor still reviews my pieces."

Ying grunted. "I'm sure he does."

She let that one pass. "What about the printing room, Mr. Ying?"

"I'll get to that. First, you go back, down to the dungeon, look in December of 1921. Week of the twelfth, that's the Monday. Once you've done that," he pointed at the floor, "you come back here and I'll explain."

She did the math. "December, twelve years ago? Is this why you, what, retired? Quit? Got fired?"

Ying ushered her out of the shed.

"Wait. Why me, Mr. Ying?" She waved her hand in the vague direction of downtown. "Why not Zhuang or Poon or even Chang? She's the current City desk ace."

Ying smirked. "Exactly. They're all known quantities. But you, you're not Chinese. No chance you're owned by the Tong, right? Unlikely you've got family ties to any of them gangs. You're new enough they haven't got to you yet. Plus you don't do the crime beat."

Ria raised a brow. "Have you even read any of my stories?"

"Oh yes, the one about my neighbour's daughter and her Ghost saving the family dog. Very touching. Inspiring, even. How do you think I found you?"

"So you just scanned the bylines until you saw a *gwai*

name?"

He shook his head. "Of course not. I saw you. When you came to speak to Mrs. Chao next door. One simple question and here we are."

"Just hold on a damned minute." Ria pulled her arm from his grip. "I'm not going haring off on your say-so, mister. What's your history at the Crescent City Herald got to do with some special invention?"

Ying flapped his hands at her. "Keep it down, for gods' sake." He searched the surrounding yard, took a step closer. "Have you ever heard of a portable movable type machine?" he whispered.

Ria frowned, shook her head.

"It allows a person to create an entire document by using cast characters, just like we do for printing presses, instead of writing by hand."

Ria suppressed a sigh. "Mr. Ying, I hate to break it to you, but typewriters have been around for years."

He jabbed a finger in her direction. "Yes, for English and other European languages, but not for Chinese. Too many characters to put in one machine." He raised his chin. "Ours is not a language easily broken down into a palm full of letters."

"So you've done it?" The old man nodded. Ria peered around him. "Where is it? Can I see it?"

Ying shook his head. "No. You do your research first. Then come back. I need to know you can follow instructions."

Ria stared at him for a few beats. "What's in it for me to jump through your hoops?"

"The story of the century. Weren't you listening? Now," Ying tapped his pocket watch. "You better go. You'll have to be up early to catch Woodie in the dungeon. And you'd better do it before you file your story on...the swimming octogenarian, isn't it? Your editor will be sending you out on another scintillating story afterward, I'm sure."

"Yellow today, huh."

Dinwoodie Kwong touched his bowtie, offered Ria a shy smile.

"Good morning, Miss Monteverde. Is there something I can help you with?"

"Got a line on a story." She gave him the dates from Ying. "Not sure what I'm supposed to find, but." She shrugged, rubbed her fingers over the dark teak countertop. It was smooth and cool.

Woodie nodded. He pushed back from the counter, surveyed the shelving underneath, turning in a slow circle to encompass all sides of the square structure within which he spent his days.

He brought up a thick black ledger, grunting at the weight. Ria set herself up at one of the reading tables, close to the pool of warm light thrown by a brass-shaded lamp. Woodie piled dark grey ledgers on the tabletop for her, clicked on another lamp farther down the long table. She saluted him.

The ledgers were the same size as a regular newspaper, nothing unusual there. They were collated together by day, stitched into a cardboard cover, with hand lettered dates. She opened up the archived papers for December twelfth. The pages were yellowed and she wondered idly if she ought not to wear gloves.

Since Ying was a typesetter and his supposed talents were in printing, she reasoned she ought to pay close attention to appearance rather than content. She scanned the characters, the placement of columns, anything she could think of in terms of how the newspaper had been typeset.

Thirty minutes later, she had acquired dirty hands, a headache, and a new appreciation for how far women had come in twelve years.

She closed the last ledger for that week, pushed it away. Mindful of getting ink on her face, she considered Ying's boast again. But how would the speed of his printing prowess show up in the papers themselves?

When she saw the flaw in her research, she just about planted an inky palm print on her forehead.

"Woodie, can I see the weeks before and after?" She thought for a moment. "Hells, just gimme the whole damn month wouldya?"

It took him four trips.

Ria eyeballed the stacks in front of her.

"Who had Tam's job when these were fresh ink?"

"Mr. Tam did."

"He's been here that long?" She paused, considering. "D'you know when he started?"

"He was the head City desk reporter before becoming editor-in-chief. But I don't know how long he's been with the Herald."

"Easy enough to ferret out," Ria muttered.

"Is there anything else I can help with?" He glanced at the ornate clock above the entrance. Ria followed his gaze, then pushed back from the table with a curse.

"Ah, sorry for the mess, Woodie. I'm late."

"That's all right, Miss Monteverde. I'm used to it."

Ria sat back, tossing down her pencil. She shuffled the pages back into order and started re-reading. While her brain reviewed the words in front of her, she shook out her hand, rotated her wrist, rolled her shoulders and neck. She grabbed her pencil, made one quick change, set it back down with a small smile.

"Nice work, kitten. Now you gotta run it to the setters."

Ria jumped in her seat, then cursed herself inwardly. She allowed herself one quick grimace before smoothing out her features.

"Aren't you gonna review it?" She twisted slightly in her chair, looked up over her right shoulder.

Tam shook his head. "Been reading it over your shoulder the last fifteen minutes." He grinned, his handsome face becoming boyish. "Looks pretty tight to me." He leaned forward, reaching out with his hand.

Ria slid her chair to the side, thankful for smooth casters.

Brushing past her shoulder, Tam picked up her pencil. He smoothed out her handwritten article then planted a hand on her desk, pencil hovering over the paper. He struck a few things out, rearranged some others with arrows and circles and coded scribbles. "You can explain those easily, hmm?"

Ria nodded, keeping her expression calm. She casually swiveled her chair side to side, while subtly moving farther away. "They gonna listen to me?"

Tam laughed. "Of course. I told 'em you'd be coming." He tossed the pencil on top of the papers. "Good job, kid. Quick work."

"Thanks."

He raised his brows. She suppressed a scowl. "...boss."

Tam grinned, saluting her. "That's the spirit." He made shooing motions. "Better hurry now."

Ria nodded curtly. "Excuse me."

Tam, still smiling, stepped back half a pace. Ria placed the papers between herself and his chest as she slid past him, bumping into the corner of Shen's desk behind her. She walked as quickly as she could for the stairs, lips pressed tightly together.

"Oh and Valeria?"

She turned.

"Tell Chang to use those long gams of hers to get back up here. I need to talk to her about the Ming interview."

Ria nodded and whirled back around before she said something she really wanted to say. She forced herself to concentrate on the piece she held tightly in her hand. She was here to learn, wasn't she, for gods' sake? She read everything over, had to admit that the changes were all improvements. Damn him.

She jolted to a stop two floors down. Evidently, her feet knew where she was going, even if her mind did not. She walked briskly down the left corridor. The sounds of metal clanking and voices shouting became louder as she approached the large green door at the end.

Shoving the sheaf of pages beneath an arm, Ria turned the lever handle clockwise, feeling the heavy mechanism within the door disconnect from its mooring. She pulled the metal door outward, freeing the smell of ink and hot paper into the hall. She cursed as the door continued on its arc, smashing into the wall with a crash she felt deep in her bones.

Her apology was lost in a chorus of shouts.

"Chang, you better teach this one fast. We won't have any wall left."

"Hey, *a gwai leuy*, how long've you been workin' here now?"

"How long's it gonna take before you remember how to open a door?"

"Yeah, yeah." She waved the crumpled papers. "Tam said you were expecting this? Who do I talk to?"

"Boss Man sent down his pet today, eh?" The woman sat on the corner of the nearest worktable, her legs crossed and swinging idly. Full lips, sporting deep pink lipstick, almond eyes, and glossy black hair pulled into a simple twist at her nape. She hopped off the table, brushed off her wide-legged trousers, pushed up the narrow sleeves of her striped sailor shirt.

"I'm not his pet." The rebuttal was lame by any standard, but it was all Ria had. She sold it with an icy glare.

"Hm. You may not think so, but it's not your opinion that really counts, is it, pet?"

"Cut it out, wouldya. I don't have time to flap jaws with you." Ria jerked a thumb. "He said he wants to talk to you about Ming."

Chang stared at Ria for an extra beat. She called back over her shoulder. "See you later, boys. Boss Man's calling and I've got a new Commissioner of Gaming to interview." She brushed past Ria on her way out. Ria stood her ground, waiting until she heard the massive green door clank shut behind her. She raised her chin.

"Well? Who's setting the human interest section today?"

A wiry man with a moon face waved. His forearms were corded with muscle, his shirtsleeves grimy with ink. A smear of grease darkened his chin.

He worked in front of a long slab of workspace, scratched and gouged, the wood long turned grey. Behind him, cube shelving held stacks of metal casts. Ria stepped past the smirking man working at the closer end of the table. A quick glance showed he was working on the finance section.

Moonface beckoned her to hurry. "How long is it?"

She thrust the sheaf at him. He snatched it, fingerprints darkening the edges of the papers as he swiftly skimmed her piece. She noted that he kept his prints away from her writing, though. She didn't know the typesetters and printers much at all, but she guessed this one was at least a journeyman. To her right, down a little ways, the smirker gave her the once over. Twice.

She gestured to the tray of set characters in front of him. "Mind your numbers, genius. Or you're liable to cause another market crash."

The man startled, then frowned. His lips moved as he scanned his typesetting work so far. He dug out two sets of characters and switched them, scowling.

"You're welcome." Ria turned back to her typesetter. "Good?"

Moonface nodded absently. "Ignore Mah. We all do." He pointed, his fingers tapping lightly. Two faint smears of grey bloomed beside her writing. "Does he want these two switched, or these two?"

"Those."

Moonface inhaled sharply. "Good. It'll be in." He brushed some sweat off his face with a forearm. "Murder! You like to cut it close, eh? This is gonna take me at least twelve minutes."

"Sorry about that. Got caught up by an old man with the story of the century."

He shook his head. "You gotta learn to put 'em off gently without taking out your notebook, rookie. That just encourages 'em."

"Thanks for the tip."

He shrugged. "Suit yourself." He pulled a wood-framed tray toward him, held it in the crook of his right arm, and then turned toward the shelves behind. Ria watched as he rapidly selected characters and laid them into the tray. He referenced her papers a few times, but for the most part, he zipped from one side of the shelving to the other, filling the wooden tray with a clatter of metal casts.

He slid the full tray back onto the heavily scarred tabletop.

"You still here?" He raised his chin at her.

"Curious to see how quickly you can work."

Moonface laughed, his fingers nimbly righting some characters and aligning others. "Here? Plenty fast. I trained on these shelves. Put me somewhere else, though, and I'd be as lost as you." He snatched up Ria's article and compared it with his tray. "For a few weeks, that is."

"So every press has its own system? Of storing casts?"

He tossed the papers aside, gave his tray some final adjustments. "Maybe you're smarter than Chang says."

"Everybody's smarter than Chang says. She's got a low opinion of the rest of humanity."

The typesetter laughed again. "Right on the nose."

"When did you start your training here? Who was your mentor?"

"We don't have mentors." He sniggered. "Why are you asking me these questions anyway? If you're already that desperate for another story, you won't last long here, doll."

"Do you know Henry Ying?"

Moonface hefted his tray, walked it over to the large press. Ria followed him. He nodded, handing it off to another ink-stained man in greasy coveralls and shirtsleeves. He turned, grunting as he stopped short from bumping into her.

"Everybody here knows Ying. Why?"

Ria shrugged. "Just trying to dig up some background. He says he has a story for me."

"He's your old man with the story of the century?" Moonface waved dismissively. "Doll, that river's been fished dry. Old Man Ying is a loon, full of crazy schemes."

"Such as?"

"Taking all of this—" He swept his arm at the twelve-foot tall shelving behind him. "And rearranging it, for gods' sake. Said it was too slow, our mnemonic was too complicated. Said he had a machine could get us to print twice as fast."

"It was a typesetting machine then? Not a press of some kind?"

Moonface nodded. "Damn thing was a ripper, I'll give him that. But it made all sorts of mistakes we had to correct anyway."

"So it ended up taking the same amount of time."

"Hey," said Mah, sidling over, "they still gave him a week, though, didn't they?"

Ria eyed the short little smirker. "What did you typesetters think of it?"

"It's gone, idn't it?" Mah's smile was filled with yellow teeth.

Moonface grinned. "And we're still here."

"Oh gods, what happened to you?"

Ying smiled, then winced. "Tripped and fell down the stairs." He held the door open for her, ushered her into the sitting room, offered to take her coat.

She shook her head. "Can I make you some tea? Get you an ice pack? Or a Healer? When did this happen?"

Ying made his way arduously to a well-worn, wingback chair. Bracing himself on the arm, he sank gingerly to the seat. "Bah. Healers are expensive. Don't need magic for bumps and bruises, just bandages and ice."

"At least let me make you some tea."

"Yes, yes, if you promise that will end your fussing."

Ria bustled around in the old typesetter's kitchen, found a package of almond cookies and the tea things. She filled the kettle for two and clicked on the gas stove with a *whoomph*.

Ten minutes later, she returned to find Ying, eyes closed and breathing shallowly. Her alarmed shout caused him to open one eye and squint.

"Hush. You're making my head hurt." He pushed up to sitting, let her pour him tea, and settled back against the cushions with a sigh.

Ria saw his hands, watched the tea slosh ever so slightly in his mug.

She said, "I saw the archives. You were able to add another 50 per cent, I'd guess, to that week's editions, weren't you?" Ying stared into his tea. Ria saw his knuckles turn white around the cup. "I talked to a coupla typesetters. They remembered your experiment. So I concede. You know your way around machines and printing. Do I qualify to see this invention of yours now?"

After a few noisy sips, he looked at her. "I've changed my mind. This...story is nothing more than an old man's vanity. I'm sorry for your trouble."

Ria frowned, pondering the about-face. Ying watched her with a bland expression, the picture of calm imperiousness marred somewhat by the deep purple bruising and puffy right eye.

"That's quite a coincidence," she said. "You getting hurt and then changing your mind."

"No coincidence at all. I could've been dead, or dying. At the bottom of the stairs with no one to hear me calling for help. Really makes an old man reassess his...obsessions. His life." His gaze shifted. "Or what's left of it."

"Uh-huh. And nobody came by to talk to you after they got wind of this story?"

"Why? Who did you tell?" He grimaced. "It doesn't matter. What about Tam? Did you speak to him?"

Ria shook her head. "Chang's his top crime reporter. I'm a lowly rookie and certainly not allowed to tramp around on her beat. I'll be lucky to get to the City desk in a year as it is. Who knows how long it'll take if I'm on his bad side?" She paused, frowning again. "Did he do this to you?"

"I told you already, I fell." Ying laughed then, a wheeze that degenerated into a series of groans and rapid breathing. "Listen, I'm sorry I wasted your time." A faint grin. "Got your heart pumping though, eh? Dreaming of bigger, better things?"

Ria shrugged. She watched the old man for a few silent seconds, then placed her tea down, and stood. "Well, guess I better be getting back to the land of nonagenarian mah-jongg champs then. Those stories don't write themselves, sadly."

"Yes, of course. Sorry for your trouble." Ying shuffled her quickly to the door. She heard him slide the bolts in behind her.

Blinking in the bright sunlight, Ria clattered down the front steps and headed for the back of the house. No matter how rapidly the old man shuffled, she'd still have a few minutes on him. Plenty of time to pick a lock if she had to. Walking briskly along Ying's buckled cement driveway, she mentally reviewed the lessons given her on locks by her best friend, the private gumshoe.

But it was moot. She found the lock on the brown grass next to Ying's workshop, shattered and useless. She eased open the narrow double doors, flinching at the screech as they swung unevenly on dented hinges. The cherry tree blocked most of the sunlight through the window, but Ria could tell things were awry even without the bulb on.

The shadows were all wrong.

She heard the slam of a door and the scrape of slippers on cement.

"Damn it, I told you I was done."

Ria spared a glance at Ying, wheezing next to her. He leaned on a cane, cradling his left side. The ointment around his black eye was shiny in the sunshine.

She turned back to the inside of the shed, surveyed the shredded papers and smashed machinery. The worktable lay on its side, two of its legs ripped from their joints.

"Did they tune you up before or after they made you watch this?"

He grunted. "After."

Ria picked up a stack of trampled schematics, smoothing out the tears and crumples. She thought of what he'd said about her Chinese colleagues. "Was it the local sugar boys?"

Ying shook his head. "I've always hated that term."

Ria pushed aside a torn table leg with her foot. "Aw c'mon, Tong, *tohng*, they're almost identical sounding. The irony is too rich to ignore."

"Irony is over-rated." Ying stayed in the doorway.

Ria discarded her attempt at light-heartedness. "So why would anyone threaten you now? It's been twelve years. I was told your experiment was a bust. I mean, I saw it myself, in the archives. The Herald went back to its normal length the following week."

Ying grumbled.

"Drop it, Miss Monteverde. It's not worth my life. Or yours." He raised his cane, jabbed it at the ground. "And you learned your Cantonese all wrong. Tong doesn't sound like *sugar*. It's a homonym for *butcher*."

"Woodie, didn't you refile those archives I was looking at?"

"Yes, Miss Monteverde. Right after you left."

"So they oughta be on this shelf, right? I saw you take them from right here."

"Which...? Yes...they should—"

"But they're not."

"I...don't know where they could be. I just tidied up. The tables are all empty."

"Never mind. One way or another, it'll be sorted."

This time, she pulled the green door open just enough to slide inside, then hauled it closed behind her. The presses were in full swing, working on the evening edition. Ria carefully searched the cavernous space, mindful to keep out of the way of the frantic printer operators.

In the end, she stopped back where she'd started.

The long scarred worktables were still smeared with ink, trays stacked chockablock at the edges. The metal casts laid tidily in their cubbyholes. Scraps of paper were stuffed into a tall metal bin. No matter how long she stared, however, no one appeared.

"Why the long face, pet?"

Ria startled at the voice in her ear. "Chang, damn it, stop being a sneak."

"You need better ears. I've been following you for the better part of five minutes. Who are you looking for?"

"A typesetter. The wiry one with the moon face."

Chang shook her head. "They're *union*, pet. Strict hours."

"Union?" Ria frowned. "We don't have any unions here."

"It's the polite term for gangsters, pet. The sugar boys." Chang looked at her sideways. "I thought you were City-born and bred."

Ria assessed Chang openly as she mentally recalculated her options. She decided to go with her gut, changing tack.

"Then I guess I'll have to settle for you."

"I'm no one's second choice, pet."

"You've been here over ten years, right? Did you know Henry Ying?"

Chang laughed, surprised. "Are you mixed up with one of his crazy inventions?"

"Why did he leave? Was he fired? Or did he quit?"

"Quit. Right after one of his inventions cranked up production so high, it broke the presses. Literally."

Ria cocked her head. "They didn't fire him for that?"

"The owners loved him. He was a real live Poindexter. A genius with anything mechanical. Saved 'em a lotta dough on repairs and new presses. Aside from which, he was their best typesetter. Fast and accurate."

"But why did he leave?"

Chang shrugged, palms up. "You'd have to ask him. Listen, let me give you some advice. Tam and Ying used to be real tight, but when Ying left, Tam soured on him fast. If you're snooping around a story on Ying, don't. Tam won't print it anyway." Chang turned away.

"Wait. What were you doing? Back when Ying reigned here? What kind of stories were you getting then?"

"Me? I was a custodian. Put myself through secretarial school. Joined the pool on the first floor. Six years of that and then finally up to the reporters' floor. I'm a regular success story, fifteen years in the making." She raised a finger. "But if he likes you, there is a fast track here, pet." Chang's smile didn't reach her eyes. "The question is what you're willing to pay for it."

Ria stood, hands on her hips, staring at the shelves of grey-bound archives.

"So you're telling me they're all back."

Woodie nodded.

"When?"

"This morning. I went up to tell you straightaway, but Mr. Tam had some urgent research he needed from me."

Ria shook herself. "Well, I guess I'm glad the mystery got solved."

Woodie helped her pull down the archives for the entire month of December of 1921 again and left her to it. She started in order, reading every headline and checking all bylines. Going by instinct, she either skimmed or read articles, and she kept notes on intersecting names and events. Every now and then, she heard voices and footsteps, chairs being dragged across the floor, the heavy thump of other ledgers being set down. But she stayed invisible, tucked away in her corner, working steadily through thirty-one days of old news.

Two hours later, she found herself at her desk upstairs, staring out a far window at the darkening twilight. She had the shadow of a revelation skipping at the edges of her mind. Chasing it around in her thoughts countless ways, she came to the same conclusion each time.

She picked up her telephone.

"I checked the archives again, Mr. Ying."

The old man sighed heavily. "I told you, it's over."

Ria kept her voice low. "I noticed a hitch in an evening edition. Friday the sixteenth. Columns were out of alignment and the spacing was choppy. I'm no expert, but it seemed to me there was some quick and dirty editing." She paused, giving him a chance to explain. Then, "It's not about the printing press at all, is it? You excised a story after a print run, didn't you? Had to go back and reset the page, re-run the entire thing."

"It's no use now, dredging up the past."

"He paid you off, didn't he, to cut out that one story? About Ming?"

"Listen to me good—"

"And your comment about the Tongs and the other reporters here. That was really about Tam, wasn't it? He's the one connected to them. Did you discover that when your typesetting machine became a threat to *the union*? Did he threaten you then too? Convince you to quit for your health?" She paused. "Or maybe you just couldn't stand being reminded that you have a price."

"If you keep this up, girl, you won't ever live long enough to regret your choices." He cut the connection with a crash.

Ria winced, jerking the receiver away from her ear.

"Your winning personality again, pet?"

Ria whirled around, trying to get a handle on her racing heart.

Chang smiled toothily at her. "One of your sources jam out on you?" She shrugged. "It happens. Someday," Chang paused, reconsidering. "Eventually, you'll learn to cull the rats." She sauntered away toward the stairs.

Ria shrugged off Chang's condescension. What choice did she have, after all? She was a rank newcomer, barely trusted to deliver paper copy to the print room, for gods' sake. Chang was the head reporter on the City desk, given first pick of the best leads because everyone knew Chang had killer instincts.

Ria sat up straight, her stray thoughts coalescing into a vague plan. She frowned, thinking hard about her next steps. Pushing aside her misgivings, she called out. "I need to talk to you about Ming." A pause. "And Tam."

Chang stopped, turning back. "Oh, are we bosom friends now?"

Ria made a rude noise. "You've been on this Ming story for over a week, since it leaked that he would be appointed the new Gaming Commissioner. That's plenty of time for you to do your magic."

"Flattery now, is it, pet?"

"But all you've written are fluff pieces. Not that Tam's seemed to mind."

Chang cupped an ear, forced a surprised expression. "Do I finally hear some rusty wheels turning? Is there life in that pretty little head of yours after all?"

Ria waved the comment away. "I know I can't trust you, but I think your self-interests might work in my favour this time."

"A resounding vote of confidence."

"It's the best you'll get from me. Now, are you interested in a career-making story or not?"

Chang raised a brow. "I'm way ahead of you, pet. The real question is, are you?"

Tam's club was in a six-story brownstone, in the European style. It was gentlemen only, but the butler was civilized enough to show her into a small sitting room off the entrance. She supposed she ought to be grateful he hadn't simply shut the door in her face.

Ria paced the length of the room, clenching and unclenching her fists. She whirled as the door opened.

"Valeria. To what do I owe this unexpected pleasure?" Tam smiled, his handsome features warm and open. He nodded to the butler, who withdrew, closing the door silently. Tam gestured to the caddy in the corner. "Care for a sherry?"

Ria held back her grimace at the thought of the sickly sweet liqueur he undoubtedly had in mind for her. "No, thank you. I'm sorry to bother you during your off hours...boss."

"Burning the candle at both ends, are we?" Tam chuckled. "I admire your ambition and work ethic, Valeria, but you must be careful not to overdo it." He looked down, brushed something off the breast of his blue silk smoking jacket.

"Just trying to make a good impression. Like Chang. You've got her interviewing Commissioner Ming plus she's still covering that bank heist. I thought it best to step up my efforts too." She did her best impression of a demure smile.

"Of course, of course. What do you need from me?"

"Well, it's about Commissioner Ming, actually. You wrote about him when he was a mah-jongg parlour owner, up for election as a City councilor. Twelve years ago."

"Some of my best work. What of it? Chang has you doing her grunt work, has she?" Tam poured himself a finger of amber into a cut crystal tumbler, adding two ice cubes. He shook his head, expression indulgent.

Ria took a deep breath. "What did he offer you? To get an article taken out? You had to bribe Henry Ying too, I assume?"

Tam stilled.

"Aside from the fact that you've just made a dangerous accusation, Valeria, I have no idea what you're talking about." He sipped his drink. "But I'm fond of you, so I'll let you explain before I have you thrown out."

"You were writing a series investigating Ming's past as a parlour owner. You dug up everything you could find about his years in China, his early years in the City, his murky beginnings as a parlour boss. I mean, you had a real talent for explaining complicated bylaws and by-election regulations. You went after Ming, hammer and tongs, for a solid week, but then, three days before the civic by-election, you didn't write a single thing about him."

Ria circled slowly, keeping Tam in her direct line of sight as he sauntered to the fireplace.

"The editor, Shin, lost interest." Tam shrugged. "You'll learn that the longer you work in this business, the less control you actually have. The editor-in-chief has all the power, Valeria. I learned that back in '21." He watched her over the rim of his glass as he took another drink.

Ria shook her head. "Ying told me everything," she lied. "You shouldn't have destroyed his workshop."

"You think anyone's going to believe a senile old man, notorious for his whacky inventions? Or you, for that matter? Another pretty face, trying too hard to prove herself in a man's world? And a *gwai* to boot." He paused. "Not that I need to prove anything."

"You want to play it this way, then?"

"Did you think I'd quake in my boots? Confess to you?" Tam laughed. "Those articles have been archived for years, for anyone to read. I've got nothing to hide."

"But you weren't sure, were you? You heard from one of the typesetters that I was asking about Ying. You found out from Woodie that I was looking at those archives. You intimidated an old man by destroying his life's work. Then you took those archived papers so no one would know you were looking at them. You checked the dates, you thought you were safe, so you returned them."

Tam frowned. "I know Ying didn't talk." He put down the tumbler on the marble mantle with a soft click. "And you cannot prove a negative."

Ria took a step back. "True enough. The excised story is long gone. What was it, just out of curiosity? Was it about Ming's second wife? The one with palsy? The one Number Three Wife drowned in the bath? But everyone thought it an accident."

Tam's frown deepened as he considered Ria's words. Then: "Chang."

Ria nodded. "She's tenacious and cunning. She discovered everything Ming tried to hide twelve years ago. You were smart to promote her, but stupid to put her in Ming's path. Or perhaps it was just arrogance."

Tam stared at her for several moments, then

shrugged. "Commissioner Ming's past has no bearing on me. You can try accusing me of failing to uncover that sordid tit-bit, but the worst I'll look is incompetent. And it was so long ago, I was just a callow youth. I've more than proven my worth as the City's best newspaper editor."

Ria took another step backward, felt for the doorknob. "I guess we'll both take our chances, won't we?" She opened the door.

Chang stepped inside. "Your butler is doing a deplorable job of keeping the riff raff out, Boss Man."

Ria closed the door and leaned back against it.

Tam glared. "Neither of you will work for a decent paper again. I promise you that."

Ria raised her chin. "I'd rather work for a third-rate rag than you any time."

"Well, I wouldn't," said Chang. "Besides, pet, Tam here won't fire us. He can't."

"You've got nothing on me. I'm too smart for that." Tam picked up his drink, sipped it, the very picture of elegant ease, even slipping one hand inside the pocket of his smoking jacket.

"Actually, little Miss Valeria here gets the credit for keeping our jobs safe."

Ria kept her expression neutral, her mind whirring into high gear to figure out Chang's meaning.

"She's actually quite a good investigator, Tam. Killer instincts."

Tam narrowed his eyes.

"You can't fire us, see, or else we show the coppers your deep and long-standing ties to the Central City Tong. Your uncle runs that gang, doesn't he? Adopted uncle, but still. It's not your fault you were sold into the family before you were even born."

Ria struggled to keep the shock from her expression. She forced her brain to work out all the angles, but she was clearly miles behind Chang.

"Now before you say it's not a crime, to be related to bad people," said Chang, "just think how it will look to have the police swarming all over you. Do you honestly think dear Uncle Boss Man won't be just the tiniest bit suspicious? I've never met the man, of course, but I'd guess he's somewhat mistrusting. Perhaps even paranoid."

"You can't talk if you're dead." Tam pulled his hand out of his pocket. Ria blinked. He was pointing a gun at them.

She froze, even as her heartbeat ratcheted up, thundering in her ears.

"Oh, it's the kiss off, is it?" said Chang coolly. "I hardly think your butler will help you cover up a double murder. Besides, I forgot to mention I sent your uncle a little bird. Apparently, someone's been skimming from Commissioner Ming's weekly payoffs."

Tam paled.

"Maybe your uncle's willing to believe the coppers are a smokescreen. But numbers don't lie, Tam. You'd best be thinking to your own future." Chang gestured to Ria. "Let's go."

Ria opened the door, mind numb, hands slick with sweat. She fisted them to still the trembling as she left the club through the front door. She turned left, unwilling to look Chang in the face, and strode away into the night.

"Good morning, pet. You're tougher than your delicate looks suggest. I thought you'd call in sick today too."

Ria dropped into her chair. "I had a legitimate day off yesterday. And you can cut the chauvinist remarks, Chang."

"Oh so you'll take them from Tam, but not from me, eh? Why? Because he's a man?"

"Just your luck, I finally relocated my spine."

"Actually, it's your lucky day today, pet. You're being moved." Chang gestured with her chin.

"Stop calling me that." Ria followed the gesture to a cluster of desks in the far corner. She looked up at Chang, frowning. The other woman nodded.

"Big changes today, Monteverde."

Ria swiveled around. Tam's office door stood open. A workman in navy blue coveralls was scraping away the painted name on the glass.

"A new editor-in-chief? Where's Tam?" Ria lowered her voice. "Did he resign?"

"In a manner of speaking."

"Who's the interim boss?"

"No interim. He named a successor. The owners approved unanimously."

"Quick work. Who is it?"

Chang grinned broadly.

"Oh gods." Ria groaned, cold blooming in the depths of her stomach. "How long have you been planning this?"

"Since I left the secretarial pool."

"And you were just waiting for the right sap to show up."

Chang's smile was fierce with satisfaction.

"All to get Tam fired." Something in Chang's expression pinged Ria's radar. "What?"

"They found him this morning." Chang watched Ria

closely. "Looks like suicide."

Ria's stomach roiled. She clamped a hand over her mouth and ran for the restroom. After, she rinsed her mouth out with cold water, splashed her face liberally. Staring at her pale reflection, she ran through fifty ways to tell Chang no. Every one threatened to empty her stomach again.

She returned to find her things in a box, sitting atop a desk in the far corner. She sat down gingerly, smiling wanly at Zhuang and Poon. They eyed her askance.

The telephone on her desk rang. She stared at it, eyes wide.

Poon said, "You gonna answer that, rookie?"

Ria slowly picked up the receiver.

"Monteverde." She swallowed. "City desk."

A DEAD RECKONING
ROBERT BOSE

Boone didn't look both ways before crossing the street and it killed him. Stifling an annoyed curse, he stared down at his body and watched the black BMW SUV speed off, the rear lights vanishing into the drizzle like the last moments of a dying Marlboro.

A well-dressed man, the same one Boone had spent the night following from chophouse to bar to nightclub, walked out of the shadows. Arnie Gerste, small time import-export broker and self-important wiseguy. He pocketed the 9mm in his hand and nudged his wingtips into Boone's oozing ribcage. Finding no response, he went through the dead man's pockets. Car Keys. Phone. Beer Money.

Clinging to the mortal realm as a tattered shade, Boone helplessly watched Arnie's antics. The man strolled up and down the street spinning the key on his finger, pausing every few meters to press the alarm. He'd find the car, dammit, and Boone couldn't do much of anything about it. There just wasn't enough of him. He was scraped thin, soul flapping in the ether, a fading memory. The black SUV came back around the block and stopped. A hulking Neanderthal got out and opened the rear door. Arnie got in and they drove away.

Boone bent down and examined the watch on his limp and outstretched arm. 9:04 PM. Three hours to complete the job. He sat on the curb, leaned against a rusting fire hydrant, and waited. The meter was running.

After some time, an ornate black hearse edged with glittering chrome, pulled up. A small robed figure got out, walked over to the remains, and set down a red enamelled toolbox. It bore the device of a laughing skull, one eye socket cavernous, the other, tiny. The figure examined the body with expert precision and turned its cowled head towards the lounging spirit.

Boone stood up and began to pace. "Couldn't you have gotten here sooner? A right bastard stole my car keys. It's a 67' Mustang for God's sake. I pay the Guild for prompt service. You Fixers need to be fixing!"

It shrugged and began pulling tools out of the box.

"That busy? Really? Sorry, I had no idea."

The Fixer probed the eight quarter sized holes perforating the dead man's chest and gave Boone an inquiring tilt of his head.

"They were good shots, I'll give them that. I haven't seen a grouping so tight in years. Do you remember that incident at the Cecil?"

The figure shook its head and pulled a ledger from within its featureless robe.

"I should still have three lives on account." Boone

took the little wire bound book and ran his spectral finger down the page. "Two? Oh right, Christmas Eve." Poisoned absinthe. Quick, painless, and forgettable as murderous deaths go.

He touched a smudged crimson thumbprint and watched the tally drop to one. He'd have to do something about that. The closer he got to the final swan song, the harder it was to return to the mortal coil. He'd contact his rep once this job was over.

The Fixer got down to business. It sat before the body and blew into a rune-encrusted flute, carved from weathered bone. Human, no doubt, the guild acolytes always tended towards the authentic. Eerie wailing cut the air. It was rhythmic and soothing. The pitch increased, a cloud of golden fog coalesced and settled into the bullet holes. Boone felt his essence drawn back into his body with a wild surge of light and fire. He hit the wall. Hit it and pushed through. It was like coming to a complete stop after travelling at a hundred miles an hour, then flooring it again. The speed of life.

When Boone opened his eyes he was alone on the street. He coughed and spit out a bit of something that tasted like cotton candy. He hated that stuff. And dammit, his back hurt.

Sirens blared, heading in Boone's direction, providing some impetus to get a move on. It wasn't a busy part of town but someone must have heard the shots and called it in. He was well down the nearest alley when he realized he'd left his hat. He cursed, but it wasn't worth going back for. Not like it was a Borsalino or anything.

With his head down, Boone plowed through a young couple, dressed for the nightclubs and having a quick smoke. He stumbled back to help the girl to her feet, mumbling an apology, and felt a paper pressed into his hands. A twenty. He grinned, nodded a thank you, and barrelled on down the alley. He did appear pretty down-on-his-luck. With a quick check to make sure he wasn't being followed, he ducked into the Nelson.

The light was turned so far down Boone had to stop and let his eyes adjust. He missed the old days, when it was legal to smoke indoors, and you could cut the murk in here with a sword. I guess they compensated by keeping it as dim as possible. He made his way to the bar, intent on a stiff drink before he faced his client.

A slim arm pulled Boone into a booth. Lien Hua draped herself over him, arms sliding around his neck like a couple of velvet snakes. Then she recoiled, pushing him away in disgust. "Ugh, you smell like death."

"You have no idea. It's been a rough night."

She noticed his torn, blood soaked shirt and ragged trench coat. "I see. You look like death as well. Did you find Gerste? We don't have much time."

"I was on his tail until some guardian angels showed up."

Lien Hua picked up a fork and thrust it deep into the tabletop. It stuck there, quivering. "You lost him? After all that work..."

"Not quite, the bastard slipped up and stole my phone. Once I get back to the office I can trace it."

"Good. It's critical we learn where Gerste made that delivery. A dark presence nears. Old, powerful, and dangerous. I'll need to lend you my strength." She crinkled her nose and cuddled back up. Boone felt a hand on his thigh.

"Whoa princess, none of that now. I'm not sure how old you are, but it isn't old enough."

"That's not what you said last night." She snuggled closer.

Boone conjured up some elusive memories. Jazz? Tea? A messy hotel room? Terminal trauma tended to mess with his mind. "I appreciate the thought. I really do. But I need to get moving. We can celebrate after I find your honourable ancestor."

Lien Hua pouted and then sighed. "Of course. You are right. Nothing is more important than freeing Master Wu. If you can't release him before midnight, he will be trapped for another hundred years." She touched her watch. "That leaves you two and a half hours."

"I'm still a bit hazy on what exactly I'm looking for."

"Did you get hit in the head? We've been over this multiple times. A Mandarin relic."

Ah yes, an ancient Chinese artefact, that was it. In a town bursting with cowboy collectables, it should stick out like a sore thumb.

The princess pulled on a heavy overcoat and hat, hopped over his lap, and slid out of the booth. She paused to run her hand down his stubble and into his blood matted hair. Boone groaned as she grabbed a handful and yanked him up off the bench, kissing him hard enough leave scorch marks.

"I'm a lot older than I look," she purred before vanishing into the gloom.

He had to admire her. All the right bits in all the right places. The air was thick with the scent of flowers on a rainy day.

Boone chugged a beer, grabbed a coffee to go, and made it back to his office. It was just around the corner and down a block, tucked above the mouldering ruin that was once the Owl's Nook used bookstore. He noticed that the landlord had boarded up the broken windows. Progress, of a sort, after four years of complaints.

The outside light turned on as he dragged himself up the stairs, illuminating the metallic stencil on the door. Lust and Pound. Dammit, some lowlife scum had messed it up again. Next week he'd hang around with a baseball bat and nip that in the bud. It was getting tiresome. He used his bloody sleeve to fix the o and the F.

Boone checked on the whereabouts of his lost phone. It showed up at a residence in the sleepy community of Ramsay, just across the river. Convenient. He probed his ribs and winced. Time to find some help.

He made a call. Five rings before it picked up.

"Yes?"

"Ragnar, it's Tagger Boone. I'm looking for your boy. Bjorn. I have a job that requires his expertise."

"Tagger, this is a really bad time."

"Rags! Sorry man, but it's a matter of life and death."

"It's always life and death with you, but he's busy." Echoing gunshots filled the background. "Why don't you try Galan, I hear he's back from Barcelona."

"Thanks, appreciated." The call cut out.

Galan Arlington, also known as Galan Hammerhand. The son of a bitch was a hard-drinking, skirt-chasing, knee-capping bundle of trouble. He was also an old friend, one that owed Boone big time.

Boone found Galan at the Drum and Monkey, following the booming voice and twisted laugh all the way in from the street. He had sober second thoughts. Did he need this kind of crazy? Boone brushed the thought aside and pushed through the crowd at the door. There he was, all three and half feet, standing on the end of the bar wearing the black tuxedo like he meant it. He was holding a terrified patron by the front of his shirt. The man's feet dangled in midair.

The dwarf gave Boone a quick glance. "Boone! Long-time no see. Still dressing like a friendless vagabond I see. Don't you have any pride man? Let me take you shopping. I know this righteous tailor."

"I might have to take you up on that, but right now I need a favour. You have a minute?"

The dwarf smashed his forehead into the dangling man's nose, splattering it across his face in an explosion of blood and cartilage before dropping the unfortunate fellow in a crumpled heap. Galan hopped down off of the bar and took a ring off the groaning man's hand. "Sure, but I have to catch a flight in..." He looked at his watch. Some sort of jewel encrusted Rolex. "...116 minutes."

"This shouldn't take long. I just need a bit of muscle while I collect some intel for a client. It's over the river in Ramsay."

"Ok, wait here, I'll grab my ride."

He disappeared around back and pulled up few seconds later in a red glistening Italian roadster. Boone whistled. "Maserati Spyder? Nice."

"It's all about image, Boone, one day you'll figure that out." He laughed.

Galan pulled up a block down from where the phone was. His Mustang was sitting along the curb and a black SUV was parked next to it. Boone pointed it out, mentioned the owners were armed and dangerous. Galan shrugged, unconcerned. "This is going to be fun."

He handed Boone his jacket, picked up a rock, and crept over to the BMW. The rock went through the passenger window and the alarm blared.

Two huge identical goons in black suits charged out

of the house. The first one hefted a pistol. "Kid, what the hell are you doing?" He grabbed Galan's shoulder and spun him around.

The dwarf flashed a twenty-four carat grin and punched him in the groin. Just the sound of it hurt. The stunned goon fell to his knees and started to throw up. Galan ran up the side of the car, spinning acrobatically through the air, to plant both polished leather shoes into the side of the man's head. The thug hit the dirt with a meaty thud.

The second goon backed away, digging for a weapon. Galan, still airborne and moving, tucked, rolled, and scythed through his knees in a whirlwind of bone-crunching fury. The man fell back screaming. The dwarf clambered up the collapsing thug's body and flung himself straight up in the air, twisting in slow motion as the pull of gravity dropped his elbow onto the man's chest. The effect was terrible, like an axe hitting a side of beef.

Galan picked up the car keys, turned off the alarm, and straightened his shirt. Twenty seconds. He wasn't kidding around.

The open door led to a well-appointed entryway. A shoe rack held a pair of expensive and familiar wingtips. Three hats hung from a coat stand and a drying umbrella leaned in the corner. Strains of Hockey Night in Canada bounced down the hall. Galan followed the music.

Arnie was sitting on a rich leather recliner. Black silk pyjamas, prissy ascot, slippers. A regular fashion statement. Pabst Blue Label cans crowded a coffee table. He drained the one in hand, placed it with the rest, and picked up a stack of papers. "Hans, grab me a beer on your way in."

"No can do."

The man scrambled up, papers scattering. He noticed Boone behind the dwarf. "You. You're dead!"

"I get that a lot."

"You took eight bullets!"

"Where did you make that delivery last night?"

He clammed up and started inching towards another doorway. Galan did a little flip and put both feet into the man's groin. Arnie crashed against the wall, heaving and gasping.

Boone cringed. "Do you have to keep doing that?"

Galan wasn't listening. He launched himself off an ottoman, got his legs around the Arnie's neck, and used his weight to spin the flailing man in a complete three sixty. The man crashed through the coffee table, cans spinning across the room. Sticking the landing like a pro, the dwarf grabbed Arnie's throat and squeezed.

"The nice hobo asked you a question."

Arnie gurgled and choked out a name. "Slate Resources." Galan slammed the man's head into the floor and jumped up.

"There you go Boone, nothing to it."

"Thanks."

"No problem. Not sure you want to get into it with Nathaniel Slate though. The man's treacherous."

"You know him?"

"We've done business."

"I don't have much choice."

Galan scratched his head. "A word. Keep an eye out for hired help. Slate doesn't like to get his hands dirty.

"Good to know. Are we squared?"

"That's not how I see it. There is still one thing." The dwarf paused and reached into his jacket.

Boone instinctively put a hand in front of his groin.

Galan chuckled and pulled out a thick billfold. He peeled off a few high denomination bills and tucked them into Boone's pocket. "Please," he added, "go visit my tailor. Bespoke Henry's in Marda Loop. I meant it about your image."

"Once this business is taken care of," he lied. "I guess we should do something about all of this."

The dwarf made a call. "Clean up on aisle six."

Boone raised his eyebrows.

"My guy will erase everything. Part of the service." Galan said, and he was gone.

That was bit of a relief, all things considered. Boone dug around and located his stuff. He also found a Slate Resources key-card and a brand new Glock 9mm. A plan formed. Not a clever plan. Not a cunning plan. More of an out-of-options-lets-wing-it kind of plan. He commandeered one of Arnie's suits. It even fit. The man loved his pinstripes. Boone tucked his hair under the black fedora from the entryway and splashed on some of Arnie's fragrant aftershave. He didn't even recognize himself.

The Mustang roared to life. 11:02 PM. Time to put this job to bed. He roared downtown and parked in a cheap lot three blocks from Slate Tower, then ran to the base of the towering obelisk of black granite and polished steel. He used a few tricks to get past security and into the executive elevator. It's amazing what the right access pass and some fast-talking can get you if you look the part. Boone guessed he wasn't the first late night visitor to enter the premises.

The top floor, home to Nathaniel Slate's personal suite, was dark and deserted. Boone stopped and cursed under his breath. Traditional Chinese lithographs lined the walls. Vases, urns, and statues filled shelves and display cases. The bastard was some kind of Mandarin art collector. Boone examined each piece but nothing stood out. The clock ticked, trudging closer towards midnight.

A spiral staircase climbed up to a penthouse. Boone padded up the stairs and found a black door inlaid with a silver mountain. It stood open a crack, leaking a sliver of light. He pulled out the Glock, crept to the door, and listened. Voices. Boone recognized Slate's from a recent newscast. It was stern and a bit clipped, in an old English sort of way.

"I will help you deal with Umbra once this current business is concluded. Those scientists have twice interfered with my own development plans."

"Don't underestimate them. They have hidden resources." Another man, this one with a strong East Asian accent.

"So do I."

"I appreciate your offer. I do. But I shouldn't require your assistance. In a few minutes my power will exceed the..."

Boone felt a presence behind him. A silky female voice said, "Boo!" before everything faded to black.

He returned to consciousness tied hand and foot to a carved wooden chair. He blinked away a bit of double vision and fought past the raging headache. Nathaniel Slate sat across from him, behind an expansive obsidian-topped desk. "Mr. Boone. You are alive for one reason. One. My business associate wishes to ask you a question. You will answer that question."

"Boss, Gerste and the twins said they put a full clip of widowmakers right through this one's heart." An attractive young Japanese lady in skin-tight ballistic nylon rested the business edge of her katana on Boone's shoulder. "I would have aimed for the head."

Boone recognized her. Lady Chiyome, executive bodyguard and sword-for-hire. He'd seen her once, long ago, at an industry mixer on Pump Hill. Galan, ever the charmer, had fallen in love. They'd left together.

"Of course dear Lady, of course. Now where were we? Mister Boone, let me introduce you to Ping Ji." Out of the shadows shuffled an enormous, hulking man-shaped thing with tattooed alabaster skin, long wild hair, and a ratty loincloth. Slate smiled. "I should mention that PJ is a *Yao Guai*, a demonic celestial from the lowest level of Chinese hell."

The creature stopped in front of Boone. It bent over until they were eye to eye. The scent was overpowering, thick with dust, snakes, and forgotten crypts. It sniffed. "Lien Hua."

There was a memory of flowers on a wet day.

"Answer the question." Lady Chiyome slid her blade to the edge of his throat.

"That didn't sound like a question."

The demon picked up his chair and slammed it down hard. The frame cracked and Chiyome's blade bounced, drawing blood.

"Lotus Blossom. Where is she?"

"Who?"

"I smell her. In your hair. On your skin. She thinks she is clever, but she is nothing." A clawed hand reached for him but stopped short. "Fah. It's not worth my time to break her petty wards. In a few minutes I will be a god." The *Yao Guai* pulled back a long curtain, opened a tinted window, and let the light of the full moon fall across the room. "Slate! It is time."

Nathaniel Slate watched the exchange with a wry grin. "Lady C, if you wouldn't mind." The lithe bodyguard floated over and placed an ornate wicker casket on the desk. Slate opened it and pulled out a large ginseng root. It had tiny arms, legs and a head, and resembled a shrivelled doll. "A Greater Root of Power." He held it to his nose and inhaled. "Maybe the greatest. PJ, are you really sure you want to eat this thing?"

"I must devour it at the stroke of midnight, when the full moon weakens the bonds. Only then will the soul within be vulnerable."

"The soul of Wanyan Wu."

"My ancient nemesis. I will gain his power and burn my foes in the fires of *Avīci*."

"*Our* foes."

The demon bared its teeth and nodded. "Our foes."

Slate tossed Lady Chiyome a small leather bound book. "Six minutes. Get comfortable and she will make the necessary preparations." Ping Ji nodded and assumed a classic meditative pose.

The bodyguard moved furniture and copied pictures onto the floor with white chalk. Circles and lines. Stars. The sun. They glowed, illuminating one by one when kissed by the moonlight.

Boone considered his options. He could make a break for it, give the princess a sob story, and lie low for a while. With only one get-out-of-jail-free card left, he could even justify it. Couldn't he? No? No. He sighed. Five minutes. Time to play his card.

Muscles flexed and the chair creaked. It was an antique and not accustomed to being abused. The demon had broken the frame and shocked the glue holding it together. Boone rocked forward and surged up, yanking his arms and twisting his legs. The chair burst apart, the back and seat crashing to the floor. He scooped up the root and ran towards the window.

Slate's eyes went wide. "Chiyome! Stop him."

"With pleasure."

Boone still didn't know what he was supposed to do. The princess had said it would be obvious. Right... Hold on. What was that? A faint whisper in the back of his skull. Wait. He retreated until his butt pressed against the windowsill and held up the root like a shield. "Stop, or-"

"Or what?" Lady C unsheathed her katana and in one elegant motion sliced through his outstretched arm at the elbow. Boone's severed hand fell, still clutching the little ginseng man. He did a little jig and caught it with his left. Goddammit.

Ping Ji roared and barrelled across the room. "Imbecile. You must not damage the root!" He brushed her shoulder with a spear of crackling fire, blasting her into the nearest wall. She fell with a thud, pictures tumbling to crash onto the floor around her.

"Three minutes." Slate, unfazed, tapped his watch.

The *Yao Guai* held up a clawed hand and said a word. Semi-translucent lotus petals shimmered into existence around Boone. The demon dug his nails in and tore them away.

"You," said the reaching *Yao Guai*, "the soul. Now!"

That whisper again. Wait.

Wait for what? A big smelly demon was going to rip his head off? He felt faint. Maybe he'd die of blood loss first.

Ping Ji shuddered and spun around, spraying ichor from a deep wound in his back. Chiyome danced behind him, a tornado of biting steel. She spit out some blood. "I don't care who you are. Nobody touches me without my permission."

The blade met spear. Chiyome strained, muscles

popping, but the demon was far stronger. With a triumphant grunt, he wrenched the sword from her grasp, flipping it behind him. Towards the window. Towards Boone.

The blade impaled Boone's remaining hand, the root, and his heart. Time stopped. Free.

A crackle of light burst from the ginseng. It coalesced into the form of an ancient Chinese man in elaborate phoenix robes. Master Wu. It had to be. The sorcerer nodded and bowed before dissipating in a wild display of multi-coloured fireworks.

Boone had one last glimpse of the room. Stoic Nathaniel Slate leaning back in his chair. An enraged Ping Ji sheathed in flame. Lady Chiyome pulling a wicked knife from her boot. Tagger Boone toppled backwards through the open window and fell forty-two stories to the street below.

The decaying shade sat on the hood of the car and struggled to keep from slipping over the edge. Not much left, just threads of soul stuff and chaotic thoughts. Boone pulled himself together the best he could. He'd never been this close to oblivion before.

The car itself was totaled, the roof cratered in and dripping blood onto the pavement. The sword still transfixed his chest. He needed to get out of the area before Lady C came looking for it. Out of the city. Out of the country. Maybe they would all kill each other. That was a pleasant thought.

Sirens echoed in the distance. It would only be minutes before the authorities showed up. He willed the Guild get there faster. It was hard to spin a dive like that as a near death experience.

Boone didn't wait long. The hearse pulled up, and

the Fixer went right to work, inspecting the mashed and mangled corpse. Boone received a long, hard stare.

"Yeah, yeah, don't give me that. It's not like I plan these things."

The acolyte searched for something around the crushed luxury vehicle.

"My arm? I left it upstairs."

With an exaggerated shrug, and a soundless sigh, the figure faded out of sight. Fire surged and flashed forty-two floors up. Ping Ji was still in the game. Still angry.

Another spirit materialized next to Boone. It was the old man from the root. He gave a deep bow. "Your sacrifice was great. I am forever in your debt."

Boone returned the bow. "My pleasure."

"How did you come to be there, in the end, at the perfect moment?"

"A descendant of yours, a girl named Lien Hua."

"Ah yes, the Lotus Blossom. I must find her and thank her as well."

Boone thought about the princess. They were warm thoughts. He'd have to collect for services rendered before he got the hell out of Dodge.

The old man eyes crinkled. He knew, or guessed what Boone was thinking. "I will settle your account with these... creatures. It is the least I can do for now."

A scorched and smoking Fixer reappeared. It clutched Boone's arm and brushed off patches of rippling flame. The acolyte saw Master Wu and stopped dead. Energy crackled. Raw power permeated the ether. The old man rubbed his hands and smiled. "Such petulance from youth." He walked over, patted the little robed figure on the head, and got into the passenger seat of the hearse.

The Fixer shook for a long moment. Boon had never

seen one so... flustered. It shrugged at last, put out the remaining flames, and went to work. Out came the flute, a small cloth bag leaking silver dust, and a roll of duct tape.

"Duct tape? I thought it would be bark flayed from the world's oldest tree or something. Not practical? Really? And while you are in there, could you fix my back? I think you gave me the wrong spine last time."

The acolyte ignored him and used the tape to reattach his arm. It sprinkled the dust along each limb and over his leaking skull. Lots of eerie wailing. High pitched. Penetrating. The resulting golden cloud was expansive, surrounding and infusing his entire body in a cocoon of blazing light and pulsing fire.

The wall, this time, was damn near impenetrable. Boone hit it hard and bounced back. He hit it again. And again. Each time making a small dent, a crack, a hole. The wall fractured and he broke though. To Life.

His back still hurt.

THE WORKMAN'S FRIEND
JANICE MACDONALD

Harold might tease her about being friendly with workmen, but it was just a matter of getting things done properly. Susan always made sure the coffee went on just as the plumber or the carpenter was expected. Her grandmother had said that you could catch more flies with honey, and Susan knew that she got quality work out of the people she hired to work on the house. If it meant listening to their particular ideas on politics and the state of the world over the occasional cup of coffee, it was a small price to pay.

The house was going to be wonderful when it was completed. They'd got it for what passed as a song these days. More like a freakin' aria, Harold had grumbled, but he'd gone along with Susan's dream of refurbishing the old place. It had been the original farmhouse of the area, before the city had encroached and annexed all the land into boxy little blocks. At present, it stood among the squat bungalows like a fat trawler surrounded by pleasure craft. In her dreams Susan saw it gleaming on its double allotment, the old trees a reproachful comment on the neighbouring shrubs.

Some impressive changes had already been implemented since they'd started, but it was only now that noticeable differences were beginning. The basement had been re-dug, the foundations jacked up, new plumbing had been installed, and rewiring and roofing completed before the winter had set in. Now the craftsmen had turned to the finishing touches.

Already the kitchen had been modernized, with its workstation for Susan's computer fitted into the niche left by the old storeroom. Larry had done a great job of creating cabinetry that evoked "old farm kitchen" while hiding all sorts of modern gadgetry from view. There was a pull-out drawer for garbage and recyclables, a shelf that stored the toaster, and a glass-fronted wine rack cupboard that allowed room for corks to be dropped between the panes. The microwave, dishwasher, range and fridge all had yellow coloured fronts, adding a cheeriness that was picked up in the yellow and white floor tiles.

The pine flooring in the large living room was echoed in the lintel, window mouldings and mission-style furniture that Susan had always favoured. Just last week the dust from the dry-walling had settled enough that she'd been able to bring out her collection of Santa Fe scatter rugs.

Larry was upstairs now, setting in the mirrored sliding doors that fronted the new closet in the master bedroom. That was the one problem with old houses, no closets. Susan had opted for creating one along the dormer wall. It was slightly shorter than standard, but neither she nor Harold were of basketball build, and it was long enough to house all the shoes and sweaters in the shelves at either end. The mirrors would also pick up the western light through the window, making it airier. At least, that was the idea.

If Larry had ideas of his own, he'd offered them shyly, and Susan had incorporated a few, but she was firm in most of her visions for the house. Larry was easy to work with. It had been an uphill slog with Andy, the plumber who'd installed the half-bath and laundry area in what had once been the covered back porch. Mind you, he wasn't annoying to listen to, like Remy the electrician had been. Remy was always harping on about the little lady checking things out with her husband before giving the go-aheads. As if Harold really wanted to be consulted on where to put the razor plugs in the back bathroom.

When he got home each evening, Harold listened with tolerant amusement to Susan's accounts of dealing with "her workmen" as he called them. He seemed to like the changes being wrought around him, as long as his dinner was on time, but had no real interest in being part of the planning. He spoke approvingly of Susan's improvements being property enhancements, and suggested that the resale value would be enormous when she was done, but Susan just brushed aside these comments with vague smiles. This was her dream home and she knew in her heart that she'd never be leaving it. She just nodded and signed when Harold devised various complicated insurance schemes concerning mortgages, deadlines, fatalities, accidents, and acts of God. If Larry hit his thumb on the site, they were covered.

Oftentimes, Harold would phone from the office and make teasing remarks about "her workmen" in a voice she knew other people there could overhear. She'd heard him at parties, too, commenting that Susan would chat up the milkman if she was up before six-thirty. He had a theory that women at home and freelancers in general must get abnormally lonely during the day. When she thought about it at all, she considered Harold to be very secure in her love for him, to risk comments like that being bandied about the workplace. It was not a joke Susan herself particularly enjoyed, but Harold allowed her such leeway for her plans that she felt small about quashing his enjoyment of his own humour.

She put Harold's disinterest in the house plans down to his absorption in his own work. He owned a thriving travel agency in the centre of town, which catered to business people. Harold planned their conference trips and their yearly winter-sun holidays. He often scouted holiday spots himself, but Susan had long ago ceased to accompany him on these jaunts because she felt like an extra piece of luggage set on the beach while he was busy working out deals with hotel owners and resort managers.

She was a homebody at heart, which was probably why she'd veered toward a freelancing career in the first place. The folks who had invented modems and fax machines had probably had her in mind. She luxuriated in being able to look up from her workstation to find her own nest surrounding her. Harold was such a people person that he probably couldn't fathom the enjoyment of solitude.

She was in the kitchen, pouring herself a cup of decaf, when Larry came down the back stairs to let her know he'd be quitting for the day. He was going to leave his tools in the back bedroom as he'd be back the next morning. Susan was momentarily startled, but then recalled that Larry had mentioned the early departure sometime last week. It was something to do with his kids, an at-school afternoon or something. He had twins he was abjectly proud of; he'd mentioned them to Susan several times and showed wallet snapshots, beaming. He lounged in the archway a few minutes, going over the plans for the attic conversion he'd be starting next week. Then, after rinsing his coffee cup in the sink, he was off out the back door. Susan drifted back to work, hearing without listening for the roar of his half-ton in the alley.

She wasn't sure how much time had passed when she heard another sound from the back yard. Maybe Larry had forgotten something. She looked up from her computer, surprised to see Harold entering the kitchen from the back porch. He usually used the front entrance, closer to the driveway where he always parked.

She was also surprised to hear that he'd forgotten a file at home. Not only was he a meticulous planner, Harold almost never brought work home with him. She offered him a cup of coffee, pleased that he seemed able to take some time out to enjoy being home in daylight hours. He asked her where her "boyfriend" was, squeezing her shoulder briefly as she handed him his coffee. As she explained Larry's absence, she had a strange sense of déjà vu, as if she had told Harold of Larry's school visit plans before.

Harold, for once, seemed interested in the installation of the mirror doors. Did they actually make the bedroom as bright as Susan had imagined they would? She admitted that she hadn't been up to see the finished work yet, and was pleased to hear Harold suggest that they go up right then together to see. Seizing on his sudden interest, she moved with him up the back stairs, not even bothering to save the open file on her computer. She spoke over her shoulder of the attic plans to Harold bringing up the rear.

It took only a few minutes. Harold rinsed out his coffee mug carefully, dried it and hung it back on the wall rack. The disposable raincoat he had pulled from his briefcase on the way up the stairs was stuffed into a garbage bag he could dump in a can down the alley as he drove back to work. He scanned Susan's workspace, and decided against turning off the computer.

It would add a touch of realism when he returned that evening and called the police to tell them that he'd found his wife bludgeoned to death with a hammer in their bedroom. Lord knows, he thought, rehearsing his lines, he'd warned her enough times about being too friendly with the workmen.

Yes, he thought, looking at the gleaming new features surrounding him, even without the attic conversion, this place should bring him enough to set Consuela up in the villa she had her eye on.

He wondered briefly if she'd be remodelling.

THE COELACANTH SAMBA
AL ONIA

Darren stared at the embalmed monster behind the glass. The dull green fish hung suspended from the ceiling above its large tank. Its primitive eyes were hooded by protective armor plates but he felt he could see into them and back the millions of years the species had inhabited the oceans.

Movement, reflected in the aquarium, caught his eye. The movement stopped two feet beside him. He appraised the figure in the glass. Female. Slim, tall and watching him.

She said, "Impressive, isn't it?"

"Striking." He held up the annual report with its picture on the cover. "This doesn't do justice to the real thing. Where'd it come from?"

"President's father caught it deep-sea fishing in South Africa a decade or two ago. Preserved it and shipped it home. Hell of a trophy."

Darren circled the large tomb harboring the prehistoric specimen. "Hence Coelacanth Resources. Darren Mclean." He extended a hand.

"Molly Hatch. Investor relations for Coelacanth."

"You have a firm grip. IR must be strenuous work."

She chuckled. "I wish. I have to exercise religiously."

He took a quick glance at a well-toned calf below the hem of her skirt. "Runner?"

She nodded. "And dancer. Latin."

He moved his hips sideways, careful to keep his shoulders still. "I've done a little myself. Heck of a workout. Running's easier."

"But lonelier. What brings you to our office, Darren? Not the cha-cha, I'm sure."

"Mr. Coelacanth. Your president. The receptionist's retrieving him and a coffee."

"I'll leave you to Russell." She took a step then turned. "You should come dancing. A few of us meet at the Mocambo every Thursday evening. Tomorrow night. Do you know it?"

"Still finding my way around Calgary. Don't know if I can make it but thanks for the invite."

She pulled a cell phone from her blazer pocket. "Sorry, Darren. I have to go. Investment bankers coming in to discuss the latest reserve evaluation."

"Any oil price news is bad news, these days."

"Keep next Thursday free?"

"I will."

She shook his hand while listening on her phone. She mouthed, "See you again."

"Count on it." He watched her walk away, imagining for a moment those hips in a Latin slit skirt. Unprofessional, he told himself. Nice.

"Here's Marvin's file." Russell Formag pushed a folder across the crescent-shaped desk in the president's office.

Darren flipped past the full-size photo reproduced in the annual report. He scanned the resume of missing executive Marvin Richter. "You and he go back."

"When I started in the oil business, everybody with the right technical degree got hired. The cycles and failures have honed it to sticking with people you know. And trust."

Darren turned to the last stapled set of papers. "Trust? Seems to me you don't run security check on someone you trust."

Russell exhaled a long sigh. "Boiler plate. You notice it's clean. I'll give you a brief history lesson. I hire who I want. Including you. I'm the boss according to the annual report you have. That's the public line."

"Reality intrudes." Darren thought of his own reality. Encouraged to accept early retirement from the RCMP to work for double the money in the private resource sector in 'Fort Crack'. Then the price of the resource dropped in half and he was pounding Calgary streets looking for jobs which weren't there. Connecting with Formag was a break.

"The reality is my board of directors. We were over our bank line without enough production to service debt. One board member sat on another company's board with the opposite problem. Production but no ideas and more new prospects to invest their cash flow."

"A merger. Makes sense to survive."

"In financial terms, absolutely."

Darren caught the hesitation in Formag's voice. Not guilt. Disgust. "But you merge more than physical assets." He thought of Molly's aggressive manner. She didn't fit Formag's quiet confidence. Or Richter's from what he gleaned in his brief read. "People."

Russell tapped Richter's security report. "People. Read the others. The board agreed with my request to do all senior staff but they hired the firm, not me."

"You think I can do better?"

"Since I have a missing friend and colleague, coincident with the merger, you have to."

"Why did you request checks in the first place?"

"The company we merged with, Bluestone, had an attitude of entitlement. President inherited the firm from his dad and hired youngsters in positions over their heads. Paid 'em way too much. Every professional had a company car. German."

Darren reflected on his ten-year-old repainted police cruiser. Four doors and two and a half tons of clapped-out Detroit iron. Just the wheels to park in front of the Mocambo.

He said, "Generous."

"Generous my ass. The president and one of his VP's owned the leasing company."

"Jesus. Isn't that a conflict?"

"Tip of the iceberg, in my opinion. And in my gut."

"Richter feel the same?"

"He was digging hard. On his own. Marvin's a chameleon. Gets along with folk, even these bandits."

Darren glanced at the remaining folders. "The others?"

"The two main immigrants from Bluestone. Molly Hatch and Nik Orlaski. I had to accept them under the terms of the deal."

Darren tapped Richter's photo. "You talk to the police?"

Russell nodded. "You're ex, you know the drill."

"Right. Not long enough. No evidence of violence at his residence, according to your phone message."

"Detective Ennis recommended you."

"The respect is mutual. I owe him one." Darren opened Orlaski's file first, he'd already formed a first impression of Molly. He noted the home address. "Lives well, for a man of thirty-two. Family money?"

"Father's s butcher, mother cleans houses. Nik's first gen Canadian. As you note, he lives well. Or well above his visible means. I've been doing this for three decade and my house would fit inside his garage. His trophy wife spends six months a year in Palm Springs. I rent a fucking condo for golfing vacations."

Darren slid Molly's photo out. "I've met your IR chief. Intense."

"She works long and hard."

"Ambition's not a vice."

Russell had calmed. "No, it isn't. I'm pressing guilt by association. She had a brief affair with Bluestone's president. It's in the file."

"Richter's divorced. Any chance...?"

Russell shrugged. "Nothing obvious. I know his taste. Runs closer to his age. The homebody type."

Darren slid the folders into his briefcase. He checked his notes from the previous day's phone call. "Richter's been gone one week, three days longer than a planned fly fishing vacation."

"Which he never made. Which is why it isn't a search and retrieval case. Yet." He passed a key ring to Darren. "His house. I look in on his place when he's away."

"I'll need a cover story to talk to your staff."

"What's wrong with the truth?"

Darren thought a moment. Russell Formag was as

straight forward and elemental as the beast in the lobby. He liked him. "Nothing, Maybe not the whole truth, though."

"You judge."

One bonus of being an ex-cop. Judgment allowed.

Darren lifted the binoculars as the massive triple door rose in one wing of Nik Orlaski's country estate. He mentally tallied the exotic sports cars with the security report's list. He scanned the house in time to catch a blond head passing across a second story window.

Darren got into his car, stowed the binoculars, and headed toward the long driveway. A walk-through of Richter's place in the afternoon turned up nothing other than a man who'd expected to come home. Soon, judging by the fridge contents. The hot water wasn't turned to vacation, but how many people bothered with that detail?

Nik backed a Cobra into the sunlight and parked it as Darren drove up.

"Hi. You Nik?"

"Who wants to know?" He shifted a glance to the upstairs behind him. Nik had a hose in one hand and water bucket in the other.

"Darren Mclean."

Nik's eyes appraised Darren's ride before the driver. "Cop?"

"Ex. Just like my car." He beamed as though proud of the hulk. It couldn't run down any of Nik's vehicles in an all-out chase but it could function as a heck of a roadblock.

"The offset wheels give them away. Yours is the first I've seen in a while that wasn't a taxi, post-retirement."

"A parting gift. Better than a watch."

"So what can I help you with, ex-cop Mclean?" Nik started to fill the bucket.

"I'm looking for Marvin Richter."

"Aren't we all? I've got men and equipment on standby waiting for his okay."

Darren strolled around the Cobra. According to the security report it, like the others parked inside, was a repli-car. The classic look but far less valuable than a genuine mid-1960's original Shelby version. "Nice." He tried to look inexpert. The security firm hadn't been diligent. Or were incompetent.

"Thanks. One of those South African copies." Nik bent over his bucket.

While his attention wavered, Darren tapped his fingernails on the fender. Ting. Jackpot.

"You and Richter get along in the reborn Coelacanth? I'm working for your boss. Worried why Marvin's overdue."

"Sure. This environment doesn't offer much choice."

"Yeah. Principles and unemployment or swallow your ego and feed the family."

"You got it."

"But no idea where Richter's gone?"

Nik shook his head as he sprayed the hood with water. "Fly fishing."

"The story from Formag too." Darren glanced at the mansion. "Just you and the wife?"

"That's right." Nik rubbed a wet cloth over the car and sprayed again.

"She like cars?"

"Expensive SUV's."

"Ah." This wasn't getting anywhere. Give me an airless room and a spotlight, he thought.

Nik splashed Darren's shoes with the hose. "Sorry."

"Wife home?"

Nik stopped spraying. "Palm Springs."

"She know about your...guest?"

Nik didn't quiver. "Probably."

One of those marriages, Darren concluded. "How liberal of your both. She know about Molly?" A stab worth taking.

Nik tensed for a moment. "Brief and ultimately unfulfilling. Like a tart."

Nik poured the bucket onto the lawn. "I'm going for a drive before dark if you're done." He was already buckling the five-point seat harness. The engine fired to life with a roar.

"Enjoy," Darren shouted over the exhaust howl.

He checked his watch. He had time for the Mocambo.

The taxi dropped Darren off in front of the nightclub. A neon gaucho hat and maracas lit up the wet sidewalk. He elbowed a path through the crowd to the stand-up bar and ordered a Brasilia with lime. He sipped and observed. The dance floor was packed and in Latin tradition the heads and shoulders remained stationary, all the movement happening below, masked by the bodies themselves. He peered deeper into the mass, looking for Molly.

The music's rhythm infected him and he had to concentrate to stop his hips from swaying in time.

"*Buenas noches*." Molly appeared beside him. "Come on, park your beer on our table."

He followed, admiring the movement of her hips under the long skirt. They came to a small table with three chairs and a half dozen drinks under a woman's guard. Molly said, "You met Carla yesterday. She's the designated drink-Nazi."

Coelacanth's receptionist held out her hand in greeting. "I make sure no one adds anything."

"Keep a close watch on my beer, Carla, I don't want to wake up in the arms of a stranger, feeling like two pounds of crap in a one pound bag."

Both women laughed. Molly said, "You're fresh blood for this crowd, your fear may be more legitimate than you think." She cocked an ear. "The tempo is picking up. Do you Salsa?"

Darren pushed his beer to the center of the table. "It's been a while but let's give it a go."

Whatever moves he had forgotten, Molly soon refreshed them and muscle memory took over. He couldn't avoid constant contact with her in the milling crowd. She didn't seem to mind so he ignored his self-consciousness and enjoyed the music and the frottage of the South American experience.

"Three dances and I'm sweating. I'm going to need beer if Carla hasn't drunk it as her fee," he said.

Molly leaned closer, a hand on his shoulder. "What?"

He leaned forward and repeated his statement. She nodded and pulled him in her wake from the floor. A man sat at the table, talking with Carla. The girl stood, grabbing her date. "Your turn," she said to Molly. The pair disappeared into the dance crowd.

"You dance well, Darren. How many Latin clubs where you're from?"

He swallowed a mouthful of beer. "At this moment, none. I went to school in Edmonton and there were a few good ones there."

Molly nodded. "I did my undergrad at the University of Alberta. I wasn't into Latin then. Wish I had been, we might have run into each other then, instead of waiting all these years."

He hoisted his bottle. "To the wasted years."

"I'm serious, you're more versatile than my regular crowd. How are you on swing dancing?"

"Passable." He felt a firm hand on his thigh.

He turned to Molly, resting his hand on her exploring one. "I'm unarmed, Miss Hatch."

She continued her caress. "You're pretty good on the dance floor. How are you with the horizontal Mambo?"

"You making up for those wasted years? It's a little sudden."

She leaned close. "Sounds reasonable to me. I'll even make you breakfast, Dick Tracy."

"I'm no Dick Tracy." He removed her hand from his leg and held it. "I'm no Sam Spade, either. I'm flattered beyond belief at your proposal but professional discretion trumps my animal lust. I propose we dance our brains out tonight, I cab back to my apartment and I will come to your house for coffee in the morning. Then we will see if we still like each other." He opened his eyes and mouth wide in exaggeration of a brilliant idea. "Besides, I've had enough advances in a squad car to know a bluff when I feel one. You came here to dance."

She put her free hand on his. "Bluff called and coffee's on. Can you remember my address? I am without pen and paper in this outfit."

"I leave nothing to chance. And from dancing I know you aren't carrying anything extra." He pulled a small notebook and pen from his shirt pocket and handed it to her.

Carla and a different partner returned to exchange seats with Darren and Molly.

Molly scribbled a note and returned the pad and pen. "Now I make you earn that. Come on."

"The beat's picking up," he called into her ear.

"Shut up and dance."

"Help yourself to coffee, Darren. I'll be out in a minute. There's milk in the fridge and sugar on the table." Molly called from another room.

"Creamer?" he asked. "The detachment had creamer and I'm hooked."

"If I do it's in the cupboard left of the fridge."

Darren opened the door and found the cylinder. He noted the shelf's other contents in passing. Cornstarch, isinglass, whole oats. He closed the cupboard and stirred the white powder into his cup. What the hell was isinglass?

He wandered into the hallway. "I need to ask you about Marvin Richter. That's why I was in your office Wednesday."

"You mentioned detachment but you're not police anymore."

"No. I'm private. Formag asked me to look into the disappearance."

"What can I tell you?"

"Where he is. Then I can return to scratching for work."

"No idea. Fishing was the last I heard."

"Did you socialize with him?"

She appeared in work attire rubbing her hair with a towel. "Not really. Nice guy. Loves his work and hobby. You saw his office?"

"Yeah. The mounted trout. Another monster of the deep."

"Some work to finance a lifestyle. That was Marvin, in my opinion. I think he enjoyed work but his passion was divided now. Tough economic times encourage one to question priorities."

"And you? What's your passion?"

"Making deals. Getting the money interested in Coelacanth. Be successful more than once."

"Any thoughts on Nik Orlaski's passion?"

She frowned, pulling the towel away. "Himself. Best present anyone could give him is a full-length mirror. What was your last posting before leaving the force?"

"Port George. Vancouver Island."

She looked at her watch. Molly went back into the bathroom.

Darren finished his coffee, tidied up in the kitchen and returned the creamer to its shelf.

Molly came out with her briefcase. He followed her into the attached garage. It was cluttered with sports equipment: skis (uphill and downhill, he noted), climbing ropes and gear, kayak, mountain bike and a deflated raft. "You're very outdoorsy," he commented.

She climbed in her Teutonic convertible and pressed the starter. "This is a great climate, as long as you don't mind winter. What did you do in Port George to keep fit?"

"Stayed away from the local cafe's pastry. Run to the airport and back every second day. Twelve K round trip."

"Rain or shine?"

"There is no shine in Port George. There's rain or drizzle. Thanks for the coffee. Dinner tonight?"

"I can't. Not this evening. Business. Tomorrow if I'm not in the mountains, or Monday? Call me."

He stepped under the closing garage door and watched her drive away. He stood beside his car but didn't get in. He waited ten minutes in the fresh air, then re-entered her house through the kitchen door he'd unlocked.

Darren sat alone in Richter's office. Coelacanth was closed for the week. He checked his watch. Six o'clock. Ennis would be starting shift. Darren's phone buzzed. He opened the text message from one of Coelacanth's experts in chemical analysis. Their work normally consisted of emulsion breakdown but they turned his request around in ten hours. Impressive. The RCMP would've taken a month. He saved it and called Ennis.

"Pudge? It's Mclean. Thanks for the reference with Russell Formag. His exec's disappearance is making a bit of sense. Can you spare me some time this weekend?"

Ennis' voice shouted over the ether and Darren had to hold the phone away. "Who you calling *Pudge*, ya fat, lazy..."

Darren let his colleague expletive himself dry then said, "So? Time?"

"Yeah, I trust your judgment that much. Tell me when and where."

"Thanks. Might be a long night so bring sandwiches." He disconnected as Formag came in.

"Everyone's gone except you and me. How's it going?"

Darren closed the file and pocketed his phone. "I'm ready to include Detective Ennis. I know how and where. You supplied why. Now I need your aid to determine who."

"Name it."

"I want you to move offices."

"Like in here? To Marv's?"

"No. Move Coelacanth."

"Are you nuts? You know what it cost to break a lease, let alone re-locate?"

Darren placated him. "Not for real. Tell your executives you've got an offer you can't refuse for half the current rent with break-fees covered. Tell them tomorrow morning. I assume they all are on your text list."

"This'll help find Marvin?"

"I'm afraid it will."

Ennis nodded forward in his chair. Darren sat in the dark, his eyes on the monitors. Movement. He nudged the detective. "Look at this."

Ennis sat up, alert. "What the hell is that?" He pointed to the light grey bundle carried by the black-garbed figure.

"Watch. I think it's a raft."

"Raft? Who goes rafting in the middle of an office? On the floor?"

"No one. It's for the liquid in the tank. Let's watch the rest in person. Can you keep your knee joints quiet?"

"Look Mclean, this is the second night I've had to wait and it's what, three a.m.? I'll move real slow, I promise."

Darren turned to Russell Formag. "You stay here." Darren led the pair from Richter's office to the corridor leading to the lobby. He and Ennis stood outside the cone of light from above the Coelacanth tank. They watched in silence as the lithe figure opened the hinged side of the tank and pushed the clear hose into the liquid below. Repeated squeezing of the siphon pump soon had the preservative flowing from the tank into the raft. While the tank drained, the figure unzipped a duffle bag and removed a rope, swinging it over the beams above. Darren chanced a glance at the man beside him. Ennis looked puzzled.

The raft took shape, inflated not with air but preserving alcohol. The figure stood on a chair and pulled the rope harness into the tank. A hand dug at the gravel beside the prehistoric fish. The rope made fast, the figure stepped down and began to pull on the free end of the rope.

Ennis stroked his chin and nodded in understanding. A limp body pulled free from the rocks in the tank, then hovered for a minute to drain. The Coelacanth and the body were of similar length and similar state of death. Separated by two-hundred million years of evolution, nothing else.

Darren mouthed, *Richter*.

Ennis nodded and quietly unsnapped his holstered sidearm. He mimed, *Now*?

They separated as planned, Darren staying in the shadows until he reached the opposite side. Ennis turned on the main lights.

The figure wheeled at the sudden illumination, saw the Detective and dashed for the other entrance. Darren caught the fugitive full-bore and carried them both to the ground. Darren breathed a sigh of relief. It wasn't his dance partner. He stood and swung the captive around to face Ennis. The Detective removed the ski mask.

Darren said, "Mr. Orlaski. Hope you enjoyed your last ride in that repli-car. You and I both know it's a real Cobra, aluminum body, not fiberglass. You must've embezzled quite a fortune. Until Richter caught you. Then you tried to frame Molly. Ex-lover, still had a key to her place. Plant the first raft and the isinglass in case it went sideways."

"You can't prove dick."

Darren held him tight. "We don't need to at this point, Nik. We have you recovering Richter's body.

That's incriminating enough. Marvin demanded a late-night meeting to confront you and you killed him."

"I can plead second-degree, even manslaughter."

"This elaborate hiding of the body screams premeditation. Sure, you already had access to the raft, hose and ropes but you had to buy the siphon pump and the isinglass the day before you met Richter. Better read his rights, Detective."

Ennis asked, "What's the deal with the isinglass?"

Darren said, "It's a fining agent, adheres to tiny solids suspended in a liquid to clear it. Wine-makers use it to clear the fermenting juice. He couldn't be sure the Coelacanth tank would remain clear, after disturbing the rocks and burying Richter under them. He also didn't know if he'd start to decompose. I took a sample of the gravel and found isinglass. The raft in Molly's garage still had traces of the tank's alcohol. It was her or you."

Ennis rattled off Orlaski's rights then handcuffed him. He called the station and ordered a squad to take charge of the scene.

Darren, Ennis and Formag stood outside in the parking lot.

Molly drove up and got out of her car. "I got your text about the move late, Russell. I was hiking. What the hell is going on?"

When Darren finished she said, "You told me you weren't Sam Spade. What did you mean?"

Darren chewed his lip. "If it had been you instead of Nik, I couldn't be sure I would have been strong enough to trap you if I'd spent the night with you. Unlike Sam Spade with Bridget O'Shaughnessy."

She said, "He's not real. He's a movie character."

Darren nodded once. "Yeah, he's not real but my attraction is."

She said, "Not a promising start for a relationship."

"No. You'll be busy doing damage control for Russell and I'll be busy trying to keep busy. I will call, though. Count on it."

Ennis came close and said, "You're a good cop, Mclean. This PI crap isn't for you. If you want to go city, let me know, there's room for you."

Maybe he wouldn't be so busy after all. Darren watched Molly enter the office building. Give her time, he thought.

"I think we can work something out," Darren said. He looked around the lot. "And I have my own car."

CAPPY'S SMART MONKEY
SHARON WILDWIND

Wind rattled our boarding house window. I opened it and leaned out to check the sky. A gust blew sleet needles into my face. Welcome to Calgary.

"Close that window. Do you want me to die of pneumonia?"

"Yes." I slammed the lower window shut and opened the top a couple of inches. Our tiny attic room was stuffy.

The Honourable Crispian St. Jean Marlowe untangled his head from a towel. The steam he'd inhaled plastered his sparse blond hair to his head. He looked pathetic sitting with his feet in hot water, and a soggy towel around his shoulders. It didn't pay to be sympathetic. Sympathy made him maudlin. We couldn't afford that.

"Drink you tea, Crispian."

"Not Crispian, Christopher Loewmar. Kit Loewmar to my friends. Try to remember it."

I poured him a cup of warmish tea, doctored it with sugar, and added a dollop of strengthener from my bottle. "Why not Christopher Marlowe? Then your name would still match the initials on your trunk."

"Really, Jonathan," he said in that hoity-toity British tone he used when he though me too stupid to live. He drained the cup and pressed it against his forehead. "That's better."

I refilled his cup.

He raised it in mock salute. "To Calgary, the biggest city between Winnipeg and Vancouver. Four blocks of muddy streets, with more open spaces than buildings."

"They still have banks."

"More important, they have only three ways out of town, train, horse, or on foot. We haven't got a horse. Even if we did, pursuers can see for miles. The city cops are a joke, but leave town, and the Mounties are after you."

"They can't be as good as people say."

"What worries me is they're bored. They've been cooped up at Fort Calgary all winter."

Bored men were dangerous. Bored men with guns were worse. "Okay, we leave by train."

It would be a while before we could safely spend the bank take, but I had just enough money to move us a little further down the track.

"Train means telegraph. They'd wire ahead."

"Only after they knew they'd been robbed."

The Auld Queen was dead almost a year and a half, but it looked like her birthday was sticking around as a holiday. "Saturday is Victoria Day. Everybody will be at a parade, tea parties, or fireworks. They have tea parties and fireworks here, don't they?"

"I've heard them mentioned."

"Is there a Saturday morning train?"

"Ten-oh-seven, headed west.

"We hit a bank Friday night, and get on the train Saturday morning. By the time they discover the robbery, we're well away."

Something small and furry flew by my face. I screamed, "Rat!"

The creature wasn't a rat. It was a small, fuzzy-faced monkey that looked one step away from drowned. The pathetic creature, making frantic chattering noises, hid behind Crispian. He took the towel from his shoulders and held out his arm. "On."

The monkey jumped on his forearm. He dried it roughly with his towel.

"Don't do that. It probably loaded with fleas."

"Barney is a very clean monkey. He's bathed twice a week with lye soap."

The monkey jumped from Crispian's lap to the dresser and sat several inches from our unlit candle.

"Light the candle, will you? Fire fascinates him. But keep the matches away from him. He's almost figured out how they work."

When I lit the candle, Barney settled on his haunches, his paws folded in his lap, mesmerized by the flame. I shut the top window—the way the monkey squeezed in—and opened the bottom one wide as an invitation for it to leave.

"Mrs. Stover doesn't seem the type for monkeys."

"Barney lives at the fire hall. He's a great one for hitching rides, invited or uninvited."

I picked up the monkey, flung it into the rain, and felt a sharp pain in my finger. "Ow. The damn thing bit me." I slammed the window shut and examined my bleeding finger. "Just my luck the damn thing will have rabies."

Crispian dripped one foot out of the tub and dried it with the same towel that had held the monkey. "You shouldn't have startled him. He won't forget, or forgive."

I blew out the candle, and then added a heavier shirt over the clothes I'd worn to breakfast. "I don't like monkeys. What bank?"

"If we must, the Dominion. It's by itself at the end of the street. Fewer police patrols."

"Night guard?"

"None of the banks have night guards. The Dominion manager is a puffed up popinjay. He'd love to lord it over other managers that his bank hired a night guard."

"Where does he live?"

"North of the tracks, 207 McIntyre Avenue West. Big house, white on the bottom, green on the top, sitting all by itself. You can't miss it."

"Are there letters?"

"Beneath my undershirts."

There were two letters in an oilskin pouch. One was on light blue monogrammed paper that smelled faintly of Lily of the Valley toilet water. James Beston — at least Kit let me keep my initials — had worked as a hotel detective for the Continental Gentlemen's Hotel in Toronto. I was charming, discrete, and totally reliable. The owner's unexpected death forced his widow to close the hotel. She wished me well in future endeavours.

The second was a no-nonsense, typed referral signed by Thaddeus Jarvis Sternwood—Rosewood, Toronto. I was a solid fellow, ideally suited for working alone. Mr.

Sternwood was travelling, but could be reached *Post Restente* London or Paris. *Post Restente* translated as don't expect a reply soon.

"Works of art, Cr — Kit."

"Thank you."

I doubted fingerprint testing had made it to Calgary, but Crispian and I learned caution in Toronto. "Where did you find the typewriter?"

"The YMCA Office. Cleaned and polished after use. Always leave a machine in better shape than you found it."

And remove fingerprints at the same time. I rewrapped the letters, shoved them in my waistband, and topped off with a slicker and rain hat Mrs. Stover had unearthed in her basement. They smelled of mildew. Bank robbery schemes were already turning in my head. I had my hand on the doorknob when Crispian said, "Gideon Manchester is here."

I wanted to believe I was sweating from being overdressed in a stuffy room. "What do you mean here?"

"He was in the audience at High River."

Some men gambled; some drank. Crispian's downfall was footlights. Bored waiting for me to arrive, he'd hooked up with the Great Bostock Theatrical Company. Since the players couldn't afford train fare to High River, they'd hiked forty-five miles, carrying scenery on their backs. They disbanded after two performances, the second of which was an egg-throwing debacle. Kit hiked back to Calgary, minus scenery and theatrical companions.

"Did he make you?"

"I don't think so. I was whiskered up to play the heroine's grandfather, and listed as Christopher P.

Loewmar on the program."

"Does the railroad go through High River?"

"Yes."

"Maybe he was passing through on his way somewhere else."

"The High River track is the Calgary and Edmonton Line, not Canadian Pacific. The next train would have brought him back to Calgary."

"And then, another train could have taken him safely away," I said it with as much confidence as I could manage. "I'll be back in a couple of hours."

I headed for McIntyre Avenue West, focused on getting hired as the Dominion Bank's first night guard. The rain and wind were worse. Hard packed streets turned into quagmires. When I crossed the tracks, I sloshed my way through a couple inches of water. Even the rail bed wasn't draining fast enough to keep up with this deluge.

Crispian and I linked up with Gideon Manchester three years ago. For all his fancy clothes and elaborate rings, Gideon was a street fighter who'd graduated from Cleveland's notorious McCart Gang to being a Pinkerton thug. When the State of Ohio outlawed Pinkertons, he came north and went into business for himself in Toronto.

I'd done a lot of jobs for him, but things fell apart when he ordered me to kill a man. I drew the line at killing. Crispian and I hopped a train, pausing only to post a letter — typed, unsigned, no fingerprints — to the Toronto City Police, detailing a few of Manchester lesser known business interests. We hoped police interest would occupy him enough to prevent him from looking for us. Him being here had to be a coincidence. He couldn't have tracked us from Ontario.

Downtown Calgary was in chaos. Men on horseback and in carts dashed up and down Stephen Avenue, throwing up great muddy gouts. Men on foot all headed east. I eased myself in among them. "What's up?"

"Call went out for able-bodied men to report to Fire Headquarters. Bridges are damaged. The area below Langevin Bridge is flooding. They need help getting people out."

Would a popinjay banker consider himself an able-bodied man? Would he answer the call? Would I be wasting my time at an empty green and white house on McIntyre Avenue?

It was an ill wind that blew no one good. A disaster for others might open up what Crispian and I called business opportunities. I could go to McIntyre Avenue later. For now, I joined the crowd walking east.

Fire Headquarters was crowded and noisy. Men filled the space where fire wagons usually parked. The place reeked of wet wool, tobacco, and male sweat. Just inside the door, a man in a double-breasted blue suit with gold buttons, sat at a table, taking names. I joined the queue.

When I reached the table, the man looked up at me. I knew what he saw. Muscles on the hoof. I was tall, and strong, but I wasn't dumb. However, today, brawn was more in demand than brains.

"Name?"

"James Beston."

"Skills?"

"Teamster." If I had a new name, I might as well have a new occupation.

"Come back and see me after Cappy gives his talk."

A sudden weight struck my head. I went sprawling into the table. Papers scattered on the wet, muddy floor.

Tiny hands pulled at my hair. I screamed.

"Barney, stop that," boomed a Scottish voice. A strong hand helped me to my feet, and plucked the attacker from my head. A short, squat man, with huge shoulders, and an exquisite black moustache held Barney in his huge hand. The monkey relieved himself on my boot.

"Put him in his cage, and lock it," the Scotsman said to the double-breasted suit, who was trying to rescue papers from the floor. The man took Barney and hurried away.

The Scotsman held out his hand. "Cappy Smart. I apologize. He isn't usually like that. I don't know what got into him."

I did. "Probably all the people and noise. No harm done."

Crispian — no, Kit — we were in public now. I had to think of him only as Kit Loewmar — sidled up beside me. "Told you Barney wouldn't forget or forgive."

"What are you doing here? I thought you were on the verge of pneumonia."

"Duty called. I thought you were on your way to see a popinjay."

Cappy Smart mounted a chair and clapped his hands. The room quieted.

"I'm grateful tae ye for coming out. Before the telegraph lines went down, Banff Station sent a message. This storm goes all the way tae the mountains. We've only seen the first of it. Track is already out in both directions. Bridges are damaged. The area below Langevin Bridge is flooding. We've also have reports of basements flooding along Stephen Avenue.

"I've issued an evacuation order for everyone living below the bridge. If ye can take in evacuees, or help with food or blankets, with carts or horses, let Assistant Chief Wilson, at the table, know. Now get to work."

Kit said, "Damn."

I turned and my soul contracted. Across the room, two prosperous looking men, both in beaver hats and thick coats with lamb's wool collars, approached Cappy Smart. The larger man was Gideon Manchester. He shook Cappy Smart's hand, and gave him a card.

"Damn, indeed."

"Who's the man with him?"

"Francis Dupond. Jeweller. He has as a shop on Stephen Avenue full of bright, shiny things."

Gideon was a magpie. Shiny things fascinated him. The more they were worth; the more they fascinated him.

Gideon pointed his walking stick in my direction. Cappy Smart looked hard at me. They were talking about me, and I wanted to know what was being said. I strode across the room, just in time to hear Gideon say, "Of course, the railroad wants to keep it quiet."

I crowded in on Gideon. He took a step back. It felt like a small victory.

He smiled. His gold tooth was just visible. "What an unexpected pleasure to see you in Calgary."

He held out his hand. I braced myself for a bone-crushing grip that would break a small bone or him turning his elaborate ring inward to cut my palm, but I received an ordinary, manly handshake. Gideon intended to play with me, like a cat played with a mouse.

"I was telling Chief Smart about your remarkable good fortune on the train. Three fires and you discovered each one before they got out of hand. That makes you a hero."

It also implied I was a firebug. Coves who set fires often stuck around to accidentally discover them. "I'm just a man who notices things."

Gideon smiled his gold-tooth smile. "So do I." He nodded in Kit's direction, and reached into his coat pocket.

"Chief, I have no skill for rescue work, but I want to contribute toward feeding the evacuees." He took five dollars from his pocketbook, and handed it to Cappy Smart, who pocketed it.

"That's very generous. I'll see it gets tae the right people."

Things would be a good sight better if Gideon fed Toronto families who were going hungry because of his schemes and scams.

"And now, I shall let you continue your most laudable work. Francis, should we check your store for flooding?"

They left. Smart grabbed a handful of my shirt. I looked down at him. He might be short, but he was strong, maybe stronger than me. He pulled me close. "Listen up, Laddie. I'm tae busy tae deal with ye right now, but if there is one fire, one hint of a fire, ye're the one I'm coming for. Is that clear?"

He let go of my shirt. I pulled myself upright. "Make sure you have your facts straight before you do something you'll regret." I turned on my heel and walked back to Kit.

"I got a glimpse at Gideon's business card in his pocketbook. He's going by George Mott, Special Agent; Federated Insurance of Winnipeg."

"Insurance dodge?"

"Likely. We can get out of town in the confusion. All we have to do was hurry along, and say *rescue business*, to anyone who stops us."

"No, we can't.

And gentlemen in England now-a-bed
Shall think themselves accurs'd they were not here,
And hold their manhoods cheap whiles any speaks
That fought with us upon Saint Crispin's day."

There were times I didn't have a clue what Kit was carrying on about.

"I know the men at the YMCA Office. I'll see if I can help there. *Cry God for Harry, England, and Saint George!'"*

Assistant Chief Wilson's records were in shambles, so the queue moved slowly. When we were again face-to-face, I refreshed his memory. "James Beston, Teamster."

He found a semi-clean piece of paper. "Livery stable is on the corner of Atlantic and Drinkwater. This paper authorizes them to loan you a horse and rig, for use in town, for the duration of the emergency. After you pick up your rig, get down to Langevin Bridge."

"I'm new to town. I don't know where anything is."

"Plenty of men on the street. Ask for directions. Next."

I folded the paper and tucked it in my oilskin pouch, next to my two bogus reference letters.

The livery stable gave me a sorrel mare and a dilapidated cart with Delivery painted on the side in peeling white letters. From the way it reeked, I wasn't sure the last thing delivered in it had been alive.

Five minutes later, I was at the Langevin Bridge. The noise was deafening. I had no idea rampaging water was so noisy, or so strong. Entire trees flowed past at high speed. On the opposite bank, people crowded together on higher ground. Firemen on both sides had taken charge of creating order out of chaos.

A tall fireman in a slicker and fire hat motioned for me to lean down so he could yell in my ear. "Bridge is damaged, but she'll hold for a while. Stay to the right, coming and going. Cross over, load up, and come back. Don't stop for anything. She'll shake some."

I dug in my pockets for the watch I'd inherited from my dad, my remaining few dollars, and the oilskin pouch. "If something happens to me, these go to Kit Loewmar at Stover's Boarding House."

"Nothing is going to happen to you. Get on your way." He took my things anyway, which spoke a lot louder than his assurances.

Shake some didn't begin to describe it. The bridge had become a living thing, creaking, swaying, occasionally hiccoughing like it was fixing to turn into a bucking horse. It can't have taken me more than a couple of minutes to cross, but it seemed a lot longer.

My load of misery was a mother with five children, and two older women who, apparently, didn't speak English. The children ranged from a girl about fourteen, to a toddler in arms. The girl carried the toddler; the mother carried a heavy carpetbag, all they had managed to save. Between them, the two old women carried a wooden cage with a rooster and two chickens.

The trip back was better. Maybe extra weight stabilized the cart, or maybe having old women and kids on board, angels watched out for us. I wasn't looking forward to making the trip again empty, but I'd do it as many times as I had to. I knew what it was like to leave home with only what could be carried in a sack. What surprised me was how much the memory still hurt.

The fireman handed me my watch, money, and

letters. "Take this load to Van Horne Avenue. The CPR employees have been told to open their homes to evacuees. When you've off-loaded, come back."

At least, I wouldn't have to make another empty crossing right away.

The mother knew the way to Van Horne, two blocks south of the tracks. A wizened ancient with huge white side-whiskers stopped us at the corner. "End of the row, where the last lamp is shining."

Instead of houses, Van Horne was a row of connected brick dwellings. The door arrangements suggested four apartments to each building, two on the first floor and two on the second floor. Women or old men stood on the brick steps, holding lanterns. A few stoops were empty. Was no one home, or had the people who lived in those apartments chose not to follow their employer's orders? I knew something about that, too.

I stopped at the last building. A young woman, her black hair done up in a bun, and a shawl over her shoulders, stood on the porch, her lamp held high, like I'd seen in photographs of New York's Statue of Liberty.

I said, "Three adults, five kids, and three chickens."

"Okay, but we'll be crowded." She blew out her lantern. "Into the basement, everyone."

I'd been wrong, each building had six apartments; two in the basement. Were they flooding, too?

The children clambered out of the wagon, and down metal stairs at the building's side. Their mother yelled, "Don't touch anything."

A big man with greasy hair and thick, black eyebrows staggered around the building's corner. "Lucy, what the hell are you doing? Get away, get out of here." He flapped his arms as if that would make the evacuees vanish.

"The railroad said to. What are you doing here? You're supposed to be on a run."

"Fell asleep and missed my train."

"You'll get fired."

"You know what they say, miss a train, there will be another one along."

That likely applied to passengers, not CPR employees. I assumed this was Lucy's husband. Reeking of alcohol and other things, he smelled worse than the cart. He tried to wrestle the chicken cage from the old women. The women slipped, and fell in the mud. The cage broke open; the birds escaped; and the women tried to catch them.

Lucy put her hand on the man's arm. "These people have no place to go. The railroad said to do this."

"Damn the railroad." He put his hands around the fourteen year old who stood, shivering, in the cart. "You, missy, can stay. Got a really warm place for you."

Her mother tried to remove the man's hands from her daughter's waist. The man made a fist, pulling one arm back to hit her. I cold cocked him with one blow.

I yelled, "Everyone, back in the cart."

Children ran up the stairs and climbed on board. The two old women, who had caught the rooster and one chicken, sloshed their way back. I grabbed Lucy's arm, "Get in the cart. He's not going to be in a good mood when he wakes up."

"I have to get something."

"There's no time."

"You start out. I'll catch up."

"Hurry."

I got the sorrel moving slowly. In less than a minute, Lucy, carrying a carpet bag, stepped over her husband's body. I stopped the cart. When she came abreast, I grabbed her bag and tossed it into the back, hoping it missed the chickens and the old women. I gave Lucy my hand, pulled her into the seat beside me, and flicked the reins. The sorrel picked up speed.

I glanced over my shoulder. Lucy's husband was on his hands and knees. Even with a horse, the mud streets made it doubtful we could escape a man on foot. What scared me more was that, at the other end of the long street, Gideon Manchester, sat on a horse, watching.

Lucy said, "Turn right, and then left at the next corner."

"Where are we going?"

"To a friend of mine. She'll take us in."

"You give me directions. I'll get us there."

She held out her hand. "Lucy Blackstone."

"Johnny, ah James."

"Mr. James, you are a Godsend."

Great. Now I had a second alias I had to keep track of.

The incessant rain made our trip seem like hours, but more likely, it was about forty-five minutes. We were out of town, travelling along a narrow muddy trail. Scattered shacks dotted the prairie, the only signs of civilization.

One of the kids said, "There's a man following us."

I didn't turn around. "I know him. He won't bother us."

"He's coming closer."

I heard hoof beats. Between the muddy road and the cart's dilapidated condition, I didn't dare urge the horse to go faster. I stopped. "Let me do the talking."

Gideon pulled up beside us and tipped his hat brim. "Ladies. I'll ride escort for you, if I may? No telling what dangers there are out here."

Lucy's small hand closed around my arm. She didn't want a stranger knowing where she was taking refuge, and with good reason. I said, "Not today, thank you, Mr. Mott."

"Then I'll ride slightly behind you, shall I?"

"Go back to Calgary. Our business will have to wait until these people are safe."

"I may not be able to wait."

"You'll have to."

"I suppose all good things come to those who wait." Meaning, the longer I put off settling things with him, the harder it would go for me. He tipped his hat again, turned his horse and rode back the way he'd come.

The prairie and sky were solid grey. Pelting rain melted into soggy ground. A white dot appeared in the distance. The dot became an indistinct blur, then the shape of a woman in a white apron, standing on a cabin's porch. The small cabin, backed by a barn and a few smaller buildings, was nothing compared to Calgary houses. Grey weathered walls all but disappeared into the landscape.

The woman called out, "Lucy, is that you? What's happened?"

"The river's flooding. We had to evacuate."

The woman craned her neck. "Pippa, Verna, välkommen."

One of the older women yelled, "Anna!" They both waved furiously.

I stopped beside the porch to let my passengers disembark. There were introductions. The woman on the porch was Ann Tilton; the mother, Mrs. Weller. I forgot the children's names as soon as I heard them. Pippa and Verna launched into an elaborate explanation of something, to which Anna replied, "*Vara med lätthet.*

Gud är här," which seemed to placate them.

"Johnny James," I said, remembering both my manners and who I had to be as long as Lucy was in earshot.

Mrs. Tilton said, "Put the horse in the barn, and come inside. You need to get out of those wet clothes."

Pippa and Verna climbed back on the cart, and placed their crate between them. I had no idea why, but apparently they knew, so that was all right.

I hesitated at the barn door. I hadn't been inside a barn since I left home. One of the women got out and opened the doors. Barn and livestock odors hit me like a wave. I gagged and almost threw up. I never would have gone in, but Pippa, or maybe Verna, took hold of the bridle and led the horse inside.

The barn was somewhat wind proof. The earth inside had taken on the soft texture of over saturated ground. Every place I stepped left a boot impression. I found an empty stall, groomed and fed the horse. As long as I focused on the sorrel and a steady, rhythmical brush stroke, I was okay. I gradually managed small, covert glances, telling myself it was only a barn.

Pippa and Verna fed their rooster and chicken, and made a straw nest for them. They held a conference. One of them picked up a pitchfork. It was as tall as she was.

I took it from her, and pointed to my chest. "Me. I do this. You. House."

Both women hugged me. I smiled, and hugged them back. They left.

There was no point mucking out the stalls until the ground dried. I tossed dry straw into each one. Ann came with pig slops, a bucket of warm water, a rag, and an empty bucket. She set the last three outside the cow's stall. One look told me it was definitely milking time. I found a milking stool.

"What's her name?"

"Prudence."

I washed the udders. "Okay, Pru. I'm not your usual milker, but I'm cold and wet, and I'd appreciate it if you didn't kick the bucket or put your foot in it."

Milk streamed into the bucket.

"You know your way around animals."

"Ontario farm boy, a long time ago. Is there a Mr. Tilton?"

"Peter went to Calgary for a meeting."

"I expect it's been cancelled."

"I expect so."

"What did you say, on the porch, to the old women?"

"Be at peace. God is here."

I wasn't much for God-people, but Ann seemed all right.

"What's their story?"

"They're sisters. Pippa's grandson brought them with him from Sweden."

I would have given anything to take my grandmother with me.

"Olaus died. The Friends tried to locate other relatives, but we don't think there are any."

"You have wonderful friends."

"Capital F, The Society of Friends."

"Quakers."

"You've heard of us?"

"The rescue mission in Toronto helped me find a place to live and a job."

"We prefer to call them settlement houses."

I called them my salvation.

By the time we returned to the cabin, an early, wet evening had set. Ann offered me Peter's clothes, which I changed into while mine dried on lines strung over the wood stove. The one-room cabin had a quilt-covered double bed, wooden table, some chests, and two chairs. More important, there was hot tea, food, and a fire. It felt like heaven. At bedtime, we moved the few furnishings along the wall. Pippa and Verna, with the toddler sleeping between them, were given the bed. Everyone else made do on the floor.

Ann said, "Mr. James, perhaps it would be a good idea if we made rounds?"

The rain was lighter; the wind, stronger. Ann and I clung to one another in order to make it across the barnyard. The tool shed and chicken coop were all right. The barn looked all right — at first glance.

Ann said, "Johnny," in a tight, sad voice.

The rooster and chicken were exactly as we'd left them in their nest, except they were dead.

"Shock. Chickens are more fragile than they look."

"Turkeys are worse," I said, taking a closer look at the birds. I found what I was afraid to find. "They didn't die of shock. Somebody had rung their necks."

Ann, her hand in front of her mouth, made a small noise.

"Stay here." I searched every bit of the barn, paying special attention to the sorrel. It was easy to nick a horse's fetlock. They'd be okay when you started out, but they'd soon pull up lame. The horse was untouched.

Ann had found an old burlap sack and was putting feathers in it as she plucked the rooster. "Extra mouths to feed," she said. I sat beside her and began on the chicken.

She said, "Who was the man on the road?"

"Unfinished business."

"Are we in danger?"

"Anytime there isn't a constable in earshot, folks are in danger."

"Some people are more in danger when there is a constable in earshot."

"True. I assume, being Quakers, you have no weapons."

"We don't believe in weapons. How dangerous is this man?"

"Very, but it's me he's after. He won't bother you after I leave." I lied. Gideon did what Gideon took it in his mind to do.

"What's your story, Mr. James?"

"Actually, it's Mr. Brock, Jonathan Brock. Mr. James is, well, a misunderstanding." It felt good to be myself for a change.

"What is Jonathan Brock's story?"

"One I don't talk about." I hadn't, ever, not even to Crispian. After ten minutes of silence with Ann, I thought, why not?

"My dad got sick and died. Grief drove Grandpa crazy. He changed. He took out his anger on my Grandma and Mom. She left with my sisters. I couldn't leave Grandma alone with him."

"What happened?"

I concentrated pulling feathers. "One day, Grandpa chained me in a barn a lot like this one. All I could do was yell for him to stop beating Grandma to death. When he came to himself, he unshackled me. Told me to run to town and tell the police that a horse had kicked her. Before I left, I whitewashed on the barn wall that he'd killed her. I gathered what I could, headed for the nearest railroad, hopped a train, and left."

"What happened to your grandfather?"

"I never tried to find out."

"How old were you?"

"Fifteen."

"Where does this man come into the story?"

"Later."

I did the messier parts of dressing and cutting up the chickens. After I'd washed my hands in a puddle and dried them on my pants, I took out my money. "Is this enough to buy Pippa and Velma more chickens?"

"That's enough to buy a large number of chickens."

"Please, give it to them. Divide it up and give it to all of them."

"You don't have to do this."

"I have more where I'm staying." What I had was a Toronto bank book with a balance of less than three dollars. There was some chance I wouldn't have any use for even that amount after Manchester and I settled things.

We went back to the cabin. Ann set the chickens to cook, and then curled up on the floor next to Mrs. Weller. I stationed myself in a wooden chair pulled in front of a window.

Was Gideon out there? Since he had no way of knowing that Ann would suggest we make rounds, there had been a good chance the dead birds wouldn't have been discovered until morning. He might plan to kill us all as we slept, but I didn't think so. Gideon liked stirring up trouble, and then watched people tie themselves in knots. The worst thing I could do was stay awake fretting while Gideon had a good night's sleep in Calgary. I slept when I could.

I was awake at first light, moving quietly so as not to wake anyone. I'd gotten off the train Saturday evening. It was now Monday morning. In thirty-six hours, I'd been bitten and peed on by a monkey; encountered the one man I wanted to avoid; made a new enemy; rescued a bunch of women; and lost track of my best friend. At least, Crispian could take care of himself.

Likely, Rufus Blackstone was looking for me. If the livery stable owner reported a missing horse and cart, the Mounties wanted me for horse theft. If there'd been even a hint of a fire, the Fire Chief was looking for me as a firebug. Calgary was not growing on me.

I stepped out on the porch, quietly closing the door behind me. It was just raining, not pouring. The bone-chilling wind gusted so hard that I wasn't sure the flimsy cart would hold up all the way back to Calgary. I headed into the wind, around the house toward the barn.

Gideon waited for me in front of the barn. Not only was he better dressed for bad weather, but instead of being on horseback, he drove a dapper green and gold closed Landau. From the way the black mare daintily lifted her hooves from the mud, she wasn't accustomed to being out in bad weather.

"Get in."

"I have to return the cart and horse."

He pulled a nasty-looking Derringer. I had a healthy respect for the small gun. A gun made by Mr. Deringer killed President Lincoln. Nowadays, people incorrectly added a second "r" to the name.

"Get in. Watch your step."

If he didn't want muddy boots in his pristine Landau, he shouldn't have insisted I ride with him. I got in. It wasn't my boots that bothered him. I almost stepped on that stupid monkey, tied to the carriage's floor. Tight rope coils surrounded his small body. His eyes were closed; his mouth puffed in and out, like a fish gasping for air. I hated to see any creature suffer. I reached down to loosen the ropes.

"Leave that alone."

"He can't breathe. What are you doing with him?" I freed Barney from his rope cocoon.

"He popped out of nowhere after I left Calgary. Scared the hell out of me. I've heard he's the Fire Chief's pet. There's sure to be a reward."

"You'll get a bigger reward if you return him alive."

"Don't let him get away."

Barney didn't look in any shape to get away. He lay inert, his neck stretched so far back that his head flopped off my leg. I folded my bandana into a makeshift diaper. Not that it would do any good, but it gave me the illusion of security. In a minute, he pulled himself up. Trembling and whimpering, he hid under my arm.

When we passed the first few scattered houses, Gideon said, "In many ways, Calgary is a small town. Describe a trail to a stranger, and he knows who lives at the end of it. He'll say, 'Peter Tilton's in town, if you're looking for him.'"

I swallowed hard. Damn him.

"He'll even name Peter's hotel. 'Mr. Tilton, your wife was hurt bad in the storm. The doctor's on his way to your place. You'd better come with me.' Lots of uninhabited space to do business on the prairie. I hope Mrs. Tilton won't wait up too many nights for him."

My heart stopped racing. Gideon had killed the chickens just because he could, but he'd made a huge mistake trying to make me think he'd harmed Peter. Either he didn't know Peter and Ann were Quakers, or he didn't know Quaker ways. Peter would never need to stay in a hotel. If Friends thought Ann hurt, men and women would have gone with him to tend her; to pray for her; and to get her body ready for burial, if the worse happened. Gideon hoped to rattle me. I needed to keep up the pretence that he had. "You bastard."

Stephen Avenue was still a quagmire. Merchants cleaned windows, scraped mud from sidewalks, and piled water-damaged goods in front of their stores. A lot of basements had flooded.

Special Insurance Agent Mott had made acquaintances. Men waved to him; he tipped his hat in return. We stopped at a deeply muddy cross street to allow a heavily ladened cart to pass. Barney, who I thought was still asleep, jumped from the window to the nearest telephone pole. Still wearing my improvised diaper, he scurried up the pole, and sat on top, screeching.

Gideon said, "Damn." The cart passed. He flicked the reins. "I'm adding that to the bill you owe me." I considered jumping ship, too. The Landau moved slowly. I wouldn't hurt myself if I leapt for freedom, but I could create a disturbance, and yell for a constable.

It wasn't only the Derringer that stopped me. I was tired of running. It was time Gideon and I settled this.

At the next corner he turned right, turned right again, and entered the alley behind buildings facing Stephen Avenue. He pulled into a small shed, just big enough to keep the horse and carriage out of the rain or sun.

We walked across the alley. Gideon had his Derringer out again. In his other hand, he had a key for a glass door painted with fancy green and gold letters, Francis Dupond, Jeweller, Goldsmith, Clock Repairs. Most businessmen wouldn't label their back doors. That Dupond had told me his was a class establishment. Someone had posted a hand-lettered card inside the glass. Closed Monday due to flood. Open Tuesday.

Gideon unlocked the door and motioned me inside. It was a tidy store, worthy of the gold lettering. Milk glass electric lamps dangled over the display area. A steam radiator sat against one wall. An oak and glass counter, containing all manner of men's and women's jewelry, ran the store's length. The tall glass case behind the counter contained silver pieces, ranging from a huge tray, suitable for engraving, to teething rings and baby cups. The remaining wall space was lined with wooden, metal, and porcelain clocks.

Gideon unlocked another, inside door leading to a narrow staircase that descended into darkness. "You go first."

The black opening smelled of dank water. Like a lot of things, Dupond Jewellers appeared to be bright and shiny on top, with something rank underneath. The narrow stairs were raw wood. They still had a fresh cut smell. Behind me, Gideon struck a match, and lit an oil lamp. The sulphur smell added to the unpleasantness. By the time I reached the last stair, my feet were underwater.

The square basement was smaller than the shop. This was no hole in the ground. The walls were sandstone blocks. From the feel of the water-covered floor beneath my feet, the floor was wood. Not that it would be in good shape after being underwater.

I'd been wrong. Crispian couldn't take care of himself. He was pinioned against a wall with stout ropes around his wrists. The binding ropes went over exposed ceiling beams. His feet disappeared into the murky water, so I didn't know if he was hanging, or resting his feet on the floor. Next to him, Francis Dupond was tied in a similar position. Both men appeared unconscious; neither had a mark on him. Gideon was an expert at not leaving visible marks.

Gideon placed the lamp on a thick wooden bench that held a small smelter and ventilation hood. Smelting gold in a basement, without fresh air, was a bad idea.

I knew a fence in Toronto who had a smelter. Selling melted gold and jewels separately was safer than fencing pieces that could be identified. If the jewels were diamonds, he didn't even have to pry them out. One afternoon, for my amusement, he let me pick diamonds out of liquid gold. He didn't let me keep any.

Crispian raised his head with effort. He whispered, "Sorry, Johnny. I let my guard down."

I started toward him.

"Stay where you are. Turn slowly to your left. Keep your hands visible."

In a corner was a cast iron safe, its feet in water. I recognized the name painted on it, an old, but serviceable model. If my hands weren't so cold, I'd have no trouble opening it. From reflex, I put my hands under my armpits to warm them. I had no intention of opening that safe.

"You made an unnecessary production of drawing the line at killing. I have a deal for you. If you open the safe, I kill Dupond. If you don't open it, I kill Crispian. Either way, a man's death will be your fault."

"You're going to kill us anyway. You can't afford witnesses."

"I'll kill you last. That way, I'll have the satisfaction of you dying with a man's death on your conscious."

I already had my grandmother's death on my conscious. "What's in the safe?"

"Many shiny and interesting things."

"Which one brought you here?"

"A mourning brooch containing Albert's and

Victoria's hair, woven by the Queen's own hand, into a love knot. With Her Majesty dead, it has risen in value. Coronation Day, in London, will be the ideal place to sell it."

"You couldn't make a deal with Dupond?"

"Dupond, much like yourself, erroneously believed he was in charge. He insisted on opening the safe in private. He had no intention of allowing me to see what other indiscreet treasures it held."

Respectable men often gave their disreputable women expensive jewelry. No doubt Calgary had its share of men, women, and jewellery. A discrete jeweller was worth his weight in gold.

Kit said, "Lye baths."

Gideon pointed the Derringer at him.

"Candles and lye baths, Johnny."

Kit was hurt worse than I thought. He was delirious. I had to get both him and Francis to a doctor. My fingers were warm enough that I could give the safe a try. I squatted in front of it, and flexed my fingers. "This may take a few tries. Damp makes the tumblers go funny."

It didn't, but Gideon wouldn't know that.

"Crispian and I knew you'd catch up with us eventually. Dupond is a bystander. Let him go, and Crispian and I will come with you. We're more valuable alive than dead."

Crispian was. I was a fair cracker; he was an astounding forger. "Damn." I hoped Gideon thought the tumblers were being difficult. In reality, they had slipped into place, and the safe was open. I spun the dial. "Start over."

Gideon said, "No witnesses."

"He doesn't know who you are. I assume Federated Insurance of Winnipeg has never heard of George Mott."

136

"There is no Federated Insurance of Winnipeg."

"There you are. No way to trace you. He sure as hell isn't going to advertise how easy it was to clean out of his safe."

Gideon kept the Derringer pointed at Crispian. "I know how good you are. You should have the safe open by now. You have ten seconds. Ten — nine —

I opened it on three. I could have opened it on five, but I a small part of me shared Crispian's love of theatrics.

Inside were a dozen velvet jewelry boxes, each with a folded paper held in place on top by a green and gold paper band. Imprinted on each band were the letters F.D., inside a leaf circle.

Gideon handed me a sack. "Everything in here."

I did as I was told. In addition to the jewelry boxes, there were soft leather pouches, pebbly like they contained gold nuggets, a goldsmith's raw materials. I closed the sack and rose, holding my hands up and the sack in my right hand.

"Put it on bench and move away."

He kept his kept his gaze on me as he picked up a metal can. He moved to the staircase, removed the cork with his teeth, and poured liquid on the stairs. The raw wood soaked up the kerosene. He threw the can on the floor and went back to pick up the sack.

"I always keep my promises." Gideon turned the gun on Francis and fired. I launched myself at him to deflect his shot, but my jump went wide and I landed hard, face down in the water.

Gideon was also down. I heard all too familiar chittering. I pulled my face up and saw Barney throwing small, iron objects from the smelting table at Gideon's prone form.

Gideon was on his knees. I jumped onto his back. Rufus Blackstone had been no fight at all, but Gideon was a long-time street fighter. When he hit, it hurt. A few well-placed blows would kill me.

Behind Gideon, Barney strained to pick up a smelting cup twice as big as he was. I managed to free myself from Gideon's grasp, make it to the bench, and used both hands to heft the cup over my head. One blow would crush Gideon's skull.

Barney retreated as far away as he could. He crouched into a tiny ball with his paws over his eyes. He sounded like he was crying. What I saw was myself, crouched in a similar position, hands over my eyes, crying for Grandpa to stop. I brought the vessel down on Gideon's ankle instead of his head. He howled in pain. Kerosene fumes filled the small room.

Crispian said, "We have to get out of here."

I blew out the oil lamp. Enough daylight filtered down the staircase that Gideon became an enraged, cursing shadow, crawling across the floor. I untied Crispian. Together, we untied Francis. He had a pulse, he was hurt, but alive. I slung him over my shoulder in a fireman's carry. We barely made it up the stairs and out the door when an explosion blew us across the alley.

Dazed, I looked up to see a constable at the alley's East end. He put his hands to his mouth and yelled, "Fire!"

Rufus Blackstone, carrying what looked like a piece of railroad tie, took that moment to appear at the alley's West end. I grabbed Christian by the scruff of his neck and stuffed him in the Landau.

Thank goodness it was an enclosed carriage. By squeezing ourselves together on the floor, the carriage appeared to be empty, but I could still drive it, after a fashion. The terrified mare took off down the alley like Lucifer was after her. We sped past the constable, who changed his cry from, "Fire" to "Runaway horse." A bell clambered from the direction of the Fire Headquarters.

I steered the horse for the Langevin Bridge. Surely, by now, they'd rescued all the evacuees. I hoped the bridge was still standing. It was. More important, it was deserted, with wooden sawhorses blocking each end. Extreme Danger — Do Not Enter had been hastily painted on the sawhorses in dripping red paint. The mare dashed straight through the sawhorses as if they were toothpicks.

The bridge was worse than I remembered. It felt as flimsy as lace. I aimed the mare straight down the middle, figuring that was the safest place, and none to safe at that.

We were two-thirds of the way across when the bridge made a sharp cracking sound and the middle sank into a U-shape. Crispian, smaller and more agile that I was, stood and strained to reach the harness buckle. The horse was away like a flash, heading for the opposite shore. Crispian collapsed into the carriage.

For an instant, we hung there between wind and water. With a loud grinding noise, the bridge gave way and the carriage, with us inside, plunged into the roaring, icy water. Crispian and I clung to one another. He shouted in my ear,

"Nothing of him that doth fade
But doth suffer a sea-change
Into something rich and strange."

I yelled back, "This is no time to compose poetry."

The current threw us into a huge tree that had fallen from an eroded bank into the river. The Landau splintered. We grabbed for branches, skinning our hands, but eventually we pulled ourselves into the tree branches, and worked our way, hand over hand, to the bank. We were several miles downstream from Calgary.

As we lay there panting, I said, "What the hell happened?"

"I have no idea. Maybe Barney finally figured out how to light matches."

Unexpected grief washed over me. "Poor Barney."

"Yeah, Poor Barney."

We were quiet for several minutes, lying on our backs, looking at the sky. A tiny patch of blue appeared overhead.

"Johnny, I want to go home." He pushed himself on one elbow. "I mean Home. England. When we were in the river, all I could think of was that I'd never see England again."

He was my best friend, heck, my only friend, but he'd never been happy in Canada. I managed to sit up. "That and reciting bad poetry. I've always wondered, do you write those things you say beforehand, or do you make them up the spur of the moment."

Crispian sighed. "I write them beforehand."

"I thought so. Earning enough money to get you back to England will take a long time."

He took a leather pouch from his coat pocket. "I can use this."

It was one of Francis' gold nugget pouches.

"Where did you get that?"

"Same place I got this." He reached in another pocket and took out a worn jewellery box. He opened it. Inside was a rectangular gold brooch, studded around the edge with twelve diamonds. In the centre was a domed glass window over a hair knot.

"Where's the rest?"

"I tossed the sack away. Whoever finds it will think the explosion blew it there."

"How did you know which box to take?"

"All the others were new. This one was worn. I took a chance."

We got up, wiped what mud we could from our clothes, and started back toward Calgary. "What are you going to do with the brooch?"

"Return it to Buckingham Palace."

"You can do that, walk up to the Palace, ring the doorbell, and say, 'Excuse me, did you misplace this?'"

"It's more complicated, but my family has connections. Come to England with me."

I'd be as lost in England as Crispian had been in Canada. "I can't. Thanks to Gideon, Cappy Smart thinks I'm a firebug. I have to clear my name."

"How are you going to do that?"

"Become a fireman." Saving Francis Dupond felt good. Maybe it wasn't enough to not kill someone. Maybe it would be a better thing to save lives.

"That is the most ridiculous idea I've ever heard."

"You got a better one?"

"No."

I peeled away the oilskin pouch plastered to my skin. "I know where there's a horse and cart. It's not in great shape, but it might get you some place you can catch a train. There's a letter in here giving me permission to use the horse and cart, but only in Calgary."

Crispian took the pouch. "I can fix that."

"Do me a favor."

"What?"

"The people who have the horse and cart have a young woman staying with them. If she wants to leave Calgary, make sure she gets away safely."

We parted where the trail began to the Tilton farm. I headed back to Calgary, where I spent two nights in jail, until Cappy Smart satisfied himself there had been no fires on any CPR train. He took me on as the lowest man on the totem pole, the guy given the jobs no one else wanted, like bathing a slightly scorched Barney twice a week.

Barney hates baths. I take great pride in making sure he's squeaky clean. And, I'm teaching him to wear diapers. After all he did for me, it's the least I can do for him.

SILICONE HEARTS
BRENT NICHOLS

The problem with cutting-edge technology is that it's driven by nerds. Nasty, sexually-frustrated nerds who have yet to die out despite being non-players in the gene pool. The ones who have a little more on the ball? Well, those ones fall away from the cutting edge, don't they? They spend time in conversations, or outside feeling the touch of the sun.

You don't get to the bleeding edge by leaving your basement.

When transformative technology appeared, technology that truly changed the world, it didn't emerge from the labs of MIT. It rose from the basements of nerds, and it wasn't pretty.

I looked at the red-head in my guest chair and amended that thought. It was, in fact, pretty. Hotter than an over-cooked pop tart, and just as good for a person.

"You don't like me," she said, and pouted prettily. She did everything prettily, from leaning forward to offer me a peek down that entirely inadequate dress to squirming in her chair so more of her legs showed. "I don't know why. I only want to please you, after all."

"Try to stay on topic," I growled. She mentioned pleasure, nakedness, or release in almost every sentence. "Tell me about the missing, ah, person."

"Oh, he's wonderful," she cooed. "So big and strong! His shoulders must be this wide..."

"Tell me about the disappearance," I interrupted.

"Oh, sorry." She licked her full red lips. "There must be some way I can make it up to you!"

If I ever find the dork who invented self-replicating love bots I'm going to fold him up and stuff him into his own pocket protector. I sighed, closing my eyes to mask my irritation. Also to block out her cleavage. Just because I was annoyed didn't mean it wasn't working. "Tell me about this missing person."

"He's a Ken," she said, and reached for her purse. "I brought a picture..."

"Never mind." The Kens were all identical. "He lived with you?"

Her face lit up. "Yes! We're in love." The expression on her face was dreamy. "At night we would..."

"When did you last see him?"

"Last night. He went out for lubricant, and he never came back." Her face sagged. "Oh, I'm so worried! Won't you do something? I'd do anything." A feverish light came into her eyes. "Anything at all."

"I'll send you a bill," I told her. "Five hundred a day plus expenses." I shoved a questionnaire across the desk. Name, address, the usual. "Fill this in. Then get out."

There were nine or ten models of love bot out there,

with new ones appearing every few months. There was a shape for almost every kink. The worst were the chibi bots. I got the shivers just thinking about them.

In the eyes of the law they were things, not people. The police would do nothing. That was fine with me. More cash for Mike Mclean, Private Eye.

My client called herself Mitzi, and she lived in Burnstown, a bot neighborhood. There was a little grocery store down the street from her bungalow, and I approached a slender young man in a green apron. "Excuse me."

He turned, and I muttered a curse under my breath. He was a Juan, a slender bot with smoldering dark eyes and a six-pack that showed plainly through his white tank-top. He looked me up and down and gave me a grin that told me he played both sides of the street.

"Do you know a Ken who lives just up the block?" I consulted my notebook. "He called himself *Keanu*."

His eyes clouded with suspicion, which was unfortunate but still an improvement over unbridled lust. "Who wants to know?"

"I'm a private investigator," I told him, handing over a card. "His, ah, girlfriend asked me to look into his disappearance."

He examined the card, then pocketed it without comment.

"Call me if you hear anything, would you?"

He shrugged.

That was the pattern for the rest of the afternoon. I wandered through Burnstown, chatted with people, human and robot, and learned very little.

I finished the night in a pub called the Lovelace. All of the staff and most of the patrons were bots. The bots didn't seem to be spending much, but human customers, mostly men, were spending plenty. It was, after all, the ultimate pick-up bar.

I was wondering morosely if I'd have to give back Mitzi's retainer, and if I could do it by mail, when a slim figure slid into the booth beside me. It was a human girl, a brunette with big, serious eyes and a boy's haircut. She was too plain to be a new model of bot, and she sure wasn't there to hit on me. Not in a room full of Juans and Kens and Lances.

"Mr. Mclean?" she said. "The detective?"

I nodded. "Who are you?"

"My name's not important."

I narrowed my eyes.

"I'm here on behalf of some friends," she said. "They didn't want to come in person. They're... recognizable."

Bots, then. I don't attract a lot of celebrities.

"They're also not so good at reading people," she went on. "They get distracted. I'm supposed to decide if you're trustworthy."

I shrugged. "I can give you my mom's phone number. She'll vouch for me."

She grinned. "I'll take a leap of faith. Here." She shoved a piece of paper at me.

"22 Baker Street," I read. I raised an eyebrow.

"You might find Keanu there," she said, and stood. "You should check it out." And she walked away.

22 Baker Street looked like a crack house. Light shone between the boards nailed over the windows, and loud music pounded through the walls. The yard was full of Harleys. Not the best sign.

Well, if being a private eye was easy, everyone would be as cool as me. I took a deep breath and headed for the front door.

I crossed the creaking porch and pushed on the door. It swung open, the music got louder, and a wave of marijuana and tobacco smoke washed over me. A skinny blonde in a miniskirt slouched in the entrance hall, a beer in her hand. She gave me an incurious glance and ignored me. I could see people moving deeper in the house, burly men with beards and leather jackets.

"Seen a Ken?" I said to the blonde.

Her head turned toward me. It took quite a while for her eyes to focus. "Huh?"

"I'm looking for a Ken. You know, a bot? Have you seen one?"

Her brow furrowed. The seconds ticked past without an answer, and at last I gave up and moved past her. I made it three more steps down the hall before one of the biggest hands I've ever seen shot out of a doorway beside me and landed on my shoulder.

"Private club, buddy. Get lost." He didn't wait for an answer, just hauled me down the corridor. He reached past me to open the front door, and I distinctly heard a voice say, "Help me."

The door swung open, and a hard shove sent me staggering over the porch and down the steps. I landed sprawling on the sidewalk, my palms stinging, as the door closed behind me. It was more than time I called it a night.

But.

That voice. Had I really heard it? I stared at the house, knowing I didn't have the courage to go back in.

I'd like to pretend that altruism decided me, but it was the sour knot of fear in my stomach that did it. Fear grows when you feed it. Besides, no three-hundred-pound biker was going to believe that I'd come back after a send-off like that. So I had nothing to worry about.

Right?

Before good sense could take root and stop me, I headed back up the steps and into the house.

The blonde still stood in the hallway, staring in mute apathy. I ignored her. There was a door to my right. I swung it open, and found myself looking down a long staircase into the basement.

Someone was crying down there in the dark.

The basement was unfinished, a wide space with engine parts heaped against one wall and a furnace in the back corner. And a steel support beam in the middle of the room, running from floor to ceiling, with a bloody naked man handcuffed to it.

That, I decided, was all I needed to see. It was a police matter now. Well, technically not, since I smelled oil and hydraulic fluid, not blood. But I wouldn't mention that to the cops. I turned and hurried up the stairs.

The biker who'd thrown me out was waiting at the top. That big hand reached out, and I ducked under it and drove my head into his stomach. It hurt, but he staggered back. I shoved past him and burst out the front door.

For a big man he was appallingly fast. I made three running steps across the front yard before his foot kicked my heel and I hit the ground.

I started to rise. A boot took me in the side and I went back down, curling into a ball. A foot shoved me onto my back, and I stared up at a burly man with a handlebar moustache. He grinned, and the closest streetlight glittered on a knife in his hand. "So long, nosy," he said, and knelt.

The knife was moving toward my chest when a

booted foot slammed into the side of his face. He fell back as bright colours filled the air.

It was a hallucination. It had to be. There were five of them, faces covered in masks from chin to forehead, wearing vivid primary colours. Capes swirled as they moved. They were graceful and fast and incredibly strong.

The biker did his best. He came to his feet, the knife flashed out, and a slim girl caught his wrist in her hands. Her arms looked like delicate twigs next to the vast trunk of his arm, but she held him easily as her companions went to work. A broad-shouldered man drove a knee into the guy's stomach while a wiry man swept his legs out from under him. A fist in a bright orange glove crashed against the biker's jaw and he went limp.

The slim girl plucked the knife from his hand as he fell, then turned and hurled it into the darkness. Long seconds later, I heard a metallic clatter in the distance. I wouldn't swear that she tossed it into the dumpster I could just see at the far end of the block, but...

She knelt beside me. I knew she had to be a bot from the skin-tight outfit and the way she thrust her oversize breasts at me even as she checked my pulse. "Are you all right?"

"Yeah." I cleared my throat. "In the basement. There's a guy chained up."

"Show me." She helped me to my feet and the six of us went into the house.

The blonde was still there, and if the sight of five costumed super-heroes startled her, she hid it well. A biker behind her had a stronger reaction, grabbing under his leather jacket for a weapon, and the broad-shouldered newcomer, likely a Ken, charged him.

I took the stairs to the basement, the slim girl right behind me. I was pretty sure she was a LaTanya. She rushed past me to the guy at the pole and helped him to stand. Another Ken, I saw. She found a hammer and a screwdriver and broke the chain on his handcuffs.

Someone screamed upstairs, and furniture splintered. A gun went off, followed by the sound of breaking glass. I ignored it all, concentrating on getting the Ken's arm over my shoulder.

"Can you get him outside?" the girl asked.

I nodded.

"Good." She ran up the stairs. I heard her give a war cry, and a biker responded with a bellow of pain.

The Ken was in pretty rough shape. We tackled the stairs, one painful step at a time.

"Are you Keanu?" I said.

"Huh? What?"

I saved my breath for heaving him up another step, then said, "Do you call yourself Keanu? Do you know a Suzie named Mitzi?"

He shook his head. "No." We made it up another step and he added, "Thanks for getting me out of there."

"No problem." We managed another step.

He had one arm over my shoulder and his free hand on the railing, but he reached across to rub my chest. "You're like some hero out of a fantasy."

"That's not my fantasy. Let's just get out of here."

"Okay. Sorry." We made it to the landing and out the front door. A pair of headlights flicked on, blinding me. A huge shadow appeared, a person running toward us, and I tensed.

It was the girl, the skinny human from the bar. She took the Ken's other arm and we hustled him over to a battered silver van. We got him into a seat, and I staggered back, pressing a hand to my bruised ribs. "Thanks."

She looked me up and down. "Are you all right?"

"You almost got me killed," I said.

"Sorry." She looked contrite, too. "We heard rumours, but we didn't know anything for sure. I didn't know it would be so dangerous."

The five costumed weirdoes came out of the house, three through the front door and two bursting through the boards over the living-room window. The huge man in yellow had to be an Evan. The little one in orange was a chibi, not an inch over four feet tall with extra-big eyeholes in her mask.

The Evan had a hole in his chest, leaking dark fluid. It didn't slow him down. He had a rifle tucked under one arm, and he paused long enough to brace the gun against his knee and heave until the barrel bent. He left it lying in the weeds and hurried after the others.

The Evan clapped me on the shoulder before piling into the van. The chibi gave me a quick hug, her face pressed into my stomach, then followed. The slim girl from the bar slid behind the wheel.

Strong, slender arms went around my chest from behind, and I felt a pair of large, warm breasts against my back. "Thank you," said a husky voice in my ear, followed by a quick nip to my earlobe. It was the slim LaTanya from the basement. "We won't forget this. My name is Ella. If you ever need us, just text me." She winked behind the mask. "Or if you just get lonely." She tucked a business card into my hip pocket, then sprang into the van as it rolled away.

I hotfooted it to my car and went home.

I woke up stiff, with a bruise on my side from my

armpit to my hip bone. Getting out of bed wasn't easy, but by the time I was cleaned up and full of coffee and eggs I was pretty much fully functional.

I was doing an Internet search for hate crimes against bots when my phone rang. I didn't recognize the husky male voice with a hint of a Latino accent.

"Mr. Mclean?"

"Speaking," I said. "Who's this?"

"I met you yesterday," he said. "You were asking around about Keanu."

My pulse quickened. "Go on."

"Word is, you're okay."

"I'm a paragon," I assured him. "What can you tell me?"

"There's this car comes around sometimes," he said. "It has tinted windows, and sometimes it parks in front of my store for hours."

"So maybe it belongs to someone in the neighborhood?"

"No one ever gets in or out," he said. "It just sits there."

"I see." Probably someone with a wandering spouse, trying to catch them hooking up with a bot. Still... "Can you describe the car?"

"I can do better than that," he said. "I have the license number."

I phoned Jerry, my contact at the DMV. "Jerry, buddy! It's Mike."

"Who?"

"Mike Mclean." Doofus.

"Oh. Hey, Mike."

"Listened, Jerry, I need you to run a plate for me."

Silence. Not a good sign.

"Jerry?"

"I don't know, Mike."

"What, you don't need money anymore?"

"I have money," he said defensively. "I have a job, after all. That's kind of the point. I don't want to lose it."

"You work at the DMV, Jerry. There are better jobs." Not that I wanted him to do better.

"Not for a guy like me," he said. "I need this job."

"You need an extra fifty bucks, too," I told him. "You can earn it in about two minutes, too."

"I don't know..."

"Is it the money? I could go a little higher, just this once."

"It's not that." He blew out a gusty sigh. "I can't get fired."

"Sure you can. It builds character."

"It's embarrassing!" he snapped.

"More embarrassing than working at the DMV?"

Another sigh. "You wouldn't understand."

Now we were getting somewhere. "Try me."

There was a long silence. "There's this girl," he said at last. "In accounting. I think she likes me. But she thinks I'm a dork. If I get fired, I'll lose my shot with her."

"You really like her, huh?"

"Not really," he admitted. "She's pretty stuck up. But her tits are to die for, and I don't exactly have a lot of choice, you know what I mean?"

I did, unfortunately. "You need to find a good pick-up bar."

"Yeah, right," he said gloomily. "The kinds of bars where guys like me can score are the kinds of bars I wouldn't go into."

"You've never been in the bar I was in last night," I

said.

"Really?" He sounded intrigued in spite of himself. "Where were you?"

"Only in bachelor heaven," I said airily. "I found a bar where three quarters of the customers are bots. I've never seen so many hot girls in one place in my life."

"Aw, they wouldn't go for a guy like me," he said. He didn't sound sure, though. He would have heard the stories.

"Trust me," I told him. "You walk in that door, you're not coming out alone."

"Really?"

"Really."

"Well, where is it?"

I let the silence stretch out.

"Fine," he said. "I'll run the damn plate. Now tell me the name of the bar!"

The car, it turned out, was a green GTO owned by one Howard Mosh. I swung by his house, a run-down shack in a seedy neighborhood nowhere near Burnstown. I stole his garbage. Half an hour in my garage with rubber gloves earned me a pay stub.

He worked for ZMR Amalgamated, a wholly-owned subsidiary of Zimmerman Technology. The company had an address in an industrial park across the river, and I headed out in the early afternoon to take a look.

The place was all tinted windows and brick, a single-story building surrounded by neat strips of grass. I watched the front for a while, then headed around the corner.

On the far side of the block I found a neighborhood bar with a view of the lab from the parking lot. I set up my camera and tripod on the seat beside me, and attached a huge zoom lens. People came in and out, using swipe cards and entering a code in a number pad. My zoom lens was pretty good. Before long I had a pretty good idea of the entry code.

Just after six, a couple of guys left the lab, walked past my car, and entered the bar. I put the camera away and set out to get myself a swipe card.

It was easier than I had any right to expect. The two of them were playing darts, their coats forgotten on chairs behind them. I nicked a card from a coat pocket and headed outside.

I got the entry code on my second try. I swiped my stolen card and pushed open the back door of the lab. Lights came on as I stepped inside. Curtains lined one wall. Mysterious electronic machinery lined another wall, and I snapped a few photos with my phone.

A stainless steel table filled the center of the room, with a coffin-sized lump covered by a blue cloth. I stared down at it for a long moment, working up my nerve. Then I grabbed the cloth and pulled it away.

There was a Plexiglas case under the cloth, and inside was a Ken with straps around his arms, legs, chest, and hips. His eyes were closed, and he didn't open them when I tapped on the case.

I took out my phone and typed a quick text to Ella, the LaTanya from the super-group. Then I turned back to the Ken. "Hang on, buddy. I'll get you out of there."

I found a little sliding panel on the side of the case, just big enough for me to put a hand through. I used my pen knife to saw through the straps that held his arms, then grabbed his hand and shook it, trying to wake him up. His hand felt remarkably thick and solid in mine. I shook it, twisted it, then dropped it and prodded his ribs.

His hand reached up and closed over mine, hard enough that I gasped in pain. He started to sit up, banged his head on the Plexiglas, and lay back down. He stared at me with cold, angry eyes.

"I'm trying to free you," I hissed. "I cut your straps." I showed him the pen knife in my free hand.

Slowly his hand released its grip. I pulled my arm out and massaged my injured fingers.

"You're here to help me?" His voice was low and full of wonder.

"Yes. But I don't know how to get this case open."

"You're like my guardian angel." His voice grew warmer. "And you have such beautiful eyes, too."

I rolled my beautiful eyes and passed him my pen knife. "Here, finish cutting yourself loose." I turned, scanning the walls, looking for something I could use to break him free. A fire axe might do the trick. I went over to the curtains on the side wall and pulled them open.

And stumbled back, horror constricting my throat.

There was a tank against the wall, a vertical cylinder the size of a phone booth, and it contained a monster.

The creature was huge, and only vaguely manlike. Seven feet tall, it was thick through the chest and shoulders, with arms that would make a gorilla feel inadequate. The eyes were deep-sunk beneath a thick, overhanging brow, and only the golden hair spoiled the illusion of an overdeveloped Neanderthal.

He was naked. I say "he" because his gender was entirely too obvious. He stared down at me, then lunged at the Plexiglas, battering the surface with fists like lumpy bowling balls. He screamed, a primal sound full of hate and devoid of reason, and I flinched back in spite of myself. Everything about him was brutish and ugly and dangerous.

Except his hair.

I glanced back at the Ken on the table. It was the same hair.

"Oh, my god." I edged past the slavering brute and pulled back the rest of the curtain. There was a big red button beside the container, labeled "Release." I made a mental note not to touch it. I snapped a few more pictures, then turned back to the Ken on the table. He had his arms and legs braced against the inside of the Plexiglas, and he was pressing with all his might. I walked around the case, looking for release handle and not finding one. The Plexiglas was thick, and the metal holding it looked quite solid. I said, "I don't think that's going to..."

With a loud metallic "SNAP" the top of the case flew up, knocked bits of tile loose from the ceiling, and plunged back down. The Ken shoved it aside, then sat up, examining his own arms. "I seem to be stronger," he said.

I glanced at the freak along the wall. "You were going to get even stronger," I told him. "Do feel, um, sane?"

He gave me a dubious look. "I think so." His gaze tilted up slightly. "Uh-oh."

I followed his gaze. A red light was flashing on the wall, just below the ceiling. "Looks like you set off an alarm," I said. "Let's get out of here." I ran to the door and tugged on the handle.

Locked.

"Ken? Can you try this?"

"My name's Keanu," he said, grasping the handle.

"Oh, good. Mitzi's been worried about you. I think I'm going to ask her for a bonus."

Keanu heaved on the handle until the metal creaked,

but the door remained shut. He turned toward me. "I can't…"

The door swung inward, bumping against him, and men came pouring in. They wore helmets and military-looking uniforms, and one of them shoved a Taser against Keanu's thick upper arm. Keanu screamed, and another man joined in, pressing a Taser against Keanu's chest. Keanu fell, and the other two started toward me.

God forgive me, I sprang across the room and slapped my hand against the release button.

The monster erupted from his container. He sprang at the nearest security man, and howled as a Taser hit him in the stomach. The others forgot about Keanu and joined in the attack on the monster.

A hammer blow knocked one guard to the floor, and he didn't get up. Men in black tased the monster. He batted them away, and they charged back into the fray. They may have been amoral fascists, but those guys were brave.

I circled around the mayhem and crossed to Keanu's side. He was on one knee, struggling to rise. I helped him to his feet and we staggered out the door.

The problem with secret labs designed to create monsters is that they are really hard to get out of. My swipe card no longer worked. The back door was locked, and no amount of hammering would budge it. We gave up and went the other way, stepping quietly as we passed the door to the chamber of horrors. Judging by the noise from inside, the fight was nowhere near over.

We were staring out through a locked fire door when a silver van came barreling down the street, then swerved onto the grass and came straight at us. I grabbed Keanu's arm and dragged him back an instant before the van's bumper hit the Plexiglas and shattered it. The van backed away and the two of us wriggled out through the hole.

We weren't a moment too soon. The hulking freak, his naked chest scorched with Taser burns, reached the door a few seconds after we did. He spent a moment ripping chunks of Plexiglas from the frame, and stepped outside. He lifted his arms above his head and bellowed in triumph.

Heroes burst from the van. The freak advanced, and Keanu caught him by the forearms. The freak was stronger, but Keanu was able to hold him for several seconds. In that time, Ella slipped behind him. I didn't see what she did, but the freak collapsed suddenly to the sidewalk.

"What did you do?" I said.

Ella gave me a cool look. "I'm not telling a human where the switch is. No offense." She looked around. "What is this place?"

I shrugged. "Mad scientist's lair?" I gestured at the limp form on the ground. "I can see what they were doing, but I don't understand why."

"We'll look into it," said Ella. She looked down at the monster. "Now, what do we do with him?"

"Leave him where he's at," the costumed Evan said promptly. "He's dangerous, and he's beyond help."

Ella didn't say anything, just stared at him. He glared back, fists on his hips, then threw his hands in the air. "Fine! We'll see what we can do for him. But you can clean up the mess after he rips my arms off and beats me with them."

Four of the bots scooped the creature up and heaved it into the back of the van. I almost tried to help, as if I had anything to contribute in the area of raw strength.

Ella closed the back doors, then dusted off her hands. "We need to get out of here. Can we give you a ride?"

I nodded. Now that the crisis was past I was getting the shakes. I was in no shape to drive.

Keanu said, "Can you drop me at my apartment? I need to tell Mitzi I'm okay."

"Sure thing." Ella reached over and stroked his enormous bicep. "You're not the man you were before, though." He looked at her, and she held his gaze. "If you find you don't fit your old life anymore, there could be a place for you on the team."

She got out of the van with me when we reached my place. The sun was setting, sloshing streaks of pastel over the sky above the rooftops. She looked dramatic and dangerous and lovely in the waning light, and I felt my pulse increasing.

"Thanks for all your help," she said, and put a hand on my chest. "You've done a great service for my people."

I grinned. "It's all in a day's work for Mike Mclean, Private Eye."

That earned me a smile. The hand on my chest started to move in a stroking motion. "There must be some way I can show my appreciation."

I moved back half a step. "You've saved my neck a couple of times. I think we're even."

"All right." Her hand was still on my chest. "If you're sure you don't want to invite me in."

I thought of all the reasons I would turn her down. She wasn't a real woman. Her desires, her appetite, were programmed. However perfect her body, however dazzling her technique, she was still a machine. Sure, she was a person, in a way. That was all the more reason I had to turn her away. It would be wrong to take advantage of the desires that were programmed into her.

I reached up and lifted her hand off of my chest. Her fingers were cool and supple against mine, and I found I didn't want to let go. "Come on in," I said.

I'm only human, after all.

A LITTLE BIT EASY
THERESE GREENWOOD

Lally Thibodeaux didn't seem the kind of girl people shot at. Oh, she was different, I'll give you that, but she was a pretty, well-mannered little thing. I took to her the minute she stopped in about renting the old place on the point.

I always thought the point was the nicest spot in the county, maybe the nicest in south-eastern Alberta, with the old frame homestead on a rise about thirty feet from the river. Grandpa Allen built it before they dug the well; back then they hauled water up the riverbank. You can see clear down the river from the kitchen window, and there's a fine stand of trees along the banks. There's a nice pasture out back, too, ten acres you could hay as long as you keep an eye out and don't let the tractor wheels get too close to the river bank. It's pretty, gone to tansy and sweet clover. I wouldn't mind looking out at it every morning but the wife says I'm too sentimental. She likes the bungalow we built out near the road after our girls left home. But I liked the idea of renting out the old house. Someone ought to live there, although I wasn't sure Lally knew what she was getting herself into.

She was just a slip of a thing. I could barely see her behind the steering wheel of her big red truck the first time she stopped on our road. She hopped down to ground, tumbling out like the last peanut in the bag and pointing her little black remote control, *click-click*, to lock up her truck tighter than a drum even though the wife and I were the only people for miles.

"We aren't much for locking vehicles here," I said.

"I find you can't be too careful," Lally said. She had a funny drawl, slow and twangy, and looked about the age of our youngest, in her middle twenties. Her sweet face had a tad too much make-up but she wore clean clothes, not like some of those young people with ripped jeans and dirty shoes. She had on a nice blouse and pressed shorts like the women in banks wear, and her nails were a rosy pink. I noticed her hands because she was holding the For Rent notice we had put up at Mosier's store in early spring. Since it was into June and she was the first person to ask, we'd likely rent it to her. But for the life of me I couldn't figure out why she'd want to live out there all by herself.

"Are you sure it won't get too lonely for you?" I asked.

"Potable water in-house, clear view for a thousand yards, slight incline to slow progress, and limited access points," she said. "It's perfect."

"Planning a party?" I asked.

"Not if I can help it," she said with a smile. I could tell I tickled her and I like tickling a pretty girl, so I laid the yokel thing on thick.

"We had a family reunion out there on the long weekend last August," I said, hooking my thumbs in my suspenders. "People who were supposed to stay Saturday night were still staggering around on Labor Day. But you can't pick your family, can you?"

"No sir, you can't," she said, not smiling any more, her drawl so strong you could hardly make her out.

"That's quite an accent you got," I said. "Where you from?"

"South," she said.

"A Yankee?" I said.

Lally smiled again. "In New Orleans we'd call you a Yankee for living north of the Mason-Dixon."

"Most people call me a Canuck for living north of everything Yankee," I said. "But you can call me Jim. You sure are a long way from home."

"As far as I can get, Jim."

I fished around but I couldn't get any more out of her. Lally always was tight-lipped. That's another reason I was surprised when those bullets tore the place up. I couldn't believe she'd open her mouth long enough to make anyone want to shoot her, let alone cut loose with a machine gun. We're still picking bullets out of the old kitchen. I found one yesterday in the old radio next to Grandma Allen's pine rocking chair.

You never would have guessed Lally would be mixed up in that kind of a hullabaloo. After she got settled in I dropped by a couple times to make sure she wasn't finding it too lonely, and she always kept everything clean as a whistle. Even the wife said so. You could've ate off the floors and Lally gave the old place some touches of her own, although they weren't what I would call girly. First thing she did was put her shotgun on the rack on the kitchen wall. You're supposed to lock away your firepower these days, but that rack has been up there since Grandpa Allen shot his first mallard and, anyway, it wasn't like anyone would be around to check.

Lally kept a few more of her treasures on a corner table in the kitchen along with a bunch of wildflowers she picked fresh every day. There was a picture of a small, determined-looking woman squinting into the sun on a cement stoop, gripping a clutch purse in a hand that looked too big for the rest of her. Next to the photo was a black candle in a fancy ivory holder and a crazy statue of a skeleton in a suit. I figured it was left over from a childhood Halloween.

"That must be a photo of your mother," I said one afternoon as I dropped off another of the wife's rhubarb pies. "There's quite the resemblance around the eyes. But she's even tinier than you. Looks like she couldn't hurt a fly."

Lally laughed. "Tell that to the crack dealers who moved next door to her. They never knew what hit them when Mama Marie put the mojo on them."

"Crack dealers, that sounds like a bad neighborhood," I said. "Your mother ought to move."

"She doesn't live there anymore," said Lally, her laugh gone. "Mama Marie's passed over."

"You're young to have lost your mother," I said, thinking of our girls.

"I didn't lose her," said Lally, taking a sulphur match and lighting the black candle by the photo. "Someone took her. Shall I cut you a slice of your wife's fine pie?"

And that was all she said. She wasn't one for spilling the beans but otherwise she was a good tenant. She was determined to bring the place up to speed with two hundred amp service and a backup generator to boot. She even put in those big halogen lights to show off the place. Too bad she picked the ones with motion sensors, the raccoons tripped them all night. I didn't say anything at the time, though. I figured when she got done the old place would be better wired than the arena in town and it wouldn't have cost me a cent.

She got in her own electrician and that's when Gord McKillop met her. We thought Gord was a confirmed bachelor. He was a nice-looking lad, tall and strong as an ox, with a good job. One of the Huff girls set her cap at him for a spell but he never took the bait. We thought maybe girls weren't his cup of tea, if you catch my drift. But Gord took one look at Lally and fell like a ton of bricks. He'd find excuses to come by, little things he'd fix for her. Sometimes he'd get a job half-done and realize he needed a doo-dad he had to go all the way to town for, just for an excuse to come back the next day.

It was Gord who found the first voodoo charm. Lally and I were watching him set up an automatic skeet-shooting thing out in the pasture when he found a heart-shaped rock, polished smooth. It looked like the letter "L" had been carved into it.

"Fancy that," I said. "Nature sending you a valentine."

"It's not natural, Jim," said Lally, looking across the field, squinting so her pretty face twisted up like a monkey's. "Supernatural."

"Pardon me?" Gord and I said together. Sometimes we didn't quite follow her accent.

"It's a vengeance mojo," she said. "My mother was a Creole. She practised voodoo."

"We're United Church," I said.

"I'm a Presbyterian," said Gord. "I saw a movie

about voodoo. This corpse got up and did the limbo. It was pretty funny."

"Nothing funny about it," Lally said. "Someone put that mojo there."

Gord and I tried to tell her that a person could find all kinds of comical-looking rocks in these fields, dumped off the glaciers a million years ago. But she wouldn't hear any of it.

"Vengeance was Mama Marie's speciality," she said. "People hired her to get back at folks who wronged 'em. She'd hex a husband who laid one beating too many on his wife, or a gang-banger who shot a nine-year-old in a drive-by, or even on the butcher for keeping his thumb on the scale."

"That's one heck of a town you're from," I said. "Don't people there ever call the law?"

"In New Orleans?" Lally laughed but it wasn't the pretty girl laugh Gord and I liked. "The police down there aren't in the justice business, Jim. They're in business for themselves. They don't call it The Big Easy for nothing."

"I saw that movie," Gord said.

Lally sighed and wouldn't say any more. When Gord finished hooking up the skeet thing, she got out her shotgun and went at the targets like nobody's business. She used her little black remote control -- it amazes me how you can set almost anything to remote these days -- to launch ten targets and she hit every single one. I never saw anything like it.

"Where did you learn to shoot like that?" I said.

"Daddy was a Recon Marine." *Click-click. Bam!* Another target took to the air and was blown to smithereens. "Vietnam. Every marine a rifleman." *Click-click. Bam!* "Didn't you pass anything on to your girls,

Jim?" *Click-click. Bam*!

"Are you kidding?" said Gord with a grin. "You should've seen those girls on a tractor. You never saw anybody plough so straight."

"I don't like to brag," I said. "But Laura, our youngest, was Queen of the Furrow at the ploughing match three years running."

"You taught your girls to grow food to make people big and strong," Lally said. "My daddy taught me to kill people with advance reconnaissance and the element of surprise." *Click-click. Bam*!

I guess I shouldn't have bragged.

Lally shot and shot that day, and all night with the big lights on. You aren't supposed to shoot at night but there's no police to stop you. It takes a big deal to get the Mounties here. In fact, the last time I saw them was when the place on the point got shot-up. They didn't do a hell of a lot then. I suppose we're better off without them. Maybe we are a little bit like New Orleans. Maybe you could call us a little bit easy.

We didn't see much of Lally for a while. She kept herself busy, clearing brush near the house, white-washing the picket fence and honing the points on the stakes so they looked tidy. I thought she went a bit far putting up the electric fence along the riverbank. It didn't do anything for the view. She practiced her shooting, too, until she burned out the target-shooting thing. I watched her kick it one day and haul it into the house. Since I don't duck hunt any more, I got to use the binoculars for something.

I kept an eye on the mailbox, too. She didn't get much mail, just the electric bill and a magazine called Soldier Of Fortune. The wife thought maybe it was about how to win the lottery. When both came in at end of the month, Lally saw the flag up on the box and roared out in her big truck. She hopped out and *click-clicked* the door shut while I hustled over, and I was just hitching my thumbs into my suspenders when I saw the chicken bones at the foot of the rusty milk can holding up the mailbox.

"Damn cats," I said, reaching down to pick up the bones, which had been picked clean.

"Wait," Lally said, squatting down on her little ankles as easy as you please. She picked up a twig and poked a bone.

"Worried about rabies?" I said. "We don't get much of a scare around here."

"It's a message," Lally said.

"A message I ought to get out the .22 for those cats."

"It's for me," she said. "He's coming."

"Who?"

That's when Gord McKillop rolled up in that disaster area he calls a van, but I didn't figure she was talking about him.

"I'm worried about you spending too much time out here alone," he said to Lally through the van window. "You deserve some fun. Why don't we go in to town for dinner and a movie? There's a pretty good show at the Odeon that would cheer you up."

I liked the way Gord pretended to be doing her a favor, but he should have had the sense to turn the engine off and maybe even get out of the van. No wonder he was still a bachelor.

"I'm not up for town," Lally said.

That's when the wife came out with a plate of her butter rolls and homemade strawberry jam. The mailbox was a regular Grand Central Station that morning.

"Darn cats," the wife said. She handed Lally the plate

169

and squatted to pick up the bones. Lally started forward but the wife said, "Tut, tut." When the wife tut-tuts, you stop in your tracks.

"Lally Thibodeaux, don't you dare say you can't take those rolls," she said, picking up bones and handing them to me. "This isn't the big city, we do things different here. We don't lock our vehicles, we don't put hexes on our neighbors, and if those neighbors give us homemade rolls, we take 'em and like 'em."

"Homemade jam, too," said Gord, eyeing the plate. "You don't see that every day."

"Lally, it wouldn't hurt you to get out a bit more." I put in my two cents. "Excuse me for saying it, but you tend to mope. A pretty girl like you ought to be out having a high old time."

For a minute Lally just stood there looking at us like we had two heads each. "Are you people for real?" she said.

"Beg your pardon?" we said together.

"What's with the baking and the jam and the worrying and the advice? Why do you care?"

"Don't be silly," the wife said. "Why wouldn't we?"

Lally looked at us, at the plate in her hands, then tilted her head for a better look at Gord. "You people slay me," she said. Then she smiled her pretty smile and said, "I guess I could use some civilized company. Dinner tonight. I'll cook."

Bingo! Gord was thinking. Then Lally said, "Jim and Missus Jim, y'all come, too. I'll make you a real Creole dinner."

"Good enough," says I, putting the bones in my pocket. "With four we can get up a game of euchre. We aren't The Big Easy but we know how to have a little fun."

"Euchre," muttered Gord. "Hmmm. Maybe I'll come by early, finish setting up that generator for you, Lal."

"Why not?" she said. "You could look at my skeet machine, too. The launch mechanism is off by ten centimetres."

"I've been thinking about getting a generator," I said. "We lost power for a week in last winter's blizzard."

"I don't know why anyone with a wood-stove needs a generator," said the wife, and I knew I wouldn't be getting one any time soon. "We'll see you two tonight."

I hardly recognized Gord when we got to the point that evening. He had on a clean shirt and a tie and his hair was wet. He had an awful big grin, too.

"Got a little dirty working on the skeet launcher," he said. "Lally let me take a shower and change before dinner."

"Nice of her," the wife said.

I noticed the skeet launcher on the floor by Lally's side table. There was a screwdriver still in the barrel, like Gord had left off fixing it in a big hurry. It looked spotless to me, like all of Lally's things, not a speck of dirt or oil.

"I didn't quite get it the way I like it," Gord said, then blushed. "The mechanism, I mean. Might have to come back tomorrow with a little doo-dad to get her up and running proper."

"You don't say," said the wife.

Lally looked extra pretty. Her nails were a bright red and her blonde hair curled within an inch of its life. She was dressed to the nines in a snazzy yellow suit that reminded me of Jackie Kennedy. Gord thought the getup was for him but I got the feeling she just liked to dress up. It was the first time I saw her having fun.

Dinner was different. Spicy like you wouldn't

believe. She even put spice in the rice, and a bottle of hot sauce on the table. Lally ate it down like it was ice cream. Gord made a go at it.

"What is this called?" he said, chewing slowly.

"Jambalaya."

"Crawfish pie and a filet gumbo," I sang. "'Tonight I'm gonna see my *ma cher amio*."

Lally smiled again and the wife smiled, too. "You old flirt," she whispered. "Give Gord a fighting chance."

We were a friendly party, four people sitting around the old pine table finishing dessert -- the wife's butter tarts, best in the county--and talking about the weather and the garden and the neighbors. We were just getting up a game of cards, me explaining trump to Lally, when the power cut out. The only light in the room came from the black candle in the corner. I hadn't even realized it was lit.

"No problem," said Gord, his face spooky in the candle's flicker. "The generator will kick on in about 10 seconds."

Lally jumped up and grabbed her truck keys from the ring on the wall, tossing them on the table where the rest of us sat in the candlelight. I figured she was telling Gord to take a ride for his half-assed wiring, and I guess he did, too.

"Missing that doo-dad," Gord mumbled. "To get the generator going."

"Un-huh," said the wife.

"Hush," Lally hissed. "He's right outside."

That was when the kitchen door flung open and a flashlight cut the darkness, shining into our eyes. I squinted at the silhouette of an army man, with an army hat and army boots and a big army gun.

"Your perimeter fortifications are pathetic," said a

voice with an accent like Lally's.

"I let my defences down," said Lally. She stood back straight, hands at her sides, fingers bent.

"You three at the table, let me see your hands," the man said. We laid our cards face up on the table and fanned them out. Hearts were trump and I noticed Gord had the left bower. It's funny what sticks in your mind.

"Not the cards, you idiots." The man swore. "Put your palms on the table."

We put our hands on top of the cards and looked into the flashlight.

"They're civilians," said Lally.

"They're collateral damage," said the man. "I didn't come all this way to neutralize one witness just to leave three more."

"There's no need to neutralize anybody," Lally said. "If I was planning to testify I'd have stayed in New Orleans. There isn't a *remote* chance you'd get the needle now. Not the *remotest*."

The wife and I didn't look at Lally's remote lying on the table. We looked at Gord, hoping he wasn't giving anything away. He wasn't. Good old Gord was staring at Lally, his mouth wide open.

"This is your fault, Lally," said the army man. "Why'd you run to the police?" He said *po-leece*, like in one of Gord's movies.

"She was my mama," Lally said, "and you killed her, daddy."

"Now Lally, you know the way things go." The man's voice was soft, the same voice I used to tell my girls the rabbits chewed up the pumpkin vine and we'd have to buy a jack-o'-lantern from the store. "Your mama had no business putting the voodoo on me. Psychological advantage is the principal weapon in a soldier's arsenal."

"You beat her for twenty-five years," Lally's voice was as bitter as his was soft. "One day you killed her. You lost *control*."

That was when I lost control, too. I must have been crazy, carrying on like some hero instead of a retired dairy farmer. But I was mad as spit at this fellow who took other men's wars out on his wife and his little girl, and I heard my voice say. "You ought to be ashamed of yourself, mister."

"Ashamed of myself?" he said. I never heard a man so astonished in my life. "I'm a decorated war veteran. I served my country with distinction."

"Tell it to the Marines," I said.

"Now you are both out of *control*!" Lally said. "Now. *Now*!"

The army man was turning the gun towards me and that should have been it, but the wife hit the remote control with her little finger. *Click-click*.

The skeet machine launched out the screwdriver end over end. I expect Lally meant it to be a diversion, but I must live right because the point hit the army man right in the eye. He screamed and the old kitchen lit up like the fourth of July, sparking and popping and smoking, the machine gun bursting with bullets that flashed along the old tin ceiling. Lally kicked over the table, leaving the three of us behind it. I was glad I never bought that dainty, spindly-legged item the wife wanted from the furniture store in town. The thick old pine stopped bullets, or at least slowed them down, although the wife got hit in the leg and was bleeding like crazy. It was her scream that made Gord jump up to go for the gun. He took one in the shoulder and fell back down. He needn't have bothered, because Lally pulled her shotgun off the rack and blasted both barrels smack into the army man's head.

"So much for the element of surprise, daddy," she said.

The man looked dead to me but Lally wasn't taking chances. She kicked away his gun and frisked his body, pulling out handguns and knives and crazy-looking weapons I didn't recognize. Then she used my suspenders to throw a tourniquet around the wife's leg, pressed a tea towel on Gord's shoulder, and called the ambulance.

"She should have told us," I said to the wife as her blood soaked through my fingers. "We could have helped her hide better."

"You old fool," the wife said through gritted teeth. "She wasn't hiding from him. She was waiting for him."

Then I saw how Lally made her stand. She hadn't lit the black candle to keep that bad man away. She wanted to draw him to her. She hadn't made the old place a fortress, it was a giant booby trap. She had taken her old man's lesson about the element of surprise and done him proud.

I still think we could have swept it under the rug, most of it anyway, but Lally wouldn't take the chance. She waited till the paramedics loaded up Gord and the wife, and I drove off with them for the hospital in town. The county has its own ambulance service for heart attacks and farm accidents and allergic reactions to peanuts. But the police have to come all the way from the next county and Lally was long gone by the time they arrived.

The wife is enjoying her stay in hospital. No one around here ever got shot before -- not on purpose anyway. She's a celebrity, had her picture on the front page of the newspaper, and you wouldn't believe the people stopping by. This afternoon Gord was in, his arm done up in a sling, and he gave me a ride home after visiting hours. On his dashboard he had a heart-shaped rock with an "L" on it. Gord doesn't believe in voodoo charms but I guess he figures what the hell, maybe it will draw her back. Good luck to him, I say. I wish it was that easy.

BUTCH'S LAST LESSON
R. OVERWATER

The door flies off its hinges with a thunderous crack. I only catch a glimpse of the black boot that kicked it in, but I have a pretty good guess who's wearing it.

Shit. It's Pinner. And I know what he's here for, my heart sinking so fast it gives me vertigo.

Two hundred and seventy pounds of corpulent biker walks in, slamming a baseball bat down onto the coffee table. It collapses at one corner, spilling bong-water and empty beer cans onto the threadbare carpet.

I stand and raise my voice in innocent protest. "Fuck Pinner, you don't have to..." My head explodes in a blue flash as the bat catches me on my right ear, knocking me back onto the couch. A weighty yellow rubber bag hits my face. "What the fuck is this?" Pinner shouts.

It's my brand new scuba bag. Designed to be watertight, nothing is better for suppressing the skunky stink of marijuana.

"You couldn't have picked a worse time to try and fuck us over," Pinner bellows.

Then I notice the guy behind him. I've never seen him before. He's slender but muscular, wearing a tight black T-shirt. There's a small tattoo on one forearm. The biker-but-don't-want-to-look-like-a-biker look. His jeans are Levi 501s—the American version of that look. Shit, shit, shit. This is bad.

And it's all because of Butch. Fucking Butch.

"I'm not asking you for anything that I wouldn't do for you if the chips were down," Butch said, his lazy drawl intensified by the trebly phone line.

"Hell, I know that, Butch. But this stuff doesn't happen to me," I answered. "I could break a mirror and walk under a ladder while thirteen black cats crossed my path, and never have your luck."

Silence.

"You're still mad about Trudy," he said.

"No I am not," I said. "I heartily endorse your doomed relationship."

Butch launched into his standard defense of Trudy. The poverty growing up on the reservation. The diagnosed clinical depression. Which explained a lot about her, but didn't make her pathological lying and ballistic temper tantrums any easier to be around.

"And besides, God bless communist Canada," Butch continued. "They gave her pills for her mood swings. So we don't fight anymore."

Bullshit, I thought.

"So are you gonna do it or not?" he asked.

"You know I would. But there's no way I can get that kind of cash by Tuesday."

"Borrow it from that guy who's always talking about his Harley. He likes you."

"Pinner? He doesn't like me that much."

"Front him a quarter pound."

"I barely have two ounces right now, let alone a quarter pound. And if I did I wouldn't hand it over just because you have lousy life-management skills."

"Do the Portland Dreadlock. We'll have the cash back to you in a day."

"No way! A lot's changed, man. He's not some wannabe biker anymore," I said. "He's full-patch in the Rebels and he's all business. Remember Itchy, that guy who was always a sore loser at the pool table?"

"I'm still gonna shit-kick that guy."

"No need. He only has one good eye now, thanks to Pinner," I said. "Pinner's got something to prove—the Hell's Angels are moving up here. All the local clubs are joining up and swapping colours."

"Is that going to hurt your business?"

"Nah. I've been thinking about quitting soon anyways. So where the hell are you?"

"Lac La Biche."

"Why?"

"Trudy wants to be close to the reserve 'cause that's where her family is. It's a tiny little crap town, but we're the go-to kids for weed here."

"Great. Get one of those bus-bench advertisements like a real estate agent. You two, all smiling. *Shitville Alberta's Number One Dope Dealers.*"

"Now you're just being a dick. Anyways, I'm fucked if you don't do this."

"Call your brother."

"I did. He hung up as soon as he heard my voice."

I believed him. Butch would always burn every other

bridge before resorting to me. Because we truly were friends. So, on some level, we both knew I'd buckle.

"Fuck. Fine. Find out when the bus arrives and pick me up. It'll be cash so I'll have to bring it myself. That's if, if Pinner goes for this."

"Make sure it's cash. I can't start a bank account because then someone will figure out I'm up here illegally."

I understood. Canada was his home now, the place he wanted to live but, technically, he couldn't stay. He couldn't go back either. Not without facing an overdue student loan, a stack of unpaid fines, and the IRS.

"So we give Trudy the money," he said. "She pays the guy and he goes away happy. You stay the night. The next day, her social-services check comes in and we pay you back."

"Fine."

"I'll reimburse you for the craft store stuff."

"Sure you will."

I hated the bus station. I hated the elitism it brought out in me. Busses always hold an assortment of life's winners. Poor people, barely employable people, alcoholics waiting to get their licenses back, and me.

All I had to do was go back to school for one more year, easy if I applied myself and didn't party hard. I'd be full-on white collar; a registered retirement savings plan and a car that didn't have a grey primer door. The idea crystallized into a near-complete plan on the six-hour bus ride out. The crowd I usually associated with, they didn't have the options I had. People told this me all the time. Pinner was one of those people.

Pinner had been skeptical about loaning me the cash at first. I emphasized my reliability and the quality of the pot I was offering for collateral. Halfway through, I could tell he was buying it.

"Okay. I can do this," he said, motioning to the scuba bag. "This'll do for a deposit. But you sure as fuck better come through."

"I'm good for it, Pinner."

"The Angels are up next week and we officially swap," he said. "I barely made the cut, so God help the sumbitch that fucks this up." He sparked a pin joint, one of those skinny, little spliffs he earned his nickname from, burning half its length in one draw. He passed it over.

I took a big haul. "Not gonna lie Pinner. Those guys scare me a little."

He blew a thin stream of smoke and nodded, grinning. "They are not be fucked with. And hence," he said dramatically, "I am not to be fucked with either."

"Hence" was a big word for Pinner, even though it only had one syllable. "I get it," I said.

He flicked the roach into a filthy ashtray. "You move, what, a few ounces a week? You're too smart to be living in that shitty apartment. You could have credit at a bank and own a goddamn house someday. What's wrong with you?"

I bristled. "Maybe I'll be a dope dealer for life."

He snorted. "People who deal for life are dealers with short lives. Trust me."

I stood, folding Pinner's cash into my pocket. "Don't smoke any of my dope, please. It's promised to a guy up in Fort McMurray."

He shrugged. "It's cool. But help me out sometime when I need it. Don't forget who your friends are."

I stepped through the door. "I never do, man."

No one was there to pick me up when I arrived at the

Lac La Biche bus station. Which was actually just a laundromat with an unattended ticket counter. A faded Greyhound sign hung over a row of grey steel chairs, most of their paint worn away years ago. I got directions to the trailer park and started the long walk.

Of course, it was all the way on the other side of town. Fucking Butch. A couple miles at least, down through rows of '70s-era bungalows, past the gas stations and the car dealership, over towards a gravel and concrete yard where yellow-rusted machinery awaited some big construction project that was never coming.

The Parkwood Acres trailer park sign was face down in the ankle-high grass surrounding the entrance. Up where the road turned, I could see Idaho plates on a dented '91 Celica. The passenger side wheel had cinderblocks under it, shimmed with a hunk of two-by-four. One rim sat in the grass.

The screen door hung cockeyed from the top hinge. The door-jamb was ripped out and the door swung open when I pushed. A smashed TV lay on its side and chairs were scattered like a hurricane had blown through. Widely spaced, dried blood splats ran across the worn kitchen linoleum. Someone had been bleeding—a lot— and taking long, fast steps on their way out the door.

The bedroom dresser drawers were open, empty except for a pair of 501s and a faded WSU Cougars hoodie. A duffel bag containing some socks and boxer shorts sat by the bed. The only things in the room were Butch's.

I followed the blood splatters outside, and snooped around the trailer's perimeter. Once upon a time, the original owner had probably grown all sorts of posies in the adjoining flowerbed. But now it was crowded with dandelions and thistles with stalks like tree trunks. The skirting hung off the southwest back corner and the trailer sagged badly.

Well, what the fuck? No sign of Butch. And no sign of Trudy either. She had just as much incentive to meet me as Butch did, since she shared his debt to—who? I didn't know. But I did know that Butch would never intentionally let me down. Often, yes. But intentionally, no. I walked back around to the porch for one last look, turning the broken screen door so the front faced outwards. There was a note with bloody finger-smears all over it. "Go hang out at the Big Jug," it said.

Halfway through my second year at Washington State University, I ran out of money. Fortunately, a rough-around-the edges Idaho mountain kid and a naive Albertan small town boy made a good match. We'd become fast friends and quickly realized we were an exotic flavour for spoiled sorority chicks. Especially when we kept the jokes flowing and connected them with things they were looking for.

Butch—his real name was Stacy—was the one who showed me how to get by when the Canadian dollar slipped to 65 cents.

"Why are we working for other people's drug habits?" he asked when I announced I was moving out. "Their habits should be working for us." He pointed to the parking lot outside our window, where a drunken daddy's girl named Jeanette left her BMW the night before. "All these rich kids and dealers, hooking up at our place 'cause we throw the best parties. What's in it for us?"

Rent was due on Monday, and I was short. Butch scraped up enough dough for a keg of Coors and bought as much cocaine as he could with my almost-rent money. That night we threw a kegger, sold all the blow, got laid, made our seed money back, plus rent and food for the month, and never looked back. It took another year before things came to a head and we dropped out.

It made sense that Butch came up north with me. The ROTC wanted their money back since he never made good on his scholarship. Up here they couldn't touch him easily. There was plenty of construction work that paid under the table.

The Big Jug was one of those awful strip-mall bars where ownership changed hands every year, but the original sign always remained. I ordered the chicken strips and said I'd be right back. Running to the 7-11 next door, I bought a pack of Zig-Zag whites and a copy of the Atlantic Monthly.

I was halfway through the magazine and my third pint of Keith's when a familiar voice croaked behind me. "I knew you'd figure it out."

"Holy shit Butch!" I yelped as I turned back to look at him.

His forehead resembled a rain-soaked softball, the swollen contents straining at a stitch that began above his left eye and stretched around the right side of his head. Two puffy slits indicated the general location of his eyes, and his lower lip jutted out a good half-inch. His left temple was covered by a saucer-sized scab extending down to his cheekbone. Chunks of his black hair stuck up, blood gluing them together in thick strands. He was as forlorn a motherfucker as I'd ever seen.

I took his arm and steered him to the chair across from me, reaching back with one hand and waving to the waitress. Friends on our level don't have to waste time with pleasantries; I looked at him and he answered.

"Trudy was acting all weird. So I scooped her bank card since I had some money in there. I told her she needed to tell me what she was up to before she could have it back." He grimaced. "She went fucking apeshit. Worst freakout ever."

"I thought she was on pills for that now."

"She was. Then she figured out high-school kids'll pay fifteen bucks a pop for 'em."

I motioned for him to continue.

"She called her family and told 'em I hit her. Her brothers drove up from the reserve."

"What did they say?"

"Nothing. But I got the message."

"Okay, wait. What about the three grand you both owe this scary dude?"

The waitress arrived, clunking down a pint in front of each of us. Butch grabbed his and downed it. His slit-eyes watered. I assumed it was from slamming the beer.

"Yeah... I think that might be sorted now. She moved all her stuff to his pad in Lethbridge."

He sat for a minute. "But fuck her. It's good to see you, my brother."

"Except I'm here for no reason! Risking my ass for help you don't actually need! Jesus, man!"

His eyes had water around them again. I decided to lay off for a bit.

We owned the pool table all night and even won a few bucks. We talked the bartender into selling us a bottle of Crown Royal and got a motel room. It was old and musty and the fake wood paneling was starting to blister.

"Look what I got," Butch said slyly, pulling out a

185

small glass pipe.

"Not for me man. I steer clear of anything that can't be grown in dirt."

"Since when?"

"Since I got out of your evil clutches."

"I didn't do any of this shit when I met you either. You're giving me the bad influence trip?"

"No, Butch. But you are the ultimate enabler."

He flashed a lopsided, fat-lip grin. "You know what they say—do one thing and do it well."

I watched him fire it up, with a towel jammed under the door to keep the smell from seeping out.

I meant it when I said no, but that never stopped Butch. "C'mon," he said.

"No."

Eventually, I gave in.

I was still wide-awake with pupils the size of dinner plates when the Greyhound rolled out of town, through acres of withered bush and dead, brown crop stubble. "In the cold, grey light of dawn," as the bluegrass song puts it.

The inevitable post-crack-high depression set in as I replayed the hours of conversation. "You're the only real friend I got, brother," Butch confessed.

"And there's your only real enemy," I said pointing at the mirror above the desk. He fell for it, glancing over and seeing his reflection. He waved a middle finger.

My phone buzzed in my pocket. I ignored it. "We need to get away from this shit—all of it. It was fun when we had a future," I said. "You know, back when we were going to get degrees and careers, and wives. But it's been three years now. We're spinning our wheels." My voice was choked from trying to talk without losing the expensive smoke I'd just inhaled.

Ecstasy washed over me as I exhaled, and the room tilted on its axis. "I'm going back to school. Come with me."

I could see enough of Butch's eyes to read them. The light that used to be in them was gone. I would have said something encouraging, but I was smothering in the thick folds of a serious buzz. No longer of this earth, I floated weightlessly, my troubles suddenly far away and meaningless.

Butch was still reconciling his own failures. "I don't have your kind of willpower," he said, pausing to take a pull from the rye bottle. "And I've been having a lot of bad luck these last few years."

Looking at his swollen face, I felt authorized to lecture. "Bad luck goes hand in hand with bad decisions, brother, and you've made plenty of those."

He just nodded, holding his breath as long as he could, letting all the good stuff work its way into his bloodstream.

I shifted the conversation to good times. Portland came up, and of course the Portland Dreadlock. We laughed over our drunken stupidity. We'd flown down for a concert a few months after we bailed on school. The long and short of it is this: We were given an ounce of weed the first night to hold as a sign of good faith, while a young go-getter took our cash to obtain the proper drugs for a weekend binge. He never came back.

I was momentarily pleased when he didn't return because I'd rather have had the weed. There wasn't any weed, of course.

Unobscured by the two layers of Ziploc freezer baggie it arrived in, the contents were instantly recognizable as dyed, green paper towel, folded and fluffed into fake marijuana buds. They looked like little paper dreadlocks, thus inspiring the name.

It was a hard lesson, but Butch made good use of it. He perfected the trick, texturing specially selected paper with multiple tints of green dye, all found at the local craft supply store. He'd grind a little bit of rock salt over the still dye-damp "buds" to simulate the tiny crystals one found in good pot. For the finishing touch, he'd hide a half-smoked joint in the middle of the bag to give it a convincing odor. If you didn't look too close, the fakery was damn convincing.

But whenever Butch could, he'd get me to do it. I was the one with the artist's touch. And the pinnacle of my artistry was in a rubber bag in Pinner's freezer. Where Pinner fully believed his collateral was.

In that shitty motel, while the sun rose and my buzz slowly abated, it finally became clear; it was time to cut loose from Butch, put more distance between us. And as the bus pulled into Edmonton, I felt better. I knew I was going back to school. I knew, watching the downward spiral of people who sold prescription drugs to high-school kids, that I liked this world even less than the one I was avoiding. I was truly done with this—I wasn't just selling myself bullshit.

Butch was fucked. I'd keep an eye out for him as best I could, preferably at a distance. I hated that he was feeling low, and I knew if he didn't have someone looking out for him... well, who knew. This was the last time I'd go out on a limb for him.

I climbed out of the cab in front of my apartment, exhausted, but satisfied. I still had all of Pinner's money. Butch had wheedled for a small loan, but I knew better. Tomorrow, I'd be ready with the cash, get my scuba bag, and get on with my life.

There are only two kinds of people when it comes to

crack cocaine; those who think its buoyant, pillowy euphoria is the best feeling they've ever experienced — and those who've never tried it. Luckily, I'd proven to be impervious to its lure.

The only thing better than a crack hit is one more hit. That's a universal truth. But I could never go off the rails far enough to get evicted just because I'd blown all my rent money on drugs. I'd never get an impaired driving charge on my way to a dealer's house at four a.m. because I needed to beg for more. Or any of the stuff I saw on an almost-daily basis. I was always able to think things through — though admittedly it took a while sometimes. Butch, however, he didn't have a chance. Not without me around.

When I got home, I called my uncle and convinced him to get me a job with his crew up north. A few months of oilsands cash, and I'd have a year's tuition easy. I crawled into bed, pleased with myself.

I drifted off trying not to think about the broke illegal alien I'd abandoned in some podunk Alberta town. And I didn't dwell on the fast one I'd pulled either. I was okay. If Pinner discovered the contents of the bag now, I had his cash ready. And I had a little extra too, to settle any misunderstanding should there be one. No harm, no foul.

But now, in the face of an enraged biker — my ears ringing and a lump forming on the side of my head — it appears my self-congratulation might be premature.

Veins pop on his fat, sweaty forehead as Pinner rants. "You were set up with a guy on the inside, a friend in the business for fucking life! And you insult us by trying to put one over on us? What kind of a crew do you think you're fucking with?"

Us. He's saying "us" and looking over his shoulder at the business-biker behind him. This is a show for that guy's benefit.

"No, no, no! It's cool, Pinner!" I shout. "I've got your money right here!" I push myself up and reach for the cigar box on the side table but Pinner steps in, driving his fist into my mouth. A string of blood and saliva trails from one knuckle as he draws back and delivers a second punch to my eye. My head fragments into shards of white light.

Pinner drops the bat and grabs me by my hair. He leans into my ear, biting his words off quietly. "Dude, these boys came across the border clean. They wanted a little herb to take out on the town. I figured you wouldn't mind loaning me some for a day. I tell 'em about you, this standup guy. And then I open that bag right in front of them."

He jerks me to my feet. "Now I gotta make sure I don't look weak. Sorry, but I did warn you, stupid-ass." He punches me in the gut and I fall back on the couch sucking for air that doesn't come.

Then, the sign that this is the end.

Pinner picks the bat up and falls back two paces, his face going blank. He dangles the bat from one hand, hefting it, getting a feel for the full weight. One meaty paw hangs loose, ready to grip above the other when he finally goes for it. His intent is clear. When he winds up, he's going to lean into it with everything he's got.

There'll be no getting up. I'll be found dead on this ratty old couch, swollen tongue protruding from my bloated purple face. Fucking Butch.

Pinner steps into the swing, the bat whirling up over his shoulder, a blur as it arcs towards my skull. I'd piss myself, but I already did when I got gut punched. How did it come to this?

Pinner will be alright with the California boys—he'll save face by showing some backbone.

Butch, he's finally used up the last friend he had. That stupid sonofabitch is in for a real hard lesson.

HELL HATH NO FURY
DWAYNE E. CLAYDEN

It involved a woman. Cliché, I know, but it was about a woman. Not just any woman mind you, but the lovely Missy Garver. Long, golden red hair that shimmered with the touch of summer sun. Curves in all the right places, curves that drove you all the way up from her shapely calves to her luscious red lips. Skin so white and so smooth a guy could explore for hours and then explore some more.

She was an absolute dream. Her three brothers, on the other hand, were a nightmare. A nightmare that was currently re-enacting Ali vs Liston on my face. I was Liston. They'd thankfully moved on from using my face as a speed bag, and were concentrating their heavy bag workout on my midsection.

A roundhouse punch jerked my head near completely around, breaking my thoughts and nearly my neck. A knee to the groin seemed a fitting way to end the beating—for them, not me. The hands that had been holding me upright let go, and I crumpled to the ground like the sack of rotten potatoes I felt like. Face first into the turf, just like Liston in the first round.

"Stay away from Missy," the leader, and oldest brother said, jamming a baseball bat under my chin.

"Yeah, stay away," mimicked the next.

"Yeah, away," the third mina bird followed suit in a steadily declining level of intelligence that matched their difference in age.

"I clawed my way across the grass—not that I had anywhere I needed to be—but my face found a nice cool patch of dirt.

It was surprisingly refreshing. I did a complete body inventory. I could still feel my fingers and toes. That was the first good sign. I kicked my legs and moved my arms. All four functioned as well as they ought to. I was having definite challenges with anything close to a deep breath. Tight and sore, but not searing, wrath-of-God type pain, so I was guessing my ribs were bruised, rather than broken. I was mouth breathing like a guppy. The throbbing was centered on my nose—swollen, raw and filled with blood. Flowing like a faucet, snot and blood and misery pouring out by the gallon. It was intact—at least it hadn't been broken again. The slight curve in the middle was from another fight, another time, another dame.

I collected my thoughts—they'd been scattered around the park with what was left of my grey matter— rolled onto my stomach, pulled my arms under me and pushed. I made it into a kneeling position. So far, so good. I fumbled around, found my fedora and plopped it on my head. I stood and let the swirling of the horizon spin around me like the merry-go-round at the park on overdrive. Unlike my last ride on the horses, this time I didn't puke.

They'd caught me in the park walking home from the bar. Not that it would have been hard to find me. I walked home from that bar every night about closing time. That I'd let them catch me off guard was a testament to how much time I spent there. That I'd let them man handle me just pissed me off. I suppose the wack across the back of my head with the bat assisted.

I staggered out of the park on legs feeling like wet spaghetti. I forced my eyes to focus. No deal. The world was spinning like a top as waves of nausea fought for a release. The street lights at the park entrance burned holes in my swollen eyes. I reached for a cigarette then realized I'd quit a few weeks ago. Missy insisted. She was worth it.

I pulled my hat low over my eyes and stuck my hands in my pants pockets. I watched my feet, first one then the other, stumbling along the sidewalk. At least they knew the way home.

The chirp of a police siren stopped me cold in my tracks and kicked my brain in the ass. I lifted my head. Bright light darted outward from the cruiser. I bent low so the cop inside could see me.

"Shut that the fuck off," I yelled before the filters in my brain kicked in. I slid into the passenger seat.

Not the first time in a police cruiser, not likely the last. This was different though. The cop, Thomas Rabey, was my half-brother and I got to sit in the front— without bracelets. We shared a mom. She shared herself with a lot of different guys. He's a cop, I'm a PI. I guess we got the law angle from our fathers. They'd spent a lot of time in court, and even more time doing time.

"Oh, I suppose you want a ride."

"Since you're offering..."

"You look like shit," Thomas said.

"You're ugly like your father," I replied.

"At least I'm not stupid like your father," Thomas said.

"I gonna tell mom you're being mean to me," I said.

"Shut up. I'll drive you home." He put the car in gear and pulled away from the curb. "I see you're still wearing that stupid hat."

"Gotta look the part," I said.

"You're an idiot."

"I'm still telling mom."

"Yeah, good luck with that." He took a long pull on his cigarette and exhaled towards me. "You're a mess. Want a smoke?"

"No, I quit." I inhaled the smoke and revelled in its sweetness.

"You look like you want a smoke. How long since you quit?"

"Two weeks."

"A girl?"

"A dame."

"Whatever, Bogey. Quit talking like a fucking weirdo. You sure she's legal?"

"She's legal."

"Good for you. That's a step in the right direction."

"Fuck you."

He stopped the cruiser.

My place was a small bungalow with tall trees and overgrown lawn. Fifty years old and looking every minute of its age. Which is probably why I liked it.

"Nice place. See you've been doing some yard

work."

"Why you busting my balls? Don't you have some crime to prevent? Some widows and orphans to protect?"

"Come on, Bryce. You know I don't have time for real police work. It's a full time job scraping you off the sidewalk. Lunch tomorrow?"

"Always. Thanks for the lift."

"Get some ice. For your face, not the whiskey."

"Can't I do both?"

I closed the door and watched Tommy drive away. It was nice having somebody out there looking out for me, even if he was a cop.

I fumbled with my keys and willed my swollen eyes to focus. I was sure I had the right key, now to find the lock. Of the three I saw I went for the middle one...bingo. I flung the door open. It bounced back hitting me squarely on my forehead. Fuck.

I grabbed the bag of ice from the freezer, a glass from the sink—mostly clean—and the whiskey from counter. Important to have the necessities of life handy. I sank into the depths of the couch. The ice bag stung as I pressed it into the swollen lump on the front of my face, but after a few swallows of the whiskey, I was rewarded with that sweet, mellow numbness, spreading through my aching face like a hot barbershop towel on a cold winter day.

I closed my eyes and thought of Missy. I wanted to see her again. I needed to see her again. It would take more than a savage beating to keep me away from those dangerous curves. Missy Garver was more than worth the pain.

I woke up the next morning in agony. There wasn't a

part of my body that didn't ache. Laying my cheek on the pillow sent jots of pain deep into my brain. Each breath was a chore. It took twenty minutes in a steamy shower just to get the cemented blood and snot out of my nose. Not that it helped, with the swelling, I had to mouth breathe most of the time anyway. The redness from the night before had turned to a deep purple hew and spread across my face like a mask. Breakfast was not an option. No amount of toothpaste could remove the coppery taste of blood from my mouth.

Putting on a shirt was a whole new world of pain. I slipped one arm into the shirt sleeve and slowly pulled the shirt up the arm. The other arm wasn't so easy. I had to lift it to shoulder height, causing fire to race across my ribs. Same procedure for the jacket. Same pain. I was sporting double shiners that even my mirrored Ray-bans couldn't hide. I felt the bruising complemented my blue double-breasted suit.

I parked behind the office took the back stairs. I quietly opened the door to the reception area, saw no one, and went right for the coffee on the counter outside my office. My secretary makes a damn fine cup of coffee. I grabbed a large mug and filled it to the brim. I brought the mug to my nose and inhaled, letting the heat open up my swollen passageways and savouring what little of the fresh coffee smell made it all the way up to my skull. There's nothing better than the smell of freshly ground heaven to awaken comatose brain cells.

"About time you got here." The shrill voice of my secretary, Liz Bryant scratched and clawed at every frazzled nerve fiber in my body. I leaned away from her screeching face, holding the cup out in front of me to avoid spilling coffee on my suit—not that it was a stranger to spilled coffee.

"What the hell happened to you? Your face... No wait, I don't need to know." She glared at me over her reading glasses. She pursed her lips and scrunched her nose. "You have an appointment. She'll be here in five minutes. Your behaviour..."

I held up my hand. "Before you start—don't. I still haven't changed my ways, have no intention of changing my ways and there is nothing you can do to make me change my ways. Who's the client?"

She looked me over once more, rolled her eyes and shook her head. "Wife thinks her husband is going to kill her."

"You know I don't do domestic cases." I do have my limits and pride. Unless I needed the money. And I didn't have any cases. Unless the dame was beautiful. Unless...

"You need the money. You have no cases."

There it was.

"Fine. I'll be in my office." I sat in my chair, lay back and put my feet on the desk. My morning after pose. I opened a drawer on my left—a bottle of whiskey and my gun. After last night, I really should think about packing. A whiskey would be good. My face throbbed and with every breath my ribs protested. I grabbed the bottle, rolling it lovingly in my hands.

Two knocks and the door opened. Liz stepped inside, eyes immediately flashing on the bottle. I quickly stuffed it in the drawer. Liz moved aside and an attractive woman with the haughty air of refinement swept into the room. She was late thirties, early forties. Hard to tell. Her long brown hair was held back with a barrette. Her fingers were long and slim. At first glance, she was pretty. At second glance, there was a hardness. At third glance it was clear she wasn't impressed by any of my glances. Her sternness reminded me of my English teacher in junior high. Sexy. And fucking scary.

Liz made the introduction. "Bryce Pedley, this is Mrs. Rutledge."

"Ms. Rutledge. Rutledge is my maiden name."

"I'm sorry, this is Ms. Rutledge," Liz said, with emphasis on the Ms.

Rutledge gave Liz a look that would grind diamonds into sand.

Liz gave a pleasant nod to mask the gasoline fire behind her eyes, and shut the door behind her, maybe a little more forcefully than usual.

I stood and gestured to the chair across from me, "Please, have a seat."

She looked at the old wooden chair as if it was a piece of dog shit that she'd just stepped in. She bent straight from the hips and swept gingerly at the seat with a tissue from her purse before finally, carefully, arranging herself in the chair.

"What can I do for you, Ms. Rutledge?" I asked.

Her eyes darted around the office stopping on me. Her eyes moved from my split lips to my bruised and swollen eyes. It was clear she didn't like what she saw. I saw disgust written over her face like graffiti on the subway walls. Our eyes met, then she immediately looked away, locking in on the one item on the wall, a license from the government saying I had successfully passed the requirements to be a private investigator. She turned away, hardly satisfied with what she saw. It was okay. I wasn't impressed either. She spoke anyway.

"I believe my husband is stalking me."

"Husband? But you use your maiden name. You're separated, I take it?"

"Yes. The divorce isn't finalized. Not yet." She made

sure that was very clear. "I'm trying to move on with my life. New chapter and all."

"What makes you think that he's stalking you?"

"He doesn't like the settlement terms. He blames me for all his problems. But lately there have been a series of disturbing events."

"Such as?"

"Someone was in my house. Things moved. Things... taken."

"Such as?"

She turned her head and I could see the red flush on her neck and cheeks.

"My...my under clothes."

My mind wondered and my eyes wandered.

I looked up to another icy stare. Shit. "When did this happen?"

"Thursdays."

"Thursdays? It's happened more than once?"

"Yes, several times."

"And only on Thursdays?"

"Yes."

"Anything else?"

"It's my husband...ex-husband. I know it is. Initially, he helped out with things like yard work and minor repairs. But when things started happening, well, the children felt violated."

"Violated is a pretty nasty word." And not the kind of word kids were fond of using. Mention of her kids came pretty late in the interview—almost an afterthought. She wasn't fooling anyone. This was all about her. "You haven't mentioned the kids before."

"What?"

"The kids. This is the first time you mentioned your kids."

Now I was seeing the angle. Using the kids against the husband, and now she needed independent corroboration. Probably money involved too. Maybe big numbers.

"Yes, well, we are all afraid. I told him to stay away. I had the locks changed." She paused. I caught a slight tremble in her hands. "Then the brakes on my car failed."

That came out of left field. "That's serious. I'm guessing you've had the car checked? What did the mechanic say?"

"Well, he wasn't very helpful. Just said the fluid was low."

"So the lines weren't cut?"

"No nothing like that."

"Maybe the fluid was low. How often do you check?" Stupid question I knew, but I was still trying to size her up and figure out her angle. Looking at the perfectly manicured nails I was pretty sure she knew where all the full service gas stations were.

"What? Me! Never!"

Bingo. Pampered and paranoid.

"Anything else?" I asked, now prepared for anything and everything.

"He's been following us."

"Following you?"

"We see his car. Sometimes he is at the school. Outside the playground. I'm told he's been seen at their games, in the gymnasium."

"So he does have contact with the kids?"

"No, they've chosen not to. He just shows up there."

"Their choice, or do you have sole custody?"

"The children choose to see him only for special occasions—birthdays and such."

Dwayne E. Clayden

"Is there a restraining order?"

"No. I went to a lawyer, but he said there wasn't enough evidence. I have petitioned for sole custody."

"I see. So what do you want me to do?" I had her number now. Question was, did she have mine?

She feigned shock, as I knew she would. Then she gave me that look that every woman seems to have in her repertoire. That look that said, *how dare you?* The look that usually accompanied a totally incomprehensible request. That was the look she gave me, as if I was asking her to jump on the desk and perform a striptease for the mayor.

"I want you to follow my husband." She replied, incredulous.

She placed a picture on the table. I made no move to look at it.

"I want you to catch him doing something illegal. I want you to get him out of my life forever."

And there it was. Many's the time that these soon-to-be-divorcee's come in looking for ammo against their husbands—affairs, hidden bank accounts, gambling problems—things they can parade in front of a compassionate judge and plead for more of hubby's green. She certainly seemed the type.

I folded my arms across my chest. "About my fee..."

She'd been holding her purse firmly in her lap, like she was afraid if she let her guard down, I'd grab it and make a break for the door. Now she looked like she'd reached a turning point. A point-of-no-return. She smiled. Not a nice smile, but the corners of her mouth turned up in the right places. She opened the purse and took out an envelope. I'd half-expected to see moths escape.

"Will cash be sufficient?"

"Absolutely. But we haven't discussed how much."

"Very well, what is your fee?"

"One thousand deposit and two hundred a day plus expenses. So let's say two grand to start."

She stared, lips still curling. "Do the expenses include paying for your medical costs?" She thought she had my number now.

I rubbed at the bruises around my eyes. "Not the pre-existing ones."

"Good. You don't appear as though you live very carefully, but you came recommended. I accept your terms."

She set the envelope with the picture and slid them across the desk "My husband—ex-husband—is Chad Dawson."

She said it like I should know the name, or as if she'd already said it. Like mentioning the existence of her children, she was awfully frugal with the facts.

"When can I expect results?" Now that the money was on the table, she was all business. Fine by me.

"Two weeks. Tops."

****

The diner filled-up quickly for lunch.

It wasn't that the food was outstanding, or that the service was over-the-top, or even that the waitress was hot—unless you had stepped in from the old folks home down the street and blue-haired granny in a short skirt was your kind of thing. Maybe it was the retro 30's atmosphere. Or it was simply because this grease pit was only the restaurant for five miles. I had a reserved booth Monday to Friday. That's how good of a customer I am.

I met Tommy here for lunch at least once a week. The rest of the time I ate alone, or with clients. Usually alone.

I took the spot with my back to the wall and my face to the entrance. I knew it drove him crazy as a cop to have his back to the door. It was a small victory, but brotherly victory, just the same.

Tommy came through the front door and stopped. He took his mirrored Ray-Bans off and scanned the diner. He checked out booths and tables, then his eyes settled on me. He smiled. He did this every time we met, even though we always sat in the same booth. His way of scoping the diner. His way of being a cop.

Tommy slumped down across from me and grabbed a menu.

"Really?" I asked. "Menu hasn't changed since Diefenbaker was Prime Minister and you always order the same thing."

"You never know."

The waitress came by and filled the coffee cups. She knew cops were fuelled on coffee. And she loved a man in uniform. "You're looking good today Tommy."

"Thank you Doris."

She snuck a glance at me. "Better than your brother. Looks like he's still leading with his face."

"Bit of an improvement I think."

Doris winked at Tommy. "What'll you have boys".

Tommy set the menu down. "Burger. Nearly rare, double lettuce, double tomatoes, double pickle. Side salad."

"Sure thing, sweetie. And you?" No smile.

I stared at my brother. Like vegetables made a burger a healthy meal. "Burger and fries. Burger nearly burnt, no vegetable, just mustard and ketchup. Mayonnaise for the fries."

"You still look like shit," Tommy said.

"You still look like a limp-peckered mall security

guard. What's your point?"

Tommy smiled as he stirred his coffee. "How's business?"

"Got a client today."

"Good for you. Step in the right direction. Paying client?"

"Yup, deposit and all. Gotta follow her future ex for a couple of weeks."

"You don't do domestic cases."

"The caseload is a little thin right now."

"That's because you don't have any cases."

"I have one." I said, holding up a finger. "Speaking of which..." I slid the photocopy across the table. "I need a background check."

Tommy stared at the photo. "That's against police policy."

"I'm buying lunch. That's against my policy."

Tommy laughed, "In that case, it will be my pleasure." He pulled out his notebook and made a few notes. "I'll call you later."

I woke up to the ringing of the phone. I grabbed for it. Pain rocketed up my ribs, my arm went into spasm and I knocked it to the floor. I finally found the receiver and pulled it to my face, hitting my swollen nose. "Shit. Yeah?"

"Hey buddy, catch you at a bad time?" Tommy asked.

"Oh no, just sleeping," I wheezed, nose clogged again.

"It's two o'clock in the afternoon, grandpa."

"You calling for a reason?"

"I got the background on your case."

"Go ahead."

"Well, not a lot. Guy builds homes. Respected builder. Three crews that he runs through his own company. Seems pretty lucrative. We've only got a file because he applied for criminal records checks. He's a scout leader and sometimes football coach at the high school. No arrests, no warrants. Occasional speeding ticket. Nothing here says stalker or murder suspect."

"No domestic assaults? No calls to the cops?" Weird that the guy has no record, but plenty of guys go squirrelly when the wife takes the kids and kicks him to the curb. Some guys go a lifetime without anybody finding out what kind of evil they perpetrate behind closed doors, especially when it comes to domestics.

"Nope. About as ordinary as he can be."

"I'm missing something."

"You usually do. You gonna follow him tonight?"

"Yup."

"Be careful. You never know."

"I'll be careful. Besides, I have you to rescue me."

"There's that."

I drove by the Rutledge house. I had a least an hour to kill before I could slip in behind Dawson. It was a nice street, mature trees, five-foot hedge around the front of the place. It was well kept. No, more than that. Someone put love and attention into this yard. Not something Ms. Rutledge would deign to do. Not a dame with those perfectly manicured fingers.

The house was the usual two story with the garage out front. In the back, each house buddied right up to the next, every last inch of real estate accounted for. A six foot wooden fence separated the yards.

I had time, and I figured it wouldn't hurt to see the layout of the inside. I slipped through the front gate, up the path and rang the doorbell.

She was dressed to the nines. Hair in curls, clingy mid-thigh dress and a string of pearls looping down to a very visible cleavage.

She caught me staring — again.

Rutledge growled from the gap in the half-shut door. "What do you want?"

Not the friendliest greeting. "Just checking in," I said.

Her lips curled in apparent disgust. "You look like some kind of thug creeping around out there. What if the neighbours see you?"

"Uh, I thought I'd check out your street and yard. Maybe see the inside too. Could come in handy later."

"This isn't the best time," she said. Her face flushed.

"I'll only be a minute," I said as I slipped past her. She was hiding something.

It wasn't a something, it was a some*one*.

As I stepped through the front entrance, a man appeared from the next room. He was dressed in a dark suit. He looked to be in his 40's — brown hair, brown eyes and a pair of dark rimmed glasses that gave him a non-aggressive look — like an accountant.

I looked back at Rutledge and then to the man.

Her shoulders sagged and there was a tremor in her voice.

She handled him first. "This is the detective I told you about." Then to me, purely on ceremony, "Mr. Pedley, this is my pastor — Douglass Abernethy." I noted the way she was sure to emphasize his job title, telling me why he was there without having to explain herself.

I stuck out my hand. He took it. I was surprised by the firmness of the grip. His mousey demeanor didn't match that handshake. With my left hand I reached out and patted his arm at the shoulder. A friendly, fraternal type of pat. It also let me get another take on him. The arm was solid. This was someone who worked out. Not a muscle head, but he was toned. The kind of toned that required pain and commitment.

"Nice to meet you Douggie." I smiled.

He nodded and simply said, "Pedley." Not a pleased to meet you. Just Pedley. Like we'd say in the army. Or cop to cop.

"I'd hate to see the other guy." He chuckled. Nodding to indicate my mashed-up mug, as if I didn't know how it looked.

I broke the grip. "I was just saying to Ms. Rutledge that I was checking the yard and wanted to see the house. Could be important later."

"I see." he said. "We are all very worried about recent... events. I must say that I've never really trusted Chad."

"Why is that?"

"Can't really say. He never really fit in with the congregation. I don't like to speak ill of people..."

Here it comes, the holy rolling judgement show.

"The children at church didn't like him. Said he was too rough in sports. Women stayed away from him, were... uncomfortable around him. He just didn't fit in."

"How long have you known Mr. Dawson?"

He glanced at Rutledge, gauging how he should answer. She nodded for him to continue, "About four years. Ever since they moved here."

I roamed the bottom floor while he played the part of concerned clergyman.

"He didn't get on well with the other men. Not at all. I'm not sure any of them would consider Chad a friend."

I stopped in front of him, putting myself in his space, "And how did he get on with you?"

"Can't say I ever really trusted him." He repeated, "Sorry, but that's the way it is."

Rutledge gave me a thin smile from her spot in the doorway and nodded her approval again.

"So, the bedrooms are upstairs?" I moved in the direction of the stairs.

The preacher blocked me. "I really don't think it is appropriate for you to go to the bedrooms."

We stared at each other. He didn't back down. My first impression had been wrong. This was a man used to getting his way. Used to being in charge. Used to taking what he wanted. I decided that it wasn't important. At least not now. Let him think I was backing down. Maybe he'd slip up later. If he did, I'd be ready.

"Alright. Well, I need to be on my way." I nodded to Ms. Rutledge. "Ma'am."

Abernethy held out his hand. I left it hanging.

The next three nights I spent following Chad Dawson. I started at the building site where one of his crews was putting up at big two-story. Each night he went home, changed, grabbed a bite and then headed out. The first night he went to the high school to watch his kid practice on the football team. He stayed well back, out of sight, just watching. The second night he went across town to a different school and into the gym. His daughter was playing volleyball. Both nights he headed straight home after watching his kids. Didn't approach them, didn't even take pictures. Just watching.

On the third night, Thursday, just after dark, he came out dressed in jogging gear. This was a problem. If I tailed him in the car I'd stand out like a neon sign. If I got out and ran, I'd be out of breath by the third house—maybe four houses. Quitting smoking had done nothing for my track and field potential, let alone the bruised ribs that still wailed like a broken accordion. While I was trying to decide on a plan of action, Dawson cut through a school playground. Decision made.

I quickly circled the block and slipped in behind a line of parked cars in front of a church. I had a great sight line and I'd pick Dawson up when he exited the playground. I waited, watching intently for the man.

I leaned forward in the car. Dawson should have come out by now. I waited another minute then pulled away from the curb and drove slowly down the street. No joggers. I circled the block twice, nothing. Shit. How'd I miss him? I drove around for another 20 minutes then raced to Ms. Rutledge's house. I checked the yard. Nothing. I rang the doorbell. Rutledge opened the door. The radiant smile vanished immediately. She pulled a silk robe tightly around her body. "What are you doing here?"

I couldn't admit the truth. I was tailing her ex and lost him. I did the only thing I could. I lied. "Thursday night. Checking in. Making sure everything is A-Okay." I tried to sneak a peek past her into the dark lower level. Luther Vandross played in the background.

"I am fine. Thank you." She said, that same tight-lipped grimace curling up her lips as she tried not to look me in the face. "Shouldn't you be out making sure that Chad is not going to attack us again? Especially since it is Thursday night?"

The door was open about a foot and she was standing in that opening, blocking any view into the house. A faint aroma of scented candles drifted past.

"Don't worry," I said. "I know exactly where your husband is." I didn't have a clue. "If everything is okay I'll be on my way."

So, Rutledge is going to be entertaining. If I had to bet, I'd say the reverend is paying special attention to this parishioner. I gotta get Tommy to do another background check. Ms. Rutledge was at least three different women. Like rolling the dice. You never knew when it would come up snake eyes.

I drove around for an hour trying to find Dawson. I drove past his place a dozen times but it was dark and quiet. I circled the playground another dozen times. I headed home. The phone was ringing when I opened the door. I grabbed the phone, "Yeah."

"You better get over to your client's house now!" That was all Tommy said.

I skidded the Studebaker to a stop behind Tommy's cruiser and ran into the house. I was out of breath.

Tommy had them gathered in the living room like the usual suspects in an Agatha Christie novel. I went with the flow.

Ms. Rutledge sat on the couch with the preacher and a large woman with a severe face and hawk-like nose.

The woman was on a rant. "No good. No darn good. Knew that from the start. Something dark. He was hiding something. I always knew it. Up to no good. Double life likely."

"And who did you tell?" I asked.

"What?" she snapped. Seeing me for the first time.

"You said you always knew there was a problem. So, who did you tell?"

The preacher leaned forward. "This is my wife, Martha. She is a close friend of Kathy's."

"Kathy? Who the hell is Kathy?"

"I am." Rutledge piped up, all cool and dejected.

"Right. Sorry." I turned back to Hawknose, "So who

211

did you tell? Kathy? The police? The reverend here?" The room went silent.

Tommy said, "Someone was prowling around the yard."

"When?" Fuck. I'd lost Dawson and he'd slipped over here. This did not bode well for my reputation.

Tommy looked at his watch. "Ms. Rutledge called us about thirty-five minutes ago."

"And it took you twenty minutes to get here!" Rutledge spat. The reverend patted her arm.

"We found some boot prints in the yard. Basic tread," Tommy said. Could be anyone."

"Did anyone see the prowler?" I asked.

"No," Tommy said. "Daughter heard a noise outside. They're all wound pretty tight."

I felt a little better, but not much. I glanced at the reverend and his wife.

"Poor Kathy. She called us right away," the reverend said. "We were here before the police...and you. This is intimidation of the worst kind. Are we the only ones worried about this poor woman? Chad has money, lots of it and he won't part with a fair share. Kathy and the kids have nothing. He's leaving them in poverty. I won't stand for that. If you can't do something about this, then I will."

"I understand your frustration, reverend," Tommy said. "But we need hard evidence. There is no proof Chad has done anything wrong."

"No proof! Stalking the kids isn't enough? Invading the house isn't enough?" The pastor gripped Kathy's arm, "The police and this supposed detective are useless."

Ms. Rutledge shot me the death-ray look. "I paid you to stop this. Where the hell were you?" The look that reinforced her view that the cops couldn't organize a piss-up in a brewery. But now I was lumped in with them.

"I think that's all we can do for now. We'll have cruisers coming by your house." Tommy nodded to Ms. Rutledge, "Ma'am." Then "Reverend."

I followed Tommy outside. We stopped at his cruiser. He took out a pack of cigarettes. He offered me one. Jerk. I took it.

We smoked in silence. Then I blurted, "The boot prints were mine."

"Ya, I figured. You had your practiced stupid look in there."

"Fuck you."

He smiled. "Looks like you've got yourself into one really fucked up mess. She's a real piece of work. And her friends aren't much better."

Don't I know it, I thought. Don't I always?

Sleep didn't come easy. My mind was tumbling thoughts like a clothes dryer. All these random pieces that didn't seem to fit together. Fortunately, two fingers of whiskey finally hit my system and the tumbling stopped.

In that place between sleep and fully awake I heard a sound. It was distant. Was it part of a dream? The sound was louder. Footsteps. Someone trying to be quiet. Fuck. The Garver brothers. I reached under my pillow, slid out my trusty .38 and sprung to a sitting position as I swung the gun toward the bedroom door.

"That's a fine greeting," Missy said. She'd stopped halfway to the bed.

"I've warned you about sneaking up on me. Especially when I'm asleep." I put the gun on the night table. "What time is it?"

"Eight thirty," she said.

"You should be at work," I said.

"I called in sick," she said.

"You don't look sick," I said.

"I think I have a fever," she said. "I'm feeling very hot." She unbuttoned her blouse and threw it aside. She unzipped her skirt and with her foot, flung it into the corner. She stood before me wearing a black bra, black panties and a bright smile. I flung back the covers. She pounced on me. Repeatedly.

I lay on my back with Missy's head on my chest. My heart had finally stopped racing.

"I can hear your heart," she said.

"That's a good thing," I said.

"Yes, yes it is," she said.

She leaned on her elbow. With a finger she traced the scar on my right shoulder. "What's this from?"

"I was shot when I was in the army."

"And this one?" She traced a line along my left bicep.

"Knife. Drug dealer selling to kids. I was trying to convince him he needed to move to another city. He disagreed. Slashed me with six inch blade."

"Did he move to another city?"

"Another location."

"Where?"

"Hell. Everyone except him knew you don't bring a knife to a gunfight."

She ran her hand over the fingers on my right hand. The pinky finger had a deviation to the right at the last knuckle. "Fight?"

"Yeah. But you should see the other guy." I never got tired of saying that.

Missy rolled back on top of me. "I don't want to see the other guy, "she whispered. "Just this guy." She placed her hands on my chest. Her eyes closed and her chin rose. She rocked her hips back and forth and sighed. I hung on for another ride.

I'd decided that trying to follow Dawson was a dumb. Realistically, to follow someone you needed about a dozen guys and a half dozen vehicles. It helped if at least some of them were in good shape. Since there was just me, with one vehicle, and the only shape I was in was round, I parked down the street from Ms. Rutledge's house. Every half hour or so I'd get out and walk down the block. Looking for anything suspicious. The last four walks had produced nothing except a reminder that I really did need to get to the gym.

I poured another coffee from the thermos. Gotta have a thermos of coffee if you are on a stake out. And a large mouth mayonnaise jar. Let's just say that from experience I don't so much drink coffee as rent it. You get the idea.

Cigarettes are good too. They help pass the time. But people see the glow in the car and they think you are a creep. They call the cops. The cops come with lights and sirens and the stakeout is blown. I'd quit smoking anyway. Again.

I sipped the coffee and I tried to put the pieces together. Where did Chad Dawson disappear to? Ms. Rutledge hadn't mentioned Chad having any hobbies or other interests.

Ms. Rutledge wanted a divorce. It was almost done. Just the final arguments about who gets what and what was fair. But she was scared about a prowler or stalker or whatever it was. Really scared. That part I believed now.

Sitting in the car gets really old really fast. I decided to change the routine and take my walk a little early. I headed down the sidewalk and paused at the front of the house. I saw a shadow in the back yard. I slipped through the gate and edged down the side of the house. As I neared the back yard the hair on my neck stood. I reached for my .38. It was just clearing my coat when I heard the crunch of a footstep behind me. I turned my head in time to see an arm swinging in my direction.

The grass was cool against my face. Me and the cool grass were spending too much time together. A blade of grass tickled my nose. I was breathing through my nose. I had to, something was stuffed in my mouth. I tried to move my arms. I couldn't. My hands were tied behind my back. My feet were tied.

While the situation seemed desperate, sadly I'd been in worse. You learn a few tricks along the way. The first, was always carry a knife. The second, was carry it so you can actually use it. That was a hard second lesson to learn. But before I could use the knife, I had to get my arms in front of me. Yet again, I thought about my lack of attendance at the gym. I thought about Missy saying I needed to workout. I gagged on the cloth in my mouth. I worked it around with my tongue and jaw and finally was able to spit it out. One down.

Next I wiggled onto my side, drew my knees up tight to my chest and extended my arms downward. I couldn't breathe. My quads were cramping and I thought my arms were going to dislocate from my shoulders. Just when I thought I couldn't endure this anymore, my legs slipped backwards, and my arms came free in front of me.

It was easy to grab the knife I had clipped to my right front pants pocket. I flipped it open, reversed the grip and sawed at the rope around my wrist. Another lesson is to be sure the knife blade is always sharp, very sharp. The rope gave way. I quickly cut the bindings around my ankles. I felt the rush of blood to my limbs. At first there was pain, like when you have slept on your arm — all tingly and painful.

My hand slipped under my coat. The gun was gone. I knelt on the grass and reached around me. No dice. I crawled around, feeling as I went. New lesson. Carry a flashlight. I finally found my gun and raced to the front of the house.

The front door was closed. I was ready to use my size ten and a half on the lock but decided to try the door knob. It was unlocked. I opened the door and quickly entered the house. The lower level was in darkness. I heard movement upstairs. I moved to the stairs and hugged the wall, gun in front. Halfway up there was a small landing and then the final seven stairs. I silently kicked myself for not insisting earlier that I needed to see the layout upstairs. Someone stumbled into a piece of furniture. I heard a scream. I took the last seven stairs two at a time. As I reached the top landing I imagined the layout. I heard another scream from my left. I moved in that direction. A masked dark figure rushed at me from the room. He swung a bag at my head. I ducked and pressed up against the wall. I turned to follow and was hit across the back of my head. I dropped to my knees, then onto my face. What little vision I'd had in the darkness blurred. I rolled onto my back. Then white light assaulted my eyes. Someone had turned on the lights. I heard voices. I heard screams.

"Mr. Pedley. Mr. Pedley!"

My eyes focussed. Ms. Rutledge was standing over me dressed in flannel pajamas. A night lamp in her hand.

"Mr. Pedley. Are you alright?"

I sat up and rubbed the bruise forming on the back of my head. A nice companion to the one on the side of my head. "Yeah I'm fine. Fu... I mean golly that hurts."

"I woke up when I heard someone in my room. I screamed. He ran. I grabbed the lamp and well, I guess I thought you were the person in my room. I'm sorry."

"Did you call the cops?"

Tommy didn't want me to drive home. "You need to get checked at the hospital for a concussion."

"At least two," I said. "I'm going home."

"I'll get one of my guys to drive your car."

"No fuckin' way." I wasn't letting anyone else driving the Studebaker.

"Maybe your guys should work on actually doing some policing instead of driving me home." He didn't appreciate my advice. Not sure why I was busting his balls. I was the one who'd fucked up.

I parked in front of my house. I didn't have the energy or the focus to park in the garage. Didn't have the energy to lift the garage door. I really did need to get the opener fixed.

I stumbled up the walkway. The porch light was out. I'd have to add that to my list of things I wasn't ever going to do. Inserted the key in the lock. The lock clicked. I turned the doorknob. I was grabbed by my coat collar and spun around.

I was face to face with the Garver brothers. This was getting old. No, it was old. One of them, I think the oldest, but I really don't give a shit, said, "We told you to stay away from Missy. You didn't listen. Papa says we need to fuck you up real bad."

My arms were pulled behind my back. I could feel hot breath on my neck. I felt a rage start boiling in my gut. There was no fuckin' way I was going to get hit a third time. Older Garver stepped in front of me, lightly tapping a baseball bat into his left palm. Garver behind me tightened his grip and pulled me close. Rage burned from every pore like a rocket lifting off from a launch pad. Slowly at first then a full explosion.

I widened my stance and staggered my feet with my left foot slightly forward. I tilted my head forward, chin to chest, then flung my head backwards with full force. I heard the cartilage in Garver's nose break and felt the warm stream of blood on my neck.

Older Garver froze in surprise. My right foot swung forward with the force of a football placekicker attempting a sixty-yard field goal. I connected right between his uprights. He lifted at least a foot off the ground and then dropped like an anvil hitting the concrete of my porch, bounced once, then lay moaning. The baseball bat rolled to my feet.

The third brother, looked from one brother to the other, then to the bat. I grabbed the bat and swung upward in a low arc like I was sending a low pitch to the bleachers. The bat connected on his left knee. He cried out and stumbled forward falling off the porch onto the lawn. He limped across the lawn. The other two Garver's stumbled behind.

Tommy was already at the booth drinking a coffee. He had the good seat.

"You're early," I said.

"You're thirty minutes late," he said.

I checked my watch. Damn, he was right. "I had trouble getting out of bed."

"Late night?"

"They're all late nights." I caught the eye of the geriatric waitress and pointed at my mug. She nodded.

"Saw the Garver brothers today," he said.

"Uh huh."

"They were at the hospital."

"Our Mother of Perpetual Agony?" I asked.

"The nurses miss you. You haven't been in this week."

"Uh huh. Fuck you."

"The Garver's look like shit."

"Uh huh. They always look like shit. I think they get that from their dad."

"You don't' look so good."

"Never do."

"New bruises?"

"Thanks for noticing. Guess you got mom's looks."

"These things related?"

"Nope." The waitress filled my mug. I added sugar and cream. "What did you and your boys find out about the prowler last night?"

"Not a lot. Either a key was used or he picked the lock."

"Homebuilder would know how to get in. Maybe even how to pick a lock."

"I'll get to that. We also found some rope in the bedroom. Seems the prowler has other plans."

"Fingerprints?"

"None."

"Neighbors see anything?"

"Look Bryce, you were there. If anyone was going to see anything, it'd be you. You got clubbed."

I absently rubbed the side of my head...and the back. "So, you need to arrest the husband."

"It's not Dawson. We hauled him in last night. I know where Dawson went when he gave you the slip."

Now he had my undivided attention. Well, after I had a sip of coffee. "Do tell?"

"AA. He goes to AA meetings at the church by his place. He was out having coffee with his sponsor when all this happened."

"The sponsor might be lying."

"He's not. He's my chief."

I was sitting in my car outside Rutledge's house. The cops drove by every 15 minutes. They were finally taking this serious. Dog car came by every two hours or so and checked the yards on the block. Rutledge had sent her kids out of town, and she was holed up with the good Reverend for safekeeping. I was hoping the prowler wouldn't have figured that out yet.

Conventional thinking would lead you to believe the prowler would be spooked. But he wasn't conventional. And I really didn't know what he wanted. I was sure it was the husband. But he alibied out for each event. If it was the husband, he'd want her dead. But it wasn't him. So then who? What was the motive?

Scaring Rutledge might make sense. But not the kids. But if you assume that the stalking of the kids was their father watching their sports, and if you take that out of the equation, you're left with the house prowlings. On the last one the prowler was in Rutledge's bedroom. She was the target. He had rope. If he was going to kill her, he wouldn't really need the rope. Just kill her. So he wanted her alive. Torture? Rape? If you kept someone alive, you had to be able to control them. Rope would do that. But you also had to be able to subdue them first. And that was not easy. Not even if it was a woman. Not even if you'd had training. Strength wasn't everything, but it sure made up for a lot of other factors. It sure made things easier if you had ease of access to the premises, or if you knew the victims routine... the layout of the house... but Dawson had a pretty square alibi. So who?

It hit me like a ton of bricks. The handshake that didn't match the face, the way he called me "Pedley". How he didn't want me going upstairs, like it was his house to protect...

The old Studebaker was red lining as I flew out of the neighbourhood. How could I be so stupid?

There was a light upstairs at the reverends. I raced up the walkway. I could hear loud music blaring from inside. I tried the door. Locked. Size ten and a half key on the door lock did the trick. I was inside. I pulled the .38. My senses were on high alert. I was not taking another blow to the head. I found the staircase and moved quickly. The music was on full volume. AC/DC or Deep Purple or Queen. I really should know. It also didn't matter.

At the top of the stairs I saw the light from the front bedroom. I slipped down the hall and peeked around the open door.

Kathy Rutledge was lying naked on the bed. Her arms and legs were tied to the corners of the bed by rope. There was a gag in her mouth. She saw me, her eyes wide. She glanced to her right. Gun leading, I moved through the door. On the floor at the end of the bed lay the Reverend. Blood pooled around his head. I've seen lots of wounds and I've seen lots of dead guys and he was one of them.

My mind raced. Rutledge tied up. Reverend dead. Rutledge's eyes went wide again. She was making noises despite her gag. I followed her gaze. The reverends wife, Hawknose, was in the doorway. She was holding a military issue 9mm semi-automatic. And it was pointed at me. My .38 was at my side. I'd let my guard down when I saw the Reverend.

"Why?"

Hawknose stepped into the room. Eyes sighting down the barrel. "It was enough. I had to end it. Every place we go, it's the same. It's an illness you know. He can't help himself. But it was too much. Bringing her here so she'd be safe. He was going to take her in our house—my house. That was too much."

I had to keep her talking. The longer she talked, the longer I'd be alive. "There were others?"

"Many."

"How many?"

"I don't know how many before we married. There were some when he was in the army."

"Why didn't you do something about it? Stop it?"

"He was my husband. He loved me. It was a disease. It wasn't his fault."

It was time to bluff. "The cops are on their way. I called them when I realized the Reverend was the stalker."

"You didn't call them. You're a cowboy. You wanted to handle this on your own. Don't worry. It will be over quick."

They say in your final moments your life flashes before your eyes. Victories, defeats. Parents, grandparents, lost friends, childhood moments. The problem is that once you are dead, you can't confirm that. I have had too few victories and many regrets. I thought of Missy. That's all. She loved me for me. And that was something that just hadn't happened in my life.

I watched the hammer draw back.

Hawknose raised the gun, placed it under her chin and fired.

I cut the ropes on Rutledge and got her a sheet to cover up.

I called Tommy. A little too late, I guess. I heard the sirens long before they arrived. Guns drawn they stormed the house. Tommy got things calmed down.

I gave my story to Tommy. I gave it again to the detectives. They wanted to take me down to the station. Tommy stopped that.

I drove home. It was one of those drives where you remember leaving, and remember arriving, but you don't remember the drive.

I still hated domestic cases. No good ever came from them.

I went to the bathroom and cleaned up. The light from the hallway cast enough light into my bedroom that I could see the outline of a person in my bed. Not Goldilocks, but better— Missy.

I sat on the edge of the bed and ran my fingers through her long, red hair.

"Papa wants you to come for dinner this Sunday."

SUDDEN DEATH
JAYNE BARNARD

Game Six. The Calgary Flames were poised to win the Western Conference final on home ice. Bernie would not be in the Saddledome to see them, but he did have a recliner chair and a real colour TV, both amenities unheard-of in his village south of Berlin in 1972. During the Soviet-Canada series, a movie screen had hung from the balcony of the *Rathaus* so villagers could watch and cheer together for Mother Russia and the triumph of the Soviet system. Bernie was 11 years old when the Canadians won, and the seed of his emigration was planted by Paul Henderson's winning goal.

The Flames won the Stanley Cup the year the Wall came down, the year Bernie met his West German cousins for the first time. The year his emigration dream brushed up to reality. He took that win as a sign to move to Calgary. Fifteen years later, here he was, an expatriate *Ost* German, a Canadian citizen, getting ready to watch a Stanley Cup playoff game in his own, owned little house in Calgary. With his recliner and his little colour TV and a case of real beer from home.

He was reaching for his first beer when his nephew bounded in, bashing the back porch door against the open fridge. The ricochet caught Bernie's head on the freezer compartment. *"Schiessekopf,"* he grumbled. Holding the cold bottle against his reddening ear, he closed the fridge, turned, and skidded in the trail of melting slush from Matt's work boots. Matt saved the beer from certain destruction.

Staring up from the floor, pained in multiple body parts, Bernie snarled, "What you think you do?"

Sappy brown eyes met his. "Oh, sorry, *Onkel*. I had a great idea, is all. Need a hand up?"

"Nein." Bernie rolled over carefully, made it to his feet, and snatched the bottle back. No way was he letting the boy have his good Deutsch beer. He got safely into his recliner, grabbed the remote and turned up the pre-game commentary.

Matt kept talking anyway. Bernie swallowed the urge to shush him. If the boy had grown up a true *Ostie*, he would not talk from across the room. *Osties* kept their voices down, stood close, so a *Stasi* informer couldn't hear from the next apartment. Or the next room. But Matt was young. He had not learned all that before the Wall fell. Or, if he had, he soon forgot the safe ways in the new, unified Germany. He didn't need them in Canada either. He was more Canadian than Bernie already, just two years here. He would talk to strangers on the bus. He would yak from across the room until he was answered. In gut English learned in school, not like Bernie's construction-crew patois. But he didn't know Russian. That was from the old days.

When the smelly aftershave commercial was drowned out by the burble from the couch, Bernie gave up trying to ignore his nephew. "All right, *was ist?*"

"Enough to send to Mutti for plane ticket. We load up pallets onto your truck. "

"What do you talk about?"

"It was on the radio. Building developments left unguarded, hundreds of workers in and out. Nobody could recognize all those faces. Thirty pallets of landscaping bricks are sitting in the courtyard where I was working today. A few of those, we could sell for a buck a brick at garage sales."

Bernie glowered. "With security guards around? Cameras? Dogs? *Dumkopf.*" He turned back to the TV, where Don Cherry was yammering on like usual. Where did that guy get his jackets? Even an Italian flash-boy wouldn't wear such loud clothes.

Matt went on trying to convince him, right through the news update about the missing building inspector. Bernie had heard that a dozen times today. Last seen at a condo development yesterday, wearing a brown suit and matching loafers. What idiot wore loafers on a construction site?

"No cameras," said Matt earnestly. "The guards won't leave the game in this weather. It's a blizzard outside. It'll hide our tracks."

"Right." Bernie nodded sourly. "I leave Game Six in blizzard to steal bricks. You're some bricks missing, Matt."

In the back booth of a nearby bar, another nephew whined to his uncle. "It's a bleedin' blizzard out there.

Why tonight, anyway?"

Marco thumped down his mug and signaled the waitress. "Because it's a blizzard, Tony. No witnesses. Security will be inside watching the game."

"That's where we should stay, too," Tony pointed out, in the reasonable tones that made Marco's knuckles itch.

He controlled his urge to smack the boy and tugged at the sleeve of his new black-and white checked suit jacket instead. "Nobody will be around tonight. But the cops will sure as shit search that site for Mr. Loafers tomorrow. We gotta get it out of there. Leave after first period, do the job during second and be back to catch third."

"I wonder if they'll go into overtime," said Tony, his eyes on a TV in the corner, where Don Cherry gave way temporarily to a commercial involving a beer-stealing bear.

In the Major Crimes squad room, Kelvin Woo made a disgusted lip at his sergeant. "I can't believe you drink that crap. It's been there since this morning."

Vince Mancuso lowered his tar-filled mug onto a stack of files. "It's all coffee. You really figure this will go down tonight?"

Kelvin nodded. "Lousy weather. Big game. Security guards holed up in front of TV sets. If I can think of it, they can."

Vince looked across the deserted squad room. "Yeah, I guess," he muttered. "Damn spring snowstorm, though. That site will be a swamp. You got boots?"

"Don't need 'em," said Kelvin confidently. "We can go through the buildings. They're floored all the way, but the inside walls are only studs except for one suite where the guards hang out. We can set up in there with them. They have a TV set."

A television? Great. They'd all be watching the hockey game instead of the property. Vince levered himself out of his chair. "Let's get to the stakeout. And this time, don't offer to sign for Weims's overtime."

"Right." Kelvin slid files from the stack. "We can take these along."

Vince's cup teetered. "Watch out! Those are the robbery statements."

Kelvin shook muddy drops off the top file. "What's new since the morning?"

"Loss estimates. Jewelry was half a mill. Men's wear place wants thirty grand."

"For what was in their window?"

"They claim the shattered glass ruined all the nearby clothes."

Kelvin shrugged. "Insurance fraud's not our department. But you should see if they'll give you a new jacket. That plaid thing makes my eyes water."

The condo development's chipboard walls were lost in a welter of wet snow that deadened all sound. Bernie pushed his black wool hat up over his ears. Where was Matt with the forklift? He turned around in a slow, full 360, listening hard, staring through the whiteness, and at last heard the grumble of the little machine. After a minute he could see it, lurching over the rutted mud. He watched with reluctant approval as the boy drove up to the stacks, slid the lift's tines beneath the first pallet, backed up and swung the load towards the truck. The boy was a menace on his feet, but he knew how to run a machine.

While Matt went for the next pallet, Bernie scoped the area again, straining to see through fat white flakes. Plastic-covered window holes stared out blankly over the littered courtyard. Wind whirled, bringing snatches of the hockey game from the security room. The crowd was roaring. Bernie itched to go over and eavesdrop on the end of first period, but he did another 360 scan instead. With that mall robbery last night, right in the next block, who knew when there might be police poking around? He watched Matt wheel up to the flatbed again. Could he risk turning on the truck radio?

In the car, after first period ended, Tony was still grumbling. "Walking out before the buzzer. Flames down by two. People remember who walks out on the home team."

"Shut up and drive slower," Marco snapped back. "We smash on these roads and we're screwed."

"Not yet." Tony pumped the brakes as an intersection approached. "Afterwards, that's when we'll be careful."

Marco grabbed the dash as the Monte Carlo skated past a red light. When he finished swearing, he said, "We can't claim we were in the bar watching the game if there's an accident report with your driver's license on it."

"Oh. Yeah." Tony slowed. "So we just load it into the trunk, drop it at the garage, and get back to the game?"

"Right."

"What about fibers and all that crap?"

"It's wrapped in plastic, and it'll be frozen solid by now. Slow down, wise guy." Marco braced himself as the car skidded around a corner. "Truck!"

Tony swung the wheel. The Monte bounced off the curb and slid, just missing a flatbed truck coming out of the condo complex. "I thought all them workers woulda gone home by now."

Marco's knuckles itched. "Shut up and drive. And don't get stuck in the mud."

"It'll be frozen solid," Tony assured him.

"You hear something outside?" Vince looked towards the window.

Kelvin's eyes stayed on the guards' portable television, where figures zoomed and passed and crashed into the boards. "Too early. Not even dark. Hoo-ee! Got a breakaway! Go, baby, go. Damn!"

The sentiment was echoed by the handful of uniformed cops who had trickled in during first period. Weims, the day shift detective, was still hanging around, waiting for someone to offer to sign for his overtime. "Down by two," he grumbled as the first-period buzzer went. "What the hell's up with the Kipper? He's a sieve tonight." He gazed around with fading hope. "I guess I oughta get home before second starts. They could still pull it out."

"Hang on a sec," said Vince. "I wanna hear how you clued in."

Weims nodded. "Basic house-to-house. An old lady looked out her window at dawn and saw two guys come in here. She thought one was drunk, since the other was dragging him along. It was the only odd thing that turned up all day. So I nosed around, found the hidey-hole, and set up the stakeout."

Kelvin spared some attention for the window. "I think the snow is letting up."

Weims got up to check. "Yeah, it is. Hey,

somebody's down there!"

Bernie backed the flat-deck expertly into his shed and climbed out. "Get this off my truck tonight," he warned as he left.

"Now?" Matt whined. "What about the game?"

"We're losing. *Macht schnell.* I need this truck tomorrow." He trudged through the gathering snow to the house. Second period would start any minute. No way could he miss that. The Flames needed everybody's focus. They always played like crap the first game after a big win, but they'd be back on their skates by now. They had to be.

He and his beer were ready when the puck dropped, but the Flames weren't. They were down by two more at the ten-minute mark. Coach Sutter called a time-out just as Matt came in, dripping slush onto the carpet.

"Uh, Bernie?"

"Shh."

"Bernie?" The voice was louder, like when a little kid says he has to pee *now*.

Bernie tore his eyes from the screen. *"Gott. Was ist?"*

"You gotta come to the shed."

"I'll come when the buzzer goes."

Matt stood his ground. "You gotta come *now*."

"Did you break something?" Bernie lowered his feet and heaved himself out of the chair. "If you drop a brick on my tools, I'll—!"

But Matt was gone. Bernie glared after him and glanced back at the TV. Whatever it was could wait ten little minutes. The Flames would come out strong now. Only one Russian this team had, but there were a Czech and a Pole. Good *Ostie* stock. They could fight back. He was sinking into his chair again when Matt yelled from the back door.

"All right. I come," he muttered, swearing his way into his boots and out the door. The snow was thinning. He shoved through the shed door and tripped over a brick. "What is important?"

Matt pointed to the flatbed, where one corner of one pallet had been partly unloaded. "See for yourself."

The kid's face was dead white and sweating, more scared than Bernie had ever seen it. He scrambled up on the truck and peered. The pallet was hollow, stuffed with plastic sheeting. "*Sheisse*! Someone beat us to it! They took the bricks from inside."

"Look closer," said Matt, his voice wavering.

Bernie looked. The plastic was smeared. He pushed it flat. The object beneath came into focus: a man's brown leather loafer. A dress sock disappeared under the cuff of a brown pant leg. They were all firm under his hand. Solid, and very cold.

"*Schiesse*!" said Bernie again, backing away. He jumped down to the concrete floor. "It's him."

"Him who?"

"Don't you hear the radio?" Bernie snarled. "That building inspector? He's wearing a brown suit and loafers."

"*Ach, Gott. Die Poltzei*, they'll come after us, *nicht war*?"

Bernie cuffed him on the head. "Shut mouth." He paced the floor, breathing fast. A dead body on his truck, in his shed, with six pallets of stolen bricks. He could be deported for that. For any of that. Back to the depressed economy and depressed relatives in that little village south of Berlin. Why had he listened to Matt?

Why hadn't he stayed home in his recliner? Was the Flames' poor showing an omen? If only this whole evening hadn't happened.

Wait a minute ... "It happened *nicht*," he told Matt.

"Huh?"

"We go drop bricks back where they were. No theft. No body."

Matt stared. "But—"

"It," said Bernie, slowly and firmly. "Happened. Not."

"It couldn't happen." Tony tore away bricks. "A whole pallet can't disappear."

"Keep looking," Marco growled, shivering in his suit jacket.

"Some loser ripped off our pallet. We gotta get it back."

"Shut up." Marco cuffed him upside the head. "You want guards out here?" He paced, breathing fast. "That truck. The one you almost hit. What was on the back of it?"

"Jeez, I don't know."

"Bricks, that's what. Pallets of bricks." Marco raised his hand, lowered it sadly. Smacking the kid again wouldn't make him smarter. "No sign on the door?"

Tony shook his head mutely, keeping an eye on Marco's arm.

"Not even a magnetic job like the cheap crooks use to look legit?"

Tony shook his head again.

Marco paced some more. "There's gotta be a way to trace them. Go to the guards and say you were supposed to meet your cousin here with his flatbed truck."

"I ain't going near no guards, Marco. I don't want nobody seeing my face."

"I got a clean shot of his face," said Kelvin as the auto-winder spun. "It's Tony Watson all right. With his uncle, Marco the Mafia-wannabe. I wonder if they tried to reach their janitor buddy."

Vince grunted, eyes glued to his field glasses. "Even a London wop's not that dumb. They'd have agreed to drop off his pay once the heat dies down."

"You can't call him a wop. It's not PC."

"London wop. His momma's Italian from England, married a Canadian soldier. Like I'm a Montreal wop. YOU can't call him a wop. Nice jacket, though. Classy."

Kelvin curled a lip. "Whatever. Hell, that janitor's going down for it anyway. His bad luck that computer store across the way left its web-cam on and recorded the whole thing. Only question is whether he'll take the Watsons along." He peered out. "They still can't find it."

Weims shook his head. "How can they miss it? I saw it myself, not half an hour before you guys showed up. Should be in the third one from the left, closest row to us."

He lifted his glasses and scanned the area. "It's gone!"

Vince turned. "What do you mean, gone?"

"There were five rows, six pallets in each," Weims growled. "It's on the diagram. X marks the spot. Only now there's not five rows. Just four. Someone ripped off a whole ton of bricks during first period."

As the various cops jostled each other in the doorway, the buzzer went off, signaling the end of second. The Flames were back on their game, with two

235

goals since the time-out. The security guards stayed put, handing out snacks of cold cabbage rolls and kielbasa to each other, celebrating.

Bernie swung the truck around a corner, spraying slush. Now that second period was over, he would talk. "We put it back, nice and tidy. Then we drive away. Like we were never here."

"But we can't just leave him. We gotta call the cops."

"You want get mixed up with *Polizei*, get out my house first."

"*Gott, Onkel*," Matt whined. "I'm just saying he'll stink once he thaws out."

"Not *mein* problem."

Matt was still grumbling when he got out by the forklift. Bernie drove slowly on beneath the hundreds of leering windows, cursing the absence of the fat, wet snowflakes from earlier. He backed the truck beside the brick stacks, with both eyes on his side mirror. Then he saw the man in the loudly checkered suit, raising a hand to stop him.

Marco watched the flat-bed approach. When the driver had turned and was backing up, he stepped out from behind a pallet and held up his hand. The driver's eyes caught his in the side mirror. For a half second, Marco thought he looked scared. But the expression vanished, which was good because Marco was going to make nice until he had to do otherwise. He folded his arms and watched as the driver climbed down from his truck. He was taller than Marco by a head, and wider by a couple of barn doors. Solid, with a big square face. Built like a German. Better to not make him mad.

When the fellow came over, Marco smiled. "I'm

surprised anyone's working this late. You got business here?"

The driver's eyes narrowed. "Not your business, but *ja*, we do." He waved at an approaching forklift. "We unload these before we go watch the hockey."

Marco gave him back the look. German, for sure. Marco had not been born when Germany bombed the lettuce out of his grandfather's East London grocery store, but he knew one of them couldn't be trusted. "It is my business. Company's worried about theft. And these look like the same pallets that were here before."

The driver's square face didn't twitch. "We were told to take to the next site. We wait, but nobody come to say where to unload." He folded his arms, mirroring Marco's stance, letting Marco see how thick the muscles were beneath his plain blue workman's coat. "All this stealing, we are not leaving them there."

Marco nodded. He was almost sure the German was lying through his cold, thin lips, but then so was Marco. He watched the German trudge over to meet the forklift. Sausage fingers thumped the forklift operator's skinny chest. The shrimp got started on unloading the truck.

The truck driver came back. "Done ten minutes," he said gruffly. "So, you just work here or go all over?"

Marco thought. If he said here only, the cruddy Germans could go rip off some other construction site. "Here all night," he said. "Lousy weather, huh?"

The driver shrugged. "Wish I watching the hockey."

"Me, too." Marco squeezed his arms, wishing he could tuck his hands back into his armpits. But that could not be done with this huge burgher standing there in the freezing wind like it was a summer breeze. It wasn't dignified. "Heard the score?"

"4-2 after second."

That was all the chat. They stood and watched the unloading. When the forklift bounced away, the driver climbed into his truck and followed.

Tony came out from behind the stacks. "You're lettin' him get away?"

Marco's hand wasn't too cold to twitch. "When they're gone, you find that pallet," he growled. "We gotta load up and get out of here."

Behind a backhoe, Vince growled into his radio. "Stop that truck as soon as it's out of sight, but don't bring them back here until I say."

A faint "roger" came back. A nearby camera whirred as it wound, telling him Kelvin was still recording the Watson family outing. Tony and Marco were peeling back bricks. Vince winced as one crashed close to Marco's foot, nodded approval as a hand lashed out and cuffed Tony. Ah, they had it! They dragged out the awkward plastic bundle and stumbled with it towards their car. Then they had to drop it so Tony could open the trunk. Marco's one-handed gesture said a few dozen nasty words.

When they picked the plastic up, it was muddy. The slush promptly transferred itself to Marco's cheap checkered suit. His face was thunderous. Vince grinned. Too bad he didn't have a video camera. This would crack up the boys in the squad room. Still, any photos were better than none.

With more shoving and curses from the Watson family, the bundle slid into the trunk. Marco was wiping his fingers on a handkerchief. Tony had both hands on the car, ready to drop the lid. Vince said the magic word into his radio and stepped into view.

"Evening, fellas," he called, grinning at their stunned

faces. "You working overtime?"

Marco looked around fast, saw cops coming out of various hiding places, and put up his hands.

Vince nodded approvingly. "Watson, right? Marco and Tony. Kind uncle teaches bright nephew the family business."

Marco glared. "Sergeant Mancuso."

Tony stared. "Mancuso? The ones that own Montreal gambling?"

Marco's hand twitched.

"Uh-uh," Vince cautioned. He grinned at Tony. "Wrong family. But meet my partner, Kelvin Woo. His family holds half the book of downtown Calgary." Both detectives laughed as Tony's face paled. He would be looking over his shoulder forever, terrified that the Calgary Police were in league with Asian gambling gangs. Vince lifted his radio as uniforms cuffed and frisked the Watsons. "Okay, bring 'em in. Let's see what else we've got."

"Time to go, fellas," said the cop.

In the back seat of the squad car, Bernie glowered. Neither he nor Matt had said a word since the cop appeared, and Bernie wanted it to stay that way. *Osties* don't talk in front of the *Politzei* unless they can offer a bribe or a favour, and he had no favours useful in Canada. He glared at Matt, thinking hard about beating him to a bloody pulp if he spoke up. Like the *Stasi* would have done.

Matt seemed to get the message. He turned paler and gulped in his throat. Maybe he was scared speechless for once.

The police car rocked over the ruts towards a clump of people around those bad-luck pallets. The loud-suit security man was still there, surrounded by other suits, all watching the squad car. It arrived, and more *Polizen* opened the doors.

Bernie stepped out behind Matt. "What's the idea?" he snarled.

Matt turned. "I thought we weren't gonna—*glurg*."

While a cop helped Matt get his face out of the mud and his feet back under him, Bernie sized up the situation. Loud-suit was standing funny, with his shoulders farther back than any Communist Party Leader. His back was reflected in the tinted windows of a black car. And his hands, with pale metal glinting around the wrists. Handcuffs?

Bernie folded his arms across his chest. "What's the joke?"

One suit flipped a badge from the pocket of a plaid jacket that would have done Don Cherry proud. "Vince Mancuso. Police. I'll ask the questions."

Then he shut up. Just looked Bernie and Matt up and down.

Bernie looked at Mancuso's dark skin & pointed nose, wishing he had a hundred dollar bill on hand. More bad luck, to meet an Italian *Politzist* in Canada with his pockets empty. Still, he could play dumb. If Matt kept quiet about the bricks, they could be out of here in five minutes. They might even catch part of third period.

A young Chinese in a suit broke the standoff. Backing up, he tripped on a brick, skidded in the mud and let loose a curse. "Vince, get on with it. I'm ruining my shoes."

Mancuso's eyes rolled. Bernie's rolled in sympathy. The *Politzist* said over his shoulder, "I told you to wear boots."

About then, Bernie noticed a bunch of pallets had been torn open. There was a big, gaping hole in one stack. No trace of the plastic. His eyes skated back to Mancuso's face. More waiting.

Vince Mancuso spoke. "So, you brought these pallets. Care to tell us why?"

"*Ja.*" Bernie eased his glare a fraction. "We were told, move them to another site. We load up, drive across town in snowstorm, and those *Scheissekopfs* had left already. Nobody to sign for load. So we bring it back." He jerked his chin at Mr. Handcuffs. "He ask us the same thing."

Vince Mancuso glanced that way. "You see him before tonight?"

"Nein. Not many suits around construction site."

Marco let out his breath, but his eyes hung on the big German. Did he know what was in those bricks? The shrimpy sidekick was gawking at that empty stack right now. Better he should keep looking there, since the Monte's trunk still gaped open. Tony should have closed it before he put up his hands. It would have slowed things down, forced a search warrant, opened up opportunities for a technicality dismissal. Marco switched the look to Tony and thought about beating him to a bloody pulp if he so much as twitched a lip. Tony flinched even though Marco's itchy knuckles were out of action. Marco moved his gaze to Sergeant Mancuso, trying to look innocent.

The wind brought a rising tide of sound that hollered "breakaway". Marco and everybody else turned towards the guardroom. The announcer's voice went wild. "And it's a high shot up the middle. Rebound. Is it in? Yes! He scores!"

Tony's whole face begged Marco to let him ask. But the Chinese detective did it first. "Who? Dammit, WHO?" he yelled. "Uh, sorry, Vince. Got carried away."

Looking at the sergeant's face, Marco figured he was hurting to know, too. "Say, Officer," he suggested in his most friendly voice. "Why don't we all go find out? Can't be more than ten minutes left of third."

Vince looked around. Every cop, detective, crook, and even the short construction guy were practically on tiptoes, straining to hear. In a minute they'd be falling sideways in the mud like dominoes.

The truck driver looked at him. He looked back. "You a hockey fan, too?"

"*Ja*. Since 1972."

Vince grinned. "Soviet-Canada series? I was ten years old, glued to the TV."

The driver's square face lightened a tiny bit. "I was eleven."

"Paul Henderson," sighed Marco. When they both looked at him, he added hastily, "I was eight. He was my hero."

Vince laughed. "What the hell? Let's all go."

Tony and Marco started off, joking with the uniforms. The younger construction guy came past the Monte Carlo, looked at the open trunk, and turned white.

Vince waved back a couple of uniforms. "Bring along that evidence. And snap to it. The clock is ticking."

As they edged into the crowded guards' suite, Bernie heard the announcer's voice getting louder. Somebody was on a breakaway. "Score?" he yelled, breaking the silent habit of a lifetime.

"4-3," someone yelled back. Security guards sat on plastic patio chairs. The handcuffed Italian-Canadians were perched on upturned pails. Everyone leaned towards the portable television. A linesman's whistle went and they all leaned back. The last two uniforms slung their slushy plastic bundle onto a pile of carpet rolls. It banged against the chipboard wall with a clunk, just as the puck dropped again.

A clunk? Bernie remembered that sound three minutes later, after the Flames had tied the score and the room stopped rocking to the combined cheers of three detectives, six uniforms, four security guards, two construction workers and a pair of flash goons in handcuffs. While linesmen circled around a scrim and a coach yelled at the ref, Bernie looked into the shadows at the man-sized bundle of plastic.

It shivered. It crackled. Something roundish fell from one end. It rolled erratically across the floor. It stopped at Bernie's feet, staring upward, with eyes so lifeless they might be painted on.

Painted? By the flickering light of a beer commercial, Bernie stared down at a dummy head.

Vince hung back, keeping an eye on his collection of thugs and wannabes. A real United Nations they were, and as honest: two shifty German construction workers and Weims the overtime wonder-boy, a couple of Cockney Italian hoods, a detective whose uncles ran numbers in Chinatown, and four security guards who had let a body be stashed right under their massive Ukrainian honkers.

He turned his attention to the plastic bundle in the corner. It wasn't the missing building inspector, but there should be a pile of stolen diamond jewelry hidden inside that menswear mannequin. Unless the Germans had looted it before they returned it. Then he forgot the Germans and flat-out gaped, as the plastic shook and the dummy's head slid out to roll merrily across the floor, contaminating any evidence that might have been left on its smooth plastic surface.

Evidence issues didn't matter for long, though, as Tony Watson dodged his uncle's elbow and claimed the booty in unmistakable terms. "He's stealing our jewelry."

"Thanks a bunch, Tony," said Vince, and grinned. He whipped out his latex gloves and snapped them on like a TV surgeon. The head whispered when he lifted it, like dried pasta shifting in a box. He unscrewed the neck. A jumble of jewelry choked the hole. "Hey, Kelvin," he called. "Come take a picture. A souvenir for Marco and Tony for the next three-to-five years."

Behind him, the plastic-wrapped mannequin slid off the carpet rolls and crashed to the floor. Something back there was waving and groaning as it crawled up into view. The thing wore a brown suit, badly wrinkled, and one brown loafer. It belched and snorted and eventually asked, "Wha time zit?"

Vince pounced. "Who the hell are you?"

A security guard ambled over. "Him? Oh, the inspector. He was here last night for a poker game. What with one thing and another, he forgot to go home. We couldn't wake him up, so we dropped a tarp over him. Forgot he was there."

"You didn't tell anyone after he was on the news all day as a missing person?"

The guard scratched his balding head. "I work nights, sleep days. Missed news."

While the police grilled the idiot inspector, Bernie edged over to Matt. "*Wir gehen,*" he muttered. "We get out, right now."

"No way. They'd just pick us up later."

"You show ID card? Not me. We leave, they don't find us. I think they don't look hard. *Verstehen?*"

"But, overtime! Sudden death! We could miss the winning goal."

"*Dumkopf.*" Bernie's hand twitched, but he didn't dare smack the boy on the ear. It would attract attention. Instead he shoved Matt out into the dark, away from the TV and the guards and the *Politzei.*

They managed to get themselves outside without Matt tripping over anything or falling through a stairway hole. In the dark courtyard, the boy stopped. "We could come back tomorrow night, load up a few pallets."

Bernie's knuckles itched, all the way home and straight through 42 minutes of intense, amazing overtime. The Flames finally lost. It was that kind of night in Calgary. Still, they had one more shot at winning. Game Seven was coming in Vancouver. The Western Conference Final. He would need more beer.

THE MYSTERY OF THE MISSING HEIR

KEVIN P. THORNTON

May 2015, Fort McMurray, Alberta.

"Constable."

"Please, call me Ben."

"But not Benny right? I read in the press that there was much you didn't like about that TV series, including the way the Americans called you that, or by your last name."

"That show wasn't about me. There were similarities, true but I have never been to Chicago."

"How much did you get paid for the show?"

"Nothing." He paused. "Before you make something of that, I should tell you that I never asked them and they never offered."

"I see. Were there any other inaccuracies you wish to correct, you know, in that show about a famous Mountie from the north that was not about you? Now's your chance."

"I never had a wolf was called Diefenbaker. I wish to stress that. I have immense respect for all who hold public office in service to Canada. I would never be so discourteous."

"Yet you had a wolf?"

"Yes."

"While you were a Mountie, working in Chicago."

"Actually I was based in Buffalo."

"And your name is also Benton"?

"You have already established that."

I looked at him. I was trying for incredulous, but he was so damned Dudley Do-Right all I could do was shake my head. He was about the most famous Mountie in their history and had one of the highest arrest records ever in his thirty year career, yet still he seemed so innocent.

He continued. "I assume they changed it for the cheap laugh I assume. Diefenbaker. Dief for short, which was sensible as you always want an explosive consonant sound for an animal's name. Dief works better than Thief, for example. It attracts the wolf's attention better, especially if it is hard of hearing."

"So that part at least was true. What was its original name?"

"Farty."

"You had a deaf wolf called Farty?"

"I've had several, although I don't think they have all been deaf as much as discourteous. Wolfs are like that. As to the name, you would understand if you ever lived

247

in close proximity to one. Anyway, we're not here to talk about my history, but that of my great-grandfather. Now that I've retired I've had time to read, and his writings are proving fascinating."

"Is that why you asked me to see you? Do you want me to tell the true story about you?"

"No, I want you to help me tell the world about a string of murders he was involved in, back in 1893. Please read this," he said, handing me a folder. "It's a copy of his journal. You'll have to excuse the informal style. It is written as if he wanted to publish it."

"So how do you know that it's not fiction," I said.

"Just read it," said the Mountie. "Once you have, we'll talk."

Extract from a Constable's Journal, 1893, Fort McMurray.

When I wrote to him, back in 1890, it was to seek advice. True, I had been puzzled by the similarities of the wounds, but my corpse was 4000 miles west and some years distant from Whitechapel and its horrors.

The victim, a woman called Loretta no last name, had been found by the side of the trail leading into town. She had been eviscerated, and when the doctor examined her he found that her heart was missing.

She'd been in the community for about a year. Rumour was that she was supposed to go north to meet her husband, but she'd run out of money round about the time word caught up to her that he'd died in the Yukon. With nowhere to turn, she'd hung around the settlement, living off charity, occasional jobs and the goodwill of the single men of the settlement. And then she disappeared one night, and the next day she was dead, and I never came any closer to finding out who'd killed her. Fort McMurray was a transient town, and all I could do was question everyone, write down everything and worry at it through all my waking hours. And not get anywhere.

That was why I wrote, and I heard nothing until the report in the newspaper about his death a year later, and then near two years more before he wrote and asked if he could see me. To say I was surprised was an understatement.

I finally met him in the spring of 1893. The characteristics of my case were similar to what I had read of the fifth victim of the London terror, but I had not seen his name attached to the investigation so I presumed his involvement. As the eminent expert of his era it would have been strange for him not to be consulted. For all I knew when I first put pen to paper he had solved the mystery, they had caught the madman and I was wasting his time and the cost of a first class stamp.

But still he came.

He arrived on the train from Calgary, via the Canadian Pacific railroad from the west coast. Port Moody, although I heard they were calling it Vancouver now. Names change frequently at the crossroads of history.

The train came in to the south side of the river, a place known as Strathcona; on the north side, where the police barracks were, Fort Edmonton was evolving into the town of Edmonton. The Empire was expanding at breakneck speed.

His letter had given me a date and time, but not a

description. All I had to go on was the briefest of ideas I had gleaned from his chronicler's tales. Tall, thin, striking appearance, gray eyes, aquiline nose, prominent jawline and square chin. As I am of similar height I took to scanning over the passengers heads, looking for a like-sized man. There was no one of the right size and age. Of the three passengers topping six feet, one was an imperious looking lady, the second was an elderly man while the last looked no older than twenty-five.

I knew of his penchant for disguises and when the overly tall Madam moved into my path I was nearly taken in, but it was instead the younger of the two men I addressed.

"Mister Holmes," I said, and as he turned to me I knew I was right. The young man, as he seemed, was momentarily amused, then he gathered the other two passengers to him, gave them their due and turned to address me.

"Constable. My apologies for my duplicity. I had a run in with an opium gang in Hong Kong during my travels and I used the train trip as an opportunity to make sure I had lost my pursuers." As he spoke he used a small towel from his pocket to remove the disguise from his face, transforming within seconds into the hero of the Strand magazine articles I had read so assiduously.

"I felt sure," he continued, "you would have thought I was the lady. Pray tell how you knew which one of the three to choose?"

"The hands," I said. "There is much that can be done with stage makeup, but the older man's hands matched him, as did the lady's, marking her only as an oddly tall woman and not a man in disguise. You meanwhile, had the face of a youth but your hands are those of a mature man."

"Splendid," he said. "You have displayed more intuition in a minute than my dear friend Watson has managed in all the years I have known him. Both he and his agent Conan-Doyle are stout-hearted souls, if lacking in the ability to observe. Indeed all their combined intrigues and machinations over the years have never caught my imagination quite like your one letter. I'm sorry I took three years to answer."

"I am indeed honoured Sir, "I said, "especially given the time frame. When I first wrote to you I scarcely expected a reply, let alone a visit. I am also glad to see you are in good health, given the circumstances."

"The circumstances?" said Holmes.

"The circumstances of your death," I said, "over two years ago. It was in the Times; a report and an obituary, from April of 1891. You fell off the Reichenbach Falls, did you not?"

"As you can see, I did not," said the detective. "Constable, you would do well not to believe everything you ever read. Now, to the transport. How long will it take us to get to Fort McMurray?"

Thirteen days later, as we reached the hilltop that looked down on the small settlement at the confluence of the Athabasca and Clearwater rivers, I suspected that my companion's respect for the geography of the Empire had broadened somewhat. The spring of 1893 had been a rainy and muggy one. The three day trip from Strathcona to Athabasca Landing had taken six due to a nigh impassable muddy trail. Furthermore the barge to take us down the Athabasca River was delayed twice by swollen waters forcing us to camp by its side. By the time we had dis-em-barged and taken our horses up the last hill, still three miles from Fort McMurray, we had ridden hard for seven days, floated uncomfortably for the rest and been eaten alive by mosquitoes for all of them.

"I travelled across the Indian sub-continent quicker, "Holmes said, and when I apologized, he smiled. "This great land is not a whole country yet but that I have observed some interesting traits that seem to be predominant. You are a hardy and optimistic people on the cusp of greatness, who nevertheless feel the need to beg forgiveness all the time. The weather conditions are not of your making, yet you apologize as if they were. Interesting."

"Perhaps it is because we are thankful for how much we have," I said. "It is truly a bountiful country."

We spoke no more of it, nor the case I had sent him. Holmes was able to compartmentalize his actions and his life, and during our travails travelling he seemed content to observe and absorb the land and the experience.

The North West Mounted Police did not yet have a station this far north of Fort Edmonton. We tried to send someone up twice a year for a visit, usually me, but that created its own wave of crime. The days after I left normally showed an upturn in petty thievery and drunken arguments, and there had been much agitating for a permanent police presence in Fort McMurray since it had become a way station for one of the routes to the Yukon gold rush.

As a result though, I was known in the town, and as we rode down we met with many of the locals. There were two people in particular that I wanted Holmes to see; two Englishmen who had been in the settlement for some time now. Both men were refined and educated, yet both tried to hide it. The older one was called Bingham, while the other was known only as Bertie. Strangely they did not appear. The settlement was isolated and the visit of anyone generally brought the small community out to hear the news of the outside world.

"They're away hunting again," said Old Tom Cardinal. "They're a strange couple, those two. Always off hunting but they never manage to bring anything back. You get to wondering what they do out there."

I also wondered when Holmes would eventually ask about my case and now that he was in situ he wasted no time. We settled into camp chairs on the evening of our arrival, after we had cleaned the journey away and fed ourselves.

"Was my letter the reason why you faked your death?"

"In part," said Holmes. "There had been a concatenation of actions and reactions that meant I was becoming less useful as I became more well-known. There were also two events of earth-shaking significance that needed dealing with. One was a disruption in India that the Empire needed my brother and I to resolve. I have now taken care of that and the results of my work may delay war in Europe for another decade. Then there is the opium question; I'm still undecided how to finish that but it needs to be left for three months until certain happenings in Washington ensue."

"Ah," I said, though I had no real understanding of the geopolitics of the world.

"Finally there was your letter. The mystery of the Whitechapel Murders, or as the papers referred to them, the Jack the Ripper killings. And that, Constable, is why I am here. I believe that the reason that the Ripper stopped killing in London, the only reason mind, is that he is no longer there. The clarity of your description and the wounds that you described were such that I was convinced that my theory was correct. There has also been a conspiracy stretching right to the highest elements of the Government to hide this whole sordid mess under the misguided idea that the populace cannot tolerate the truth."

"Is that why your name was never linked to the investigation?" I said. "There were several articles in what few newspapers we receive here asking why a man of your calibre was not involved."

"Indeed. I was involved, Constable, though in a most clandestine manner. I had already narrowed it down to one likely suspect. Unfortunately he was related to the Queen, so at the request of my brother Mycroft, a request presented under the ridiculous argument that my investigation needed to be kept quiet for the defence of the realm, I was asked to disengage and Watson was forbidden to write about it.

"And what of that man, your suspect. Can you name him now?"

I can as he died last year. I believed, and so did much of the Government, that the murders were being carried out by Prince Albert Victor, the Queen's Grandson and second in line to the throne."

"My word," I said. "I disagree with why they kept it quiet, but I can understand how they would think it necessary. For such a nobleman to have killed five women in such a brutal way would have been an unprecedented scandal, were it to come out." I told him of Bingham and Bertie. He was most interested in my analysis of their attempts to disguise their education.

He paused to reflect on the information and there

was a restlessness about him.

"I have really wanted to catch this killer, said Holmes. "Such evil should be stopped, and I only wish I could have come sooner. The tally of the dead was actually much higher. "There is reason to suspect that there may have been at least a dozen deaths in London alone. Brutal murders all, clearly the work of someone deranged. The second-to-last one was a headless body in Pinchin Street, which happened three weeks before the Prince and his court coterie left for an extended tour of India. For the entire six months he was away there were no similar murders at all. Even when he came back, there was nothing for nearly nine months."

"What happened then?"

"On the 13th of February 1891, Frances Coles was murdered," said Holmes. "Less than three months later I was able to engineer my own disappearance."

"But the dates don't work," I said. "When Loretta, my victim, was killed, Prince Albert was in India."

"And he had alibis for at least three of the nights that women were killed in Whitechapel," said Holmes. "Which means that either he didn't do it, and I am wrong, or else the alibis were falsified. Having seen the lengths to which her Majesty's Government has gone to hide this entire affair, I think it is safe to assume that latter is at least feasible."

"You think they would go so far."

"I think anything is possible. My brother Mycroft is in many ways the chief policy maker of the Government, some say he is the Government. He has been instrumental in keeping me away from this investigation by finding work for me at the other end of the world. Crucial work, and dangerous, but work that could have been done by at least two of his agents."

"So he still wants you to stay away from the Ripper murders," I said.

"Indeed. Maybe Prince Albert's whole trip to India was a ruse. There is much still to know, and I believe this is where to look."

"To what end." I said. "You yourself said your suspect is dead. And why here?

"Fort McMurray is isolated, far away from the London newspapers and suffers from a lack of women. Maybe this was supposed to be a place to hide a royal problem."

"Until he conveniently died. Do you think they had him killed?"

"Quite the opposite," said Holmes. "The Whitechapel murders, the Jack the Ripper scandal, all were hidden because they wanted to keep him alive. Who would wish to do that, and have the power to do so?

"His Grandmother," I said.

"Precisely, said Holmes. Her Majesty is notoriously loyal to family. She has intervened in Europe several times for cousins and nieces. Think what she would do for her grandson."

"That would be evil," I said, "to allow a killer to keep on killing? Bloodlines covering lines of blood."

"Indeed," said Holmes. "Do you know how royalty is buried?"

"No," I said. "I do not."

"In a closed casket," said Holmes. "Which means I haven't seen a body yet."

The next day I was about my duties. Holmes wandered around the small community. Far from keeping a low profile he asked questions wherever he went, advertising his presence as a detective from

London.

There were about two hundred people in Fort McMurray, split evenly between settlers, and the transients – who were either going north to make their fortune, or south to recover from their losses. By the end of three days Holmes had spoken to most of them, and if he hadn't they certainly knew who he was.

"There is no evidence, three years later," Holmes said to me, "so I must stir the pot and see what bubbles to the surface."

That evening Bingham and Bertie came back into town. They had the equipment of people who had been out hunting, yet they brought back no skins or meat. This had happened before. They were, for this part of the world, a singularly inept couple of men.

Their home was about half a mile across the plains from where we camped. It was a spread out community nestled into the V formed by the two rivers, with rudimentary town planning in a crisscross pattern. . They had a well-built cabin that was also well-supplied, and thus a popular watering hole among the men.

It wasn't but an hour later we heard loud voices from their direction, the sound of angry argument exacerbated by drink. Holmes seemed quietly satisfied. "I don't know what I have stirred up, but I think something will happen tonight."

"The loudest voice sounds like Bingham," I said. "Do you suspect one of them to be the dead Prince?"

"I do not suspect anything or anyone," said Holmes. "I deduce and conclude."

"I see," I said, sympathizing with Watson. Holmes could be pedantic.

"If they do not come by tonight," said Holmes, "I must meet them tomorrow."

"I suspect you will not have to wait," I said. "The noise of their rowdy crowd draws nearer." I was still troubled by the possibility that I could have done more. "Is it even possible Holmes, that one of these two men is the Queen's grandson and a deranged murderer to boot? If so, why was there only one death here in Fort McMurray?

"He has specific tastes; women from the rougher edge of life. There are not many of them here. And he has only had the opportunity once."

"Why do you say that?"

"Because he has been stopped from killing. He has a minder now."

Almost as if it were timed, Bingham burst out of the twilight and headed towards Holmes, screaming incomprehensibly. In his right hand he brandished a bayonet with a blade at least eighteen inches long. I scrabbled for my revolver in its holster, but the surprise of the attack and the attacker meant I was too late. Holmes meanwhile had sprung up, his arms in front of him as a poor defence against the sharpened steel. I heard shouts from outside the circle of light, a scream as one of those following him realised what he was about to do, and a shot, so loud it silenced the air that rushed in to the circle of light. Bingham fell to the ground as if poleaxed, a large crimson hole spouting blood in the middle of his back.

"I had to," said Bertie, with a large smoking revolver in his hand. "It had gone too far."

"You are right in all details except one," said Bertie. They had been talking quietly, he and Holmes, while I went about my work. Before long I was able to draw up a chair of my own.

I had eventually cleared the small crowd away, sending them back to their homes. Bingham's body had also been taken away and stored. Now Bertie sat by the fire, a mug of Brandy in his hand, speaking to Holmes. As far as I and therefore the law was concerned, he had acted in good conscience. He would answer to no crime.

"I am not the killer. Bingham's real name is John Bingham, the Earl of Lucknow. He has been my equerry for the last five years, my personal assistant and my friend. And I have let him down badly. I should have sought help for him right at the start."

"That was back in 1888," said Holmes. "The first victim. Annie Millwood."

"Yes," said Bertie, and the anguish could be heard in his voice. "Dear God I wished I had stopped him. We were out at a club that night. Bingham disappeared for almost an hour. Later, much later, he came back to my rooms and he was covered in blood. I thought him injured. He would not say what happened and it was only because I was looking for it that I saw the report of the attack the next day, not five blocks from where we had been. But she survived, and I didn't know for definite." But his eyes betrayed his guilt

"And you didn't tell anyone," said Holmes." You kept covering for him, even as he progressed to the vilest murders I have ever investigated. You allowed everyone – including your Father and Mother, the Queen, the Prime Minister – to think that you were Jack the Ripper. Why?"

"Because it was the only way I could protect Bingham. They would have hanged him, but not me. I was trying to help him. That was why we went to India. He couldn't get treatment in England, someone would have told."

"What happened in India," I said.

"He didn't want to be cured. He escaped and came to Canada. I think he thought he could hide here. It's such a big country."

"How did you find him?" I asked.

At least he had the grace to look ashamed. "Your police report."

"Of course," said Holmes. "Who would dare refuse to help you? You had only to ask and a copy would be given to you immediately. Who would deny the Queen's grandson? Meanwhile, back in London, how did you persuade them to fake your death?"

"I didn't," he said. "That must have been their idea when I wrote and told them I wasn't coming back. They promised me a living stipend if I stayed away."

"That how you survived," I said. "But what of your hunting trips? This last one was like all the others. You never bagged anything."

Bertie--Prince Albert--paused as if trying to frame his words. "Whatever it was that drove Bingham to do what he did, there was a pressure that built up inside him. Whenever I saw it, I took him far into the bush and we shot a deer and hung it from a tree. Then he would tear it to pieces with his bare hands."

"I see," I said.

"I buried the carcasses afterwards. I couldn't bring them back." He sobbed a little. "It was horrendous to watch. The madness, the horrifying insanity of someone you loved, reduced to anomalistic fervour. I dreaded every time we went out and waited always for him to turn on me. What caused that in him? If only you knew him earlier in life. How gay and full of joy he once was."

"I suspect the nature of men's minds will be the last mystery of science to be solved," said Holmes.

May 2015, Fort McMurray, Alberta.

I finished reading it and looked up at Benton.

"Where's the rest of it?"

"The rest of what," he said.

"It, the story, the proof. Where's the rest of it? What happened next?"

"Sherlock Holmes returned to London. My great-grandfather, Robert, stayed in Alberta, eventually marrying my great-grandmother. He was based in Fort McMurray. They had my grandfather, also named Benton, who married a local woman, an only child. They had numerous children, the oldest being my Father, another Robert, who had only me. The last of the clan."

"And Bertie, the phantom prince. Did he conveniently die?"

"Eventually," said the former Mountie. "He stayed in Fort McMurray and married. They only had one child, but that daughter and her husband had numerous children."

"I thought Bertie was gay," I said. "That was why he covered for his *equeery*."

"Equerry," said Benton, "and I think you'll find, given the evidence, that Prince Albert Victor, Duke of Clarence, had enough love in him for everyone."

I looked at him strangely. There was something in his phrasing that indicated more. "Wait a minute," I said. "Are you saying what I think you're saying? That the real next-in-line descendant of Queen Victoria is Canadian and lives in the bush somewhere near Fort McMurray."

"Not quite," he said.

"So what did I miss?" I said. "I don't get it." Then I
did.

"I don't live in the bush," he said.

LINER NOTES

Many thanks and salutations should get passed around on this project, from great organizations like the *Crime Writers of Canada*, *Owl's Nest Books* in Calgary, and the *When Words Collide* festival to places like *Dickens Pub* and *Buffalo Bob's Canadian Pub*, where a number of the miscreants and troublemakers in this book made their acquaintances, sometimes at the local *#NoirBarYYC* events.

Now, let me tell you a little bit about some of these killer-dillers. I tried to run the required background checks on all of them, but most seem to be living under assumed names, hiding in government programs, or otherwise misrepresenting themselves, as criminal fictionologists will do. Still, I want to thank them—each and every one—for all of their hard work, their loyalty, and their dedication to the cause of getting Alberta crime off the streets and onto the pages! I'll thank them by the shameless flattery that follows.

Randy McCharles, author of *Murder on the Mall*, is the wickedly humorous, speculative son-of-a-gun behind numerous works like *Capone's Chicago*, *The Necromancer Candle* and *Much Ado About MacBeth*. He is a multiple-time winner of the Aurora Award for Canadian Spec Fiction, and the man behind the *Rocky Mountain Writers Retreat*, Calgary's *Taste of Local Authors* events, and the much-beloved *When Words Collide* writers and readers conference. He is an uber-mensch of the highest degree, and a damn fine inkslinger. Keep an eye out for his Chandleresque Twain homage *A Connecticut Gumshoe in King Arthur's Court*. Check him out at www.randymccharles.com

Susan Calder is the author of *Deadly Fall*, the first in her Paula Savard mystery series. She's an accomplished short story writer and poet, teacher, and a member of the board of the Crime Writers of Canada. Her story *Freezer Breakdown* was a frosty breath of fresh air in the midst of a hot summer full of dark detective tales and shady criminals. Visit Susan at www.susancalder.com

Devil's Due, a rough-and-tumble number about regrets and comeuppances. Or maybe it's about the wages of sin? Axel Howerton—Hey! That's me!—I won't wail on my own trumpet too damn much. I've got a few stories out there. I've edited a few books, including the one you're holding in your hands. My first novel, *Hot Sinatra*, is generally considered a highly entertaining romp through the hardboiled hills of L.A. It was a finalist for the Arthur Ellis Award. I love old noir flicks and smooth jazz. Come check me out at www.axelhow.com and let's be pals.

Edmonton's own S.G. Wong has a degree in Literature from the University of Alberta, is a finalist for the Arthur Ellis Award for Best First Novel, is a member of the *Crime Writers of Canada*, the *Writers Guild of Alberta*, *Sisters in Crime*, and the *Get Publishing Communications Society*. She chaired the 2015 *Words in 3D* writer's conference and her first novel *Die On Your Feet* was a local bestseller and Arthur Ellis Award finalist. Basically, she's the bomb. *Movable Type* exists in the same world as *Die On Your Feet* and the upcoming sequel, *In For A Pound*. A world full of ghosts, saucy detectives, Chinese mysticism and good ol' fashioned, hardboiled gumption. Check her out at www.sgwong.com

Robert Bose works in software. Which, I'm pretty sure, is what mobbed-up Tony Soprano types say these days instead of "waste management". Robert kicks death square in the jewels with his story *A Dead Reckoning*. He's also recently published in the anthology *nEvermore! Tales of Murder, Mystery and the Macabre* alongside no less a Canadian legend than Margaret Atwood her own damn self. He also has a wife, three kids, and a tiny sledgehammer—which is his blog, that you can check out at www.robertbose.com

I call her "The Professor", and for good reason. Janice MacDonald is the only person I know of who is quite literally a Doctor of Detective Fiction. She wrote her master's thesis on the subject, before embarking on a career that has seen her churning out mystery novels, textbooks, non-fiction titles, theatrical manuscripts, music and stories for both children and adults. Her *Randy Craig* mystery series is on book number seven with *Another Margaret*, and becomes more popular with each passing moment. She is multiple-multiple award-nominated and was the winner of the Canadian Children's Book Centers Our Choice Award for her book *The Ghoul's Night Out*. Janice is the lovely mother of lovely daughters, and her story *The Workman's Friend* is in no way a reflection of her relationship with her own gorgeous husband. www.janicemacdonald.net

Al Onia is a semi-retired geophysicist, which is a thing you can certainly be in Southern Alberta. He is also a fine writer, whose first novel *Javenny* was released in 2014. His short fiction can be found all over the Canadian spec-fic map, including *Ares*, *On Spec* and the *North of Infinity* anthology. Al is a two-time Aurora Award finalist and the man behind *The Coelacanth Samba*. Al can be found online at www.ajonia.com

Sharon Wildwind loves knitting, *Dr. Who*, and medieval games of skill. She also has an abiding fondness for Alberta's colorful history. She has written several plays set in different eras and locales in Alberta, and is currently working on a mystery set in a Northern Alberta nursing station in the seventies. She thought that Barney, the very real mascot of one of Calgary's first Fire Chief's, the eccentric and beloved Cappy Smart, would make an interesting addition to our criminal menagerie. Hot damn, if she wasn't right on the money. Go visit Sharon and check out her Elizabeth Pepperhawk/Avivah Rosen mystery series at www.wildwindauthor.com

Brent Nichols is the author of several series and standalone books that run the gamut of sci-fi and fantasy, including the *War of the Necromancer* series, the *Airship War* series and the *Gears of a Mad God* series. He also has stories in somewhere near ten-thousand and twelve recent anthologies, and stands about eight-foot-four. He is bulletproof, omniscient and his veins course with high octane rocket fuel. He recently took home the coveted Golden Skull for his reading of *Silicone Hearts* at the #NoirBarYYC event, where he was roundly acclaimed as the funniest dude in the room. Go to www.brentnichols.blogspot.ca to keep up with the machine that is Brent Nichols.

Therese Greenwood is a recent transplant from Ontario to the rural northeast region of Alberta. Before coming to AB, Therese was the co-founder of the Wolfe Island *Scene of the Crime Festival* and the co-editor of the *Osprey Summer Mystery Festival*, as well as a charter member of the *Crime Writers of Canada*. She is a two-time finalist for the Arthur Ellis Award, and winner of the Bony Blithe Award *Bony Pete* Best Short Story contest. She was the editor of the Canadian crime collection *Dead in the Water*, and has been widely published and re-published, including in Ellery Queen Mystery Magazine and the Kingston Whig-Standard.

Rick Overwater is a Calgary-based author and musician. A born-and-raised Alberta farm boy, Rick embraced the journalistic arts before turning his talents to fiction. *Butch's Last Lesson* is borne of his own experiences during his expatriate college days at Gonzaga University. He is the writer behind the indie comic *Futility*, and was previously represented in the

Coffin Hop Press anthology *Tall Tales of the Weird West.* Rick can usually be found three-beers-deep at www.overwater.ca

Dwayne E. Clayden is a paramedic, a former Calgary Police officer, and an expert on police and medical procedure, violent crime, and forensics. He is a teacher at the Alexandra Writers Centre and an internationally recognized public speaker. On top of all that, he writes a damn fine detective story. Catch Dwayne and the latest on his upcoming series of Calgary-based police thrillers by following him on twitter at @DwayneClayden

When people talk about crime in Southern Alberta—and people *will* talk about crime in Southern Alberta—one name reigns supreme. That name is Lady Jayne Barnard. In addition to being the long-standing Prairies Region VP of the Crime Writers of Canada, Jayne is the woman behind Mystery Ink, Calgary Crime Writers and most shenanigans going down at any given time in the local crime writing scene. She is the winner of the Saskatchewan Writers Guild Award and the 2011 Bony Pete for Best Short Story. Her mystery manuscript, When the Bow Breaks, was shortlisted for both the Unhanged Arthur in Canada and the Debut Dagger in the UK. Her steampunk adventure novella, *The Evil Eye of Africa* debuts in September 2015. Look her up on Facebook under Jayne Barnard, Author

Finally, the six-time Arthur Ellis Award nominee, Kevin P. Thornton, is a writer for Keyano College, chair of the local arts council funding committee and a director of the heritage society. He has been a soldier, a contractor for the Canadian military in Kabul, a newspaper and magazine columnist, a director of the Crime Writers of Canada and a board member of Northword Literary Magazine and the Fort McMurray public library. Born in Kenya, Kevin has lived or worked in South Africa, Dubai, England, Afghanistan, New Zealand, Ontario and now Northern Alberta. Some of his stories can be found in the collections *World Enough and Crime*, *How the West Was Weird Vol. 2*, and *How the West Was Weird Vol. 3*. His story *The Mystery of the Missing Heir* is the best Sherlock/Mountie mashup ever imagined. Kevin can be found online at

www.theoldfortamusingfromtheoilsands.blogspot.ca

Thanks for strolling through the shadows and traipsing through the secret hollows of our dark and delirious prairie home. We certainly hope you enjoyed the ride. If you did, come on back and see us sometime. The best thing about a book is that it'll always be waiting for you to stop by again, share a drink and an old story. Maybe help you out with an idea or two, or show you where to dig a hole deep enough to hide those skeletons, under the prairie roses, just down past that hoodoo on the other side of the lake, nobody'll miss that Oil Company executive... we swear...

Stay cool, stay warm, and stay gold.
Your pal,

Axel Howerton
Author. Editor. Hometown anti-hero.

JOIN THE CHP CREW

COFFIN HOP PRESS

First Looks!
Preorder Notification!
Advanced Review Opportunities!
Free Ebooks!
Special Offers!
Exclusive Deals and Swag!

SIGN UP FOR THE
CHP CREW NEWSLETTER
NOW!

WWW.COFFINHOP.COM

COFFIN HOP:
DEATH BY DRIVE-IN

"THE MOST FUN YOU CAN HAVE WITH THE LID UP"

Axel Howerton

Brent Abell

Katrina Byrd

Penelope Crowe

Nina D'Arcangela

Jason Darrick

Dan Dillard

Jamie Friesen

Erik Gustafson

C.W. LaSart

Claudia Lefeve

Amy K. Marshall

Jessica McHugh

Joanna Parypinski

Rob Smales

Julianne Snow

A.F. Stewart

Red Tash

R.L. Treadway

Pavarti K. Tyler

Craig Garrett
& Jeff Wilson

Nicolas Caesar

and Scott S. Phillips

A CHARITY ANTHOLOGY TO BENEFIT
WWW.LITWORLD.ORG

Coffin Hop Press

Available now in ebook and paperback
WWW.COFFINHOP.COM

A FESTIVAL FOR READERS AND WRITERS

When Words Collide is a festival for
readers, writers, editors, artists, agents
and publishers of commercial
and literary fiction

Mainstream, romance, mystery, crime,
horror, sci-fi, fantasy,
children's books, Y.A., emerging readers
and more!

Featuring informative panels,
presentations, training sessions, guest authors,
and all of the information available for
authors, editors and book lovers of all stripes
to achieve their goals and chase their dreams.

ANNUAL LITERARY FESTIVAL
EVERY AUGUST
CALGARY, ALBERTA

Would you like to know more?

Visit www.whenwordscollide.org